"**Would you care t**
God's name you're doing here?"

Lauren glowered at Alec, awaiting his reply.

"I heard you fighting with him," he said. "I heard you scream."

"Scream?" She scowled. "You mean when the chair fell over?"

"I don't know. From upstairs it sounded like he might have hit you with it. I heard you say he hurt you."

Her mouth fell open. "What were you doing, pressing your ear to the floor?" she asked furiously.

"You were both yelling," Alec pointed out. "I could hear you just fine without pressing my ear to the floor."

"Great." She drew a breath. "Look, Alec. I know your motives were decent. But I'm an adult. I can take care of myself. I've had fourteen years of other people intervening in my life, making my decisions for me, and I'm sick of it. Can you understand that?"

She looked small across the room from him, but steely, and all Alec could think was that as brave and tough as she was, she didn't need anyone protecting her at all. "I understand," he said.

ABOUT THE AUTHOR

Massachusetts native Judith Arnold, author of more than forty books, is never at a loss for new and exciting ideas. *The Woman Downstairs,* she writes, was inspired by "an image of a man sitting alone in an upstairs apartment, listening to the life of the person in the apartment below: following her movements, becoming involved merely through the sounds she made—particularly, through her music. Sometimes a single, compelling image can be strong enough to generate an entire novel." Judith Arnold is married and the mother of two sons.

Books by Judith Arnold

HARLEQUIN SUPERROMANCE
460—RAISING THE STAKES

HARLEQUIN AMERICAN ROMANCE
330—SURVIVORS
342—LUCKY PENNY
362—CHANGE OF LIFE
378—ONE GOOD TURN
389—A>LOVERBOY
405—SAFE HARBOR
431—TRUST ME

The Woman Downstairs

JUDITH ARNOLD

Harlequin Books

TORONTO • NEW YORK • LONDON
AMSTERDAM • PARIS • SYDNEY • HAMBURG
STOCKHOLM • ATHENS • TOKYO • MILAN
MADRID • WARSAW • BUDAPEST • AUCKLAND

For my mother,
who keeps on playing, anyway.

Published July 1992

ISBN 0-373-70509-3

THE WOMAN DOWNSTAIRS

CHAPTER ONE

ALEC FONTANA didn't know much about classical music. He was strictly a rhythm and blues man; he liked deep, chugging tempos and down-and-dirty lyrics, the whine of a guitar coiled around the throaty voice of a singer expounding on heartbreak, dancing, sex, revenge and other such vital matters. Alec liked music you could sweat to.

But for the third night in a row, he found himself sitting in the dusk-lit living room of his temporary digs, chewing on a mint-flavored toothpick and listening to the piano music seeping through the floorboards, drifting out the open first-floor window and up one flight into his. Slouched deep in the cushions of the armchair, his legs propped up on the battered coffee table and his eyes closed, he gnawed on his toothpick, wishing it was a cigarette, and listened as she played rich, resonant chords and smooth, soaring melodies.

He knew her name was Lauren Wyler, and she had straight black hair and pale skin. She was probably about five-four, give or take, and slim, and when she departed for the campus each morning she carried a canvas tote in her left hand and tucked her right into the pocket of her baggy beige cardigan.

He'd glimpsed her face only a couple of times, and he'd liked what he'd seen. When she left the duplex, though, all he could see from his second-floor window was her back, the sleek fall of her hair, the horizontal line of her shoulders, the tempting sway of her hips as she strode up Hancock Street.

Every evening at seven-thirty she would start playing the piano, filling his apartment with lush harmonies and slow passages. After a while, she'd try something fancy, something with trills and runs. At that point, her talent would fail her. The rhythms would falter, the notes would be wrong. It didn't take a music critic to know she was blowing it.

Then she would stop. Silence would billow up into his apartment, a strange, urgent silence that made him want to race down the stairs, pound on her door and demand an explanation for why someone as gifted as she was would stumble as soon as she got to a challenging part—and why, after just a few clinkers, she would stop playing altogether.

He couldn't, though. The silence that followed her playing was as hard and dense as concrete. He would listen for her footsteps, her voice, the thud of the lid being lowered over the keyboard. But he would hear no sign of life in the apartment under his, no curses or laughter or fuming frustration at her inability to master those difficult sections.

He would hear nothing at all.

MOVING INTO the upstairs flat had been simple enough. He'd driven out from Boston Saturday morning with his luggage—his portable typewriter and two suitcases full of clothing—stashed in the back of his Ford Probe, an Eric Clapton tape booming through the rear-mounted speakers. Mags had assured him the apartment contained everything else he might need: furniture, pots and pans, dishes and silverware, curtains, linens for the bed and bathroom, and basic cleaning supplies.

She'd made all the arrangements. "You're doing me a big favor, coming here," she'd told him when she'd telephoned him in mid-September and asked for his help. "I can't hire some outside expert to snoop around. It would attract too much attention. I realize this is going to take time away from your writing, so if you say no I'll understand. But if you say yes, I'm certainly not going to have you spending your own money on rent."

As far as his writing was concerned, he could do it in a sleepy little college town in western Massachusetts as well as in Boston's raucous, lively North End. Maybe even better. He'd have fewer distractions in Albright, less noise, no street fairs honoring this or that saint to lure him away from his desk, no tantalizing aromas wafting out of the dozens of restaurants lining the narrow streets. No unannounced inspection tours by his mother: "Why are you living in this dump, Alec? You could afford such a nice house in the suburbs." No phone calls from his sisters: "This friend of mine just got a divorce, and she's free Friday night."

Sure, he could spend a couple of months rent-free in a picture-book village nestled into the slopes of the Berkshire Mountains, nosing around a small, prestigious women's college as a personal favor to his Aunt Margaret. The change of scenery would do him good. The tranquillity would nurture his writing. The fresh air would clear his head.

He'd arrived in Albright around noon and gotten the key to the apartment from someone on the college maintenance staff. As soon as he'd finished unpacking he set out for the campus, a brief two-block walk along Hancock Street. The street was curbless and shaded with tall, leafy trees just beginning to do their colorful autumn number. Private houses shared the quiet road with duplexes; none of the buildings appeared newer than fifty years old, but with their broad porches, clapboard walls, brick chimneys and shingled roofs they exuded a quaint charm.

Hancock ended at Burke Street, which marked the western edge of the campus. Alec crossed the street to the school grounds, trying to remain detached from the "Andy Hardy Goes to College" atmosphere. The campus was picture-postcard perfect, a panorama of verdant lawns, manicured footpaths, looming brick dormitories with ivy growing up the walls, and fieldstone classroom buildings of Gothic grandeur.

Three years after Margaret Cudahy had been named president of Albright College, Alec was still amused to think his aunt had risen to such an exalted position in the academic world. Not that Mags wasn't qualified, not that she hadn't paid her dues, earning an Ivy League Ph.D., teaching on a number of faculties around the country, publishing a couple of scholarly treatises on suitably dry subjects, serving as a dean here, a vice-chancellor there before being tapped for the presidency of Albright. Despite her impressive credentials, it tickled Alec to think that good old Mags, his mother's baby sister, had emerged from a working-class Irish family from South Boston to become the head honcho at this elite women's college.

He made use of the heavy brass knocker on the front door of the president's house, a sprawling Georgian mansion perched amid terraced gardens that descended to a lake at the heart of the campus. Mags had once told him that Albright's crew team practiced on that lake.

A crew team. They hadn't had a crew team at University of Massachusetts-Boston when he'd been a student, that was for sure. Crew teams were for upper-class girls with peaches-and-cream complexions and names like Muffy and Cecily, girls who wouldn't dream of shopping at Filene's Basement, girls who didn't know the difference between a calzone and a cannoli. Crew teams weren't for people like the Cudahys and the Fontanas.

A woman in a crisp white uniform answered his knock, and Alec once again had to suppress the urge to guffaw at all the pretentious formality. "I'm Alec Fontana," he identified himself. "Is Madame President in?"

The maid frowned at his flippant tone. "Please step inside. I'll see if Dr. Cudahy is available." With a barely audible sniff, she pivoted on her heel and vanished up an opulent curving stairway.

Dr. Cudahy. It would be a cold day in hell before Mags got Alec to call her that.

When he saw her descending the stairs a couple of minutes later, relief filled him. She had on a khaki skirt with buttons down the front, a casual short-sleeved sweater and rope-soled canvas shoes. Her dirty-blond hair, liberally streaked with gray, flew about her face in untamed waves, and she wore no makeup. The august environs of Albright College hadn't changed her much; she was still his mother's kid sister, the brainy Cudahy who'd won the scholarships and brought honor to the family even if she was a spinster, poor thing. College president, fancy house, maids answering her door—in spite of it all, she was still good old Mags, a few pounds too thick around the waist and sorely in need of a proper haircut.

Alec gave her a hearty hug. "Hey, Mags!"

"You mustn't call me that here," she whispered, her green eyes sparkling conspiratorially. "I've somehow managed to hoodwink these Albright College people into thinking I'm dignified."

"Treat me right, or I'll expose you for the peasant you are," he threatened, his own hazel eyes as full of laughter as hers.

"I'll treat you as right as I can," she said, hooking her hand through the bend in his elbow. She ushered him past a vaulted great room and into a less intimidating parlor overlooking a flower garden at the side of the house. "When did you arrive in town? Did you have any trouble finding the apartment?"

"None at all," he assured her, dropping onto one of the room's damask-upholstered wing-back chairs and swinging his legs onto the polished oval coffee table in front of him.

Mags shook her head in reproach. "You can't do that here," she warned. "That's a genuine Chippendale."

Cursing mildly, Alec lowered his feet back to the plush Oriental rug. "Doesn't a cripple get special dispensation?"

"You're hardly a cripple," Mags countered. "And even if you were, a Chippendale would take priority over you. Would you like something to drink? I can ring for the maid."

Alec laughed. So did Mags, even as she reached for the silver hand bell on a side table and gave it a shake. Within an instant the starchy maid materialized in the doorway. "Mr. Fontana would like..." Mags eyed Alec questioningly.

"Have you got any beer?"

Mags grinned. "We'll take two Buds, please."

Alec relaxed in his chair. He was comfortable even though he couldn't kick up his legs. He was especially comfortable because, her posh mansion with its Chippendale furnishings notwithstanding, his aunt still chugged Budweiser.

"Now, tell me," she said, once they were alone. "You're all settled into the apartment?"

He nodded, pulled a toothpick from the breast pocket of his blue work shirt, and clenched the sliver of wood between his teeth. "When you told me you were going to put me up in a college-owned building, I thought you'd be housing me in a dorm."

"With all those high-spirited young women? Not a chance."

"Were you afraid for their safety or mine?" he teased.

Mags's response was a fleeting scowl. "The college owns a number of off-campus apartments like the one you're in," she explained. "We have so many visiting professors, people on six-month or one-year contracts, dignitaries and the like. Most of them want a comfortable place to stay on a short-term basis."

"Why'd you put me on the second floor? Those stairs are murder."

"You could use the exercise," she noted.

He grinned mischievously. "If you'd put me in one of the dorms, I would have gotten plenty of exercise."

"Alec, I'm warning you—you'd better behave yourself."

He chuckled. "Don't worry, Auntie dear. College girls are too young for me. Albright College girls are too rich."

"They aren't all rich, Alec. Over half of them receive financial aid. But you're right—they are too

young. They're also too young for Roger Phelps.
Heaven only knows what went on between him and that
student last year. Do you think you'll be able to find out
the truth about it?''

Alec shrugged and chewed thoughtfully on his
toothpick. His aunt had laid out the scenario when
she'd called asking him for help: Roger Phelps, a professor of political science and one of the faculty's lu-
minaries, was rumored to have demanded sexual favors
from a student during the previous school term, in return for which he'd gotten her into Harvard Law
School. The student herself hadn't reported the incident to authorities at Albright; however, she'd told a
friend about it, and over the summer the friend had sent
a letter to Mags detailing the affair. Enough of what the
girl had written rang true that Mags had decided the
rumor was worth investigating.

Not in a splashy way, though. If, in fact, there were
no grounds to the girl's charge, Mags didn't want Professor Phelps's reputation tarnished. Nor did she want
the media to learn of the possible scandal. Albright
College had just embarked on a major fund-raising
campaign; it couldn't afford any adverse publicity.

"I was hoping maybe you could poke around and see
if there's anything to the allegations,'' Mags had told
Alec. "You did undercover work when you were on the
police force, didn't you? If you find anything to sub-
stantiate the story, we'll take steps. I won't have a professor trading sex for law-school recommendations—
not even if he's as highly esteemed as Roger Phelps. I
won't stand for it. But until I'm sure this is more than
just a nasty rumor started by a crackpot student, I can't
risk destroying the man's good name. Phelps is one of
Albright's shining stars.''

Alec had scant knowledge about sexual harassment on college campuses. At UMass, the classes had been so huge most professors probably couldn't even distinguish the girls from the boys in the packed lecture halls. And his undercover work on the police force had focused mainly on neighborhood drug dealers, protection rackets and fencing operations.

Still, he wanted to help Mags if he could. He'd already driven over to Cambridge and found the first-year law student in question. She'd been tight-lipped enough for Alec to suspect she was hiding something. If she'd swapped sexual favors for string-pulling at Harvard Law School, it was no wonder she hadn't wanted to say anything.

Her reticence was reason enough for Alec to make the trip out to Albright College. A few weeks of quiet investigative work on the pristine college campus wouldn't land him in a hospital's intensive-care unit the way his last undercover job had. And in the meantime, he could get some writing done. Maybe the pretty autumn scenery would inspire him.

What the hell. Aunt Mags had always indulged him when he was a kid. He could indulge her now.

"So," she said once the maid had delivered their beers, "other than being on the second floor, is the apartment all right?"

"It's fine." He took a long draft straight from the bottle, then lowered it to his knee. "Who's my neighbor?"

"Let's see…" Searching her memory, Mags scowled. "You're on Hancock Street, right?"

He nodded. "I knocked on the downstairs door, but she wasn't home."

"How do you know it's a she?" Mags asked.

He chuckled. "How do you think? I checked the letters in her mailbox."

"Alec!"

"The mailbox wasn't locked," he said in his own defense. "I didn't break any laws. Her name is Lauren Wyler," he added.

Mags nodded. "Oh, yes. She's a visiting lecturer in the music department, teaching piano."

He'd noticed the piano in her living room when he'd peeked through the windows that opened onto the front porch. He'd also noticed that her furniture was as drab and sturdy as his, that she'd installed a fancy stereo system, and that she'd filled the built-in shelves along the far wall with what appeared to be a collection of teacups.

So she was a piano teacher. Probably an eccentric, addicted to tea. Probably—

"Getting her to teach here at Albright was something of a coup," Mags was saying. "She's had quite a stellar career so far. She's made two critically praised recordings, toured Europe and Asia, performed in some of the finest concert halls in the world—and she hasn't even turned thirty. But don't get your hopes up, Alec. She's very private, very shy, and single-minded about her performing career."

"I'm beginning to resent this," he muttered. "I'm not allowed to socialize with the students, I'm not allowed to socialize with my neighbor—"

"You can socialize with her," Mags allowed. "Just be forewarned—she's following a different agenda than you."

"How do you know what my agenda is?" he protested.

"I know you, Alec," Mags reminded him with an overly confident grin. "I know what goes on inside your head whenever you glimpse an attractive woman."

He glowered at her. He was a healthy single adult, not an animal. If anyone ought to show a little respect for the appetites of healthy single adults, it was his healthy single Aunt Margaret.

The truth was, he'd slowed down a great deal since his run-in with the wrong end of a lead pipe two years ago. All those months of hospital stays, operations, brain scans, casts and crutches had aged him. He'd thought things through, figured things out, come to terms with the fact that he could no longer live the kind of life he'd planned on. He'd given up police work and started writing. He'd contemplated the benefits of monogamy. He'd sold his first manuscript and made a lot of money.

He'd grown up, he'd mellowed out. He'd gotten old. Just because he'd made a joke about the delight of exercising with the cute young Albright College students didn't mean his aunt had to protect his neighbor from him.

He drank his beer and flexed his left knee to ease a crick. "I'm going to need some stuff," he told Mags. "A campus map, a directory of faculty offices and classrooms, a copy of Phelps's teaching schedule. A list of all the students in his classes, if you can manage it."

"We can get whatever you need at my office tomorrow," Mags suggested.

"Tomorrow's Sunday."

"The perfect time to go," she said. "None of the clerical staff will be around to ask us why we want all this information. Now tell me, how's your family? Are Rosie's kids over the chicken pox yet?"

Alec obediently filled Mags in on the family: the health of his nieces and nephews, the plumbing contractor who was currently wooing his widowed mother, his Grandma Cudahy's luck in the daily lottery ("She won a hundred dollars and spent it all on bingo at the church") and his Grandma Fontana's adjustment to life in a Florida retirement community. He told Mags about the new addition his sister Rosie put on her house, and his sister Mary-Beth's promotion to personnel supervisor at her company.

By the time he'd finished his beer he'd run out of news. "I've got to go buy some groceries," he said, placing his empty beer bottle on the floor so he wouldn't leave a ring on the precious Chippendale coffee table. "When should I meet you at your office tomorrow?"

"How does two-thirty sound? The administration building will be locked, so meet me at the south entrance and I'll let you in. Oh, and save next Friday afternoon at four o'clock. I'm having my annual reception for the faculty here at the house. If you haven't met Roger by then, the reception might provide you with the perfect opportunity."

"A president's reception, huh?" Alec muttered. "Sounds pompous."

"It's not," she assured him. "You don't even have to wear a necktie. But please, Alec, no dungarees."

He glanced at the faded blue denim covering his legs and sent his aunt a mocking grin. "And no belching or picking my nose. I get the picture, Auntie dear."

"You're incorrigible," Mags groaned. "Now, do you know where the supermarket in town is?"

When he got back to the duplex on Hancock Street, he considered climbing directly into his car and heading for the store to stock up on edibles. He'd eaten a decent breakfast but no lunch, and he knew his stomach would start making demands soon. But he was distracted by the lower of the two wrought-iron mailboxes on the building's front wall. He was distracted by his growing curiosity about Lauren Wyler.

Evidently she still wasn't home, since her mailbox hadn't been emptied. He flipped through the envelopes: a charge-card bill, a professional-looking correspondence postmarked New York City, a personal letter from Allentown, Pennsylvania and some glossy advertising circulars. Nothing useful.

A concert pianist, he thought as he peeked through the porch windows into the living room once more. Not yet thirty years old, and a world-famous musician.

What the hell was she doing in this teeny tiny college town miles from nowhere? Why wasn't she wowing audiences at Symphony Hall or Carnegie Hall or any of those other hoity-toity concert halls around the globe? Why was she giving piano lessons to a bunch of privileged young ladies in rural Massachusetts?

He abandoned the porch and peered through the windows at the side of the house. One offered a different view of her living room—he got a better look at the console piano against one wall, and the stacks of music books piled on top of it. From that window he couldn't see her collection of teacups—which he decided was just as well. Anyone who collected teacups had to be a little weird.

Another window opened into her kitchen, which appeared clean enough to perform surgery in, and another provided a glimpse of a small study. At the rear of the house he found her bedroom, directly below his. The double bed was made, the dresser clear, the closet door closed.

All right, what did he have? Late twenties, acclaimed in her field, used to adulation. Probably a highbrow snob, a stuck-up twit. A compulsive one at that, he decided with a parting glance at her too-neat bedroom. And with a name like Lauren Wyler, *she* undoubtedly wouldn't know the difference between a calzone and a cannoli, either.

Not much to go on, nothing promising. It was bad policy to get involved with one's neighbors, anyway. He'd be smart to keep his distance from the famous pianist.

Given what he knew about her, maybe that wouldn't be terribly difficult.

SHE CAME HOME the following evening at a little past seven o'clock. It was a warm night, and despite the drizzle Alec had left his windows open to freshen his apartment's stagnant air. He was stretched out on his couch in the living room, an open bottle of beer on the table beside him, a minty toothpick pinched between his teeth and Roger Phelps's employment file propped on his bent knees.

According to the file, Phelps had joined the Albright faculty six years ago, having been hired away from Columbia University. This struck Alec as odd. Why would a high-profile savant like Phelps leave Columbia? Surely that major university would have been able to pay him a bigger salary than Albright could. And given Phelps's prominence, his frequent appearances on televised panel discussions and news shows, Columbia's Manhattan location would have been a great deal more convenient for him in terms of access to the media. There was no indication in the documents that Phelps had been involved in any sort of scandal at Columbia.

Alec reread the letter Phelps had written to Mags's predecessor, accepting the offer of a Distinguished Professorship at Albright:

> I find the slower pace of a small college in a rural setting a most appealing prospect at this time in my life. My experience on the faculty of Columbia University has been rewarding, but my temperament cries out for a quieter environment.

Yeah, right. His temperament cried out for classrooms full of bright, eager females with nubile bodies. People were supposed to be viewed as innocent until proven guilty, but Alec had spent eight years with the Boston police department, and he knew better than to give anyone the benefit of the doubt.

His thoughts were jarred by the sound of footsteps on the porch. For a moment he thought he might have a visitor, and he set aside the folder and sat up, girding for the trek down the long flight of stairs to his front door. Then he heard a downstairs door open, and he realized Lauren Wyler had returned home.

He sprang to the window, hoping to catch a glimpse of her before she vanished inside her flat. Too late—all he saw was the door closing behind her.

He strained to follow her movements below him. She opened her front windows, then headed for her bedroom at the rear of the apartment.

He decided to go downstairs and introduce himself. After all, she was his neighbor, and he saw nothing wrong in being neighborly.

He strode down the hall to the bathroom to check his appearance before he left his apartment. The mirror above the sink threw a scruffy image back at him. His sandy-colored hair was mussed, his shirt wrinkled. His cheeks were darkened by a day's growth of beard. Sunday was traditionally his razor's day of rest as well as his own. What the heck. He'd do a quick run over his jaw with a soapy brush and a sharp blade, and then go down and present himself to the virtuoso.

At that moment the first chords rose up through the floor. She ran a couple of scales, then paused and began the chords again.

The music was far from sprightly; it lent itself more to nodding off than tapping one's toes. Even so, he felt obliged to return to the living room and listen. Something about the slow, regal progression of chords moved him. They sounded dark and resonant and melancholy, not the sort of music he'd expect from a fruitcake who collected china cups.

He would go downstairs when she was done; that would be the polite thing to do. For all he knew, interrupting a musician in the middle of her practice might be a grave breach of etiquette.

Not that he cared. Not that he felt any great urge to make a good impression on the world-class pianist. Hell, he'd written a novel that hit the bestseller lists. She ought to be worried about making a good impression on him.

He lowered himself into the armchair in the living room and propped his feet on the coffee table, taking care to avoid soiling the Phelps documents with his sneakers. He sucked thoughtfully on his toothpick, closed his eyes and listened to Lauren Wyler play.

He had no idea what particular composition he was listening to. His knowledge of highbrow music was limited to Grandma Fontana's scratchy, no-fidelity Caruso records and what he picked up watching a rented video of *Amadeus*. For all he knew, Lauren Wyler could be playing Bach, Beethoven or Brahms—or a medley combining all three.

What he did know was that, even though the music wasn't to his taste, Lauren Wyler played it with authority and style. What he knew was that as long as she was playing he would remain exactly where he was, listening.

After a while she stopped pounding out the chords. She ran a few more scales with brisk precision, and then played something a bit livelier. Still not toe-tapping stuff but it was kind of catchy in a stuffed-shirt way. He tried to picture her long, slender, agile fingers gliding across the keys. It was a surprisingly erotic vision.

Something livelier yet. Her fingers danced and pranced; the notes sparkled. And then—the first mistake, so sour he flinched.

She was supposed to be a celebrity, for crying out loud, a star of concert halls and recording studios. How could she botch a piece so badly?

He reminded himself that this wasn't a performance. She probably didn't realize she had an audience. This was nothing but a practice session; she was permitted to flub a note.

She flubbed another. And another. Her fingers seemed to be tripping all over each other, colliding, mangling the music. It was painful to listen to.

Then came silence, and that was even more painful. Alec shifted in the armchair, twirled his tongue around the tip of his toothpick and waited for her to resume playing.

Nothing.

He couldn't go downstairs and introduce himself now, not during this god-awful silence. He waited, wishing he would hear her move around, turn on her stereo—even bungle another tune on the piano, if she wanted.

He heard nothing.

And he didn't go downstairs.

CHAPTER TWO

DRIVING UP Hancock Street Sunday evening, she spotted the light in the upstairs windows and mouthed a silent curse. Someone must have moved into the apartment above hers over the weekend while she'd been in New York.

She had assumed that sooner or later someone would be taking up residence in the upstairs unit. The school wasn't about to leave a perfectly rentable apartment unoccupied for the entire year. But during the first month of her sojourn at Albright College Lauren had had the duplex to herself, and she'd grown to enjoy her solitude.

Now the building was no longer hers alone. She felt curiously dispossessed, just as she'd felt dispossessed in New York, where she'd had to camp out for the weekend at a friend's apartment because Lauren had sublet her own apartment when she'd accepted the position at Albright.

Frowning at the illuminated upstairs windows, she unlocked the front door on the left, which led into the first-floor flat. She lugged her overnight bag inside. She ought to have been hungry; she hadn't eaten anything since lunch. But she needed to play more than she needed to eat.

She dropped her bag in the bedroom, detoured to the bathroom to wash her face, and then headed for the piano. Arranging herself on the stool, she gazed at the white-and-black pattern of keys, sent a prayer skyward, then struck a few experimental chords. She ran a couple of scales, nodded at the crisp, flawless sound, and embarked on her favorite Chopin étude.

The music sounded good. She detected a mild stiffness in her right hand, but nothing she couldn't cope with. She began to smile.

When she'd visited Dr. Hayes for her monthly checkup in Manhattan the previous Friday, he had declared that she'd shown measurable improvement. Sometimes she feared the only improvements she made were in her ability to squeeze balls and lift weights, pull and flex and cause the needles on his high-tech machines to jump. When it came to what really mattered—her ability to play the piano—she worried that her right hand wasn't responding nearly as well as it ought to.

She tried not to let herself become discouraged. "I've seen amazing cures," Dr. Hayes had assured her. "I've had patients whose neurological damage has healed beyond anyone's expectations. The medical literature is filled with such cases. The nerve damage in your hand has healed remarkably so far. You've got to maintain a positive attitude if you want to keep improving. I promise, Lauren—a good attitude, and we'll get you back to where you used to be."

He'd been saying that for a long time, and she wasn't back yet. Her right pinkie and ring fingers still curled under when she wasn't consciously holding them straight, and the outer half of her hand remained weak, sometimes becoming completely numb.

But she wouldn't give up hope—not only because Dr. Hayes seemed to think optimism was her best ally in restoring the hand to full proficiency, but because...because if she gave up hope she'd have nothing.

So she played on Sunday evening, feeling her fingers warm up and her anxiety wane. She relaxed, grew confident, allowed the music to infuse her until she felt ready to cut loose.

Abruptly her right hand stalled out. The first really juicy passage, and her two outer fingers balked. So much for confidence and cutting loose, she thought with a groan.

Her annoyance at having muddled that difficult passage was aggravated by the realization that someone was upstairs, within earshot. Whoever her new neighbor was, he or she must have heard every mistake, every missed note, every blunder.

She could scarcely endure listening to herself massacre the piece. She was humiliated to think of someone else bearing witness to the mess she'd made of it.

She sat hunched on the piano stool, fighting off the anger that crept over her, chilling her and darkening her mood like one of the night's damp rain clouds. How was she going to practice when someone was upstairs listening?

She'd performed this piece in front of thousands of people. She'd received standing ovations and cries of "Brava!" And now she couldn't work through four lousy measures of sixteenth notes because of a stupid fender bender a year ago. A minor auto accident, everyone had called it. The car had incurred a dented bumper and a shattered headlight. In the back seat next to her, Elaine had suffered a bruise on her forehead. Seated in front, Gerald and Steve had been wearing shoulder harnesses and hadn't been hurt at all.

But Lauren, bracing herself with her arm as her upper body jerked forward, had fractured her wrist and damaged some nerves.

A minor accident, and she'd all but lost her reason for living.

Positive attitude, she reminded herself. *Maintain a positive attitude.*

She decided to save her practice for Monday, when she would be able to play in the privacy of her campus office. She had been assigned a small room on the top floor of the antiquated music building. The sloped ceiling, dormer windows, threadbare rug and brocade drapes made for peculiar acoustics, but at least the walls and floor were solid and soundproof. She could practice all she wanted without anyone eavesdropping.

And if the practice went poorly, she could rant and rave without some upstairs neighbor overhearing. Positive attitude or not, she'd be damned if she'd let anyone know how close she was to losing her grip on herself.

She left her apartment shortly after breakfast Monday morning, armed with her tote bag full of scores and lecture notes. It was an Indian summer day, unseasonably warm for the first week in October. She didn't really need her cardigan, but she kept it on because its deep pocket offered a convenient hiding place for her damaged right hand.

As she stepped off the front porch, she felt an inexplicable urge to turn around and glance up at the second-floor windows. She'd heard her neighbor roaming around the upstairs apartment that morning—muffled footsteps on the rug-covered floor, a clank as water flushed through empty pipes, the scrape of a chair being hauled across the linoleum floor of the kitchen.

Lauren was keenly attuned to the sounds around her; she could read them as well as she could read music.

In this case, she could read that her neighbor was a man. His tread was heavy and slightly uneven. The way he'd moved his kitchen chair implied that he straddled it backwards. The on-off-on-off of his bathroom sink told her he shaved using a blade rather than an electric razor. His movements provided a symphony of information to her trained ear.

But she didn't look up at his windows. For some reason, she didn't want to see who owned the heavy footsteps and the clean-shaved cheeks. As far as she was concerned, he was an intruder on her turf. If only he hadn't moved in, she could have practiced her piano without inhibitions last night.

As it turned out, she was unable to practice in her office during the day. She had three hour-long private lessons in the morning, then a departmental meeting during lunch, her one-o'clock seminar on performance theory, office-hours meetings with several students, and finally, at four o'clock, a visit from Bella Bronowitz, a delightful sixty-year-old professor who taught cello at the college. Bella tapped on Lauren's office door, and when Lauren opened it and saw the sweet-faced silver-haired woman, she swung it wider.

Bella was carrying two foam cups of coffee. "Black, two lumps," she said, handing one of the cups to Lauren. "I dumped the sludge and made a fresh pot." Within days of joining Albright's music department, Lauren had learned about the coffeemaker in the faculty lounge. One of the secretaries always prepared a fresh pot in the morning, and then it sat all day, evaporating and thickening until it resembled mud, at which point some generous soul took it upon him- or herself to make a fresh pot.

More often than not the generous soul was Bella. "You're an angel," Lauren said, welcoming her into the crowded office. They had to walk around the baby grand piano and duck slightly to reach Lauren's desk without banging their heads on the low ceiling. Lauren took her seat behind the desk, Bella on the piano stool. The rich aroma of coffee filled the air.

"You saw your doctor down in New York City this past weekend, didn't you?" Bella asked.

Lauren nodded and sipped her coffee. She curled the fingers of her left hand around the cup and rested her right hand in her lap. Keeping her bad hand out of sight had become a habit, even though it looked relatively normal. To Lauren it looked awful.

"So?" Bella prompted her.

Lauren shrugged. "He said he thinks I'll get back to full function—if I have the proper attitude."

"And you're getting impatient," Bella guessed.

Lauren laughed ruefully. "I'm afraid so. It's been so long, Bella."

"Less than a year," Bella argued.

"It feels like an eternity." Lauren took another sip of coffee and sighed.

"Think of this year as a vacation from touring," Bella advised. "You'll teach for nine months, and by next June you'll be ready to hit the circuit again."

Lauren grinned. "*You've* got the right attitude. Maybe you can heal me by proxy."

"I don't know a single musician who hasn't had some physical problem or other. Look at the department here at Albright—Harold Stemsky has arthritis in his neck, Louise Pelham has carpal-tunnel syndrome, Peter Villard had to have surgery done on a benign growth on his lower lip, caused by the way he positioned his trumpet's mouthpiece. And I've had chronic tendonitis for years. We're as bad as professional athletes.''

Lauren had heard Bella's pep talk before, but she listened more closely than usual this time. ''Who treats your tendonitis, Bella?''

''I see a hand specialist in Boston. Dr. Nylander. A wonderful man. Would you like his number?''

Lauren meditated. Dr. Hayes had performed surgery on her hand, repairing the torn nerves and overseeing her physical therapy. But he was a neurologist, not specifically a hand specialist. ''It couldn't hurt,'' she remarked. ''Maybe he could come up with some different exercises for me. I'm so tired of squeezing rubber balls.''

''Not once has he ever made me squeeze a rubber ball,'' Bella claimed. ''I've got his number at home. I'll bring it in for you tomorrow.''

''Thanks.'' Lauren's spirits lifted. Merely thinking about consulting with a new doctor who might hasten her recovery gave her the positive attitude Dr. Hayes had prescribed.

Her cheery disposition lasted until she arrived home. Seeing the silver sports car parked along the grass shoulder in front of her ancient Volvo reminded her of the interloper occupying the upstairs half of her building. She knew he had as much right to live there as she did, but still...she resented his presence. Unreasonable as it was, she resented him.

Her resentment swelled to unmanageable proportions as soon as she sat at the piano after dinner that night. She knew he was home—she'd heard him moving about upstairs—and that knowledge hampered her ability to practice. Hearing her mistakes was appalling enough. Knowing that someone else could hear them was demoralizing.

She played until her errors became intolerable, then stopped. If only she'd heard her neighbor moving about some more, she might not have felt so ghastly about her disastrous playing. But the lack of any noise from above indicated that he'd been listening to every note. He'd been listening, turning her failure into a communal event, a public disgrace.

She couldn't continue. She sat, waiting for some sign, any sign, that he was no longer listening to her. Silence descended through the ceiling, smothering her, denying her the freedom to heal in private.

Whoever he was, she wished he'd never moved into the upstairs apartment.

ON THURSDAY, instead of a skirt she wore well-tailored slacks. He watched as she stepped off the porch, the tote in her left hand and her right shoved into the pocket of her cardigan. When her arm shifted, the cardigan rode up enough to reveal the sweet roundness of her bottom.

A tortured laugh escaped him. He was becoming weirdly fixated on Lauren Wyler, but it was a condition he was sure he could cure easily enough simply by going downstairs and meeting the woman. They would introduce themselves, find out they had absolutely nothing in common, and then the spell would be broken.

But for some reason, he wasn't yet ready for it to be broken. He'd known a lot of smart people in his life, but never anyone he would consider artistically gifted. He certainly didn't consider himself gifted. The novel he'd written had been long on guts and short on elegance. One kind critic had referred to his prose as "utilitarian," which Alec considered as good a description as any. The story had been grisly and realistic, solidly based on experience—and readers had gobbled it up. They sure hadn't bought the book because it was "artistic."

Lauren was a certified artiste, and Alec should have found that off-putting. Instead it intrigued him. It probably would have intrigued him a lot less if she didn't have that glossy blue-black hair spilling halfway down her back, and those long slim legs, and that tight little rear end.

He'd spent the past three mornings fooling around with the outline of his new book and the afternoons hanging out on the campus, soaking up the environment. Today he planned to narrow his focus to Roger Phelps, esteemed professor and alleged philanderer. But rather than heading directly to Dwight Hall, which housed the faculty offices for the political-science department, Alec found himself strolling to the music library at the other end of the campus.

Undaunted by the eerie hush of the main room, he strode directly to the card catalogue, located the drawers listing the library's record collection, and flipped through the cards in search of a recording by Lauren Wyler. No dice; the records were listed only by composer.

He slid the wooden drawer shut and crossed to the front desk. "Excuse me," he asked the librarian in a near whisper, "but would you happen to have any records by Lauren Wyler?"

The librarian eyed him dubiously. "Only students and faculty are allowed to sign records out of the library."

"I don't want to sign it out. I just want to look at it."

Her skepticism increased. "Who are you?"

He scrambled for a reasonable answer. "My girlfriend's a student here," he said, "and she told me she was studying with this famous pianist named Lauren Wyler, and I've never heard of her. My girlfriend said if I didn't believe Lauren Wyler was famous I should check at the library, which was sure to have her records."

The librarian measured him with an incredulous gaze. Obviously she was thinking he looked too old to have a college-age girlfriend.

"A ten dollar bet is riding on it," he added, giving her a beseeching smile.

The librarian pressed her lips together, then shrugged. "Come with me," she muttered, abandoning the desk and leading him down a short flight of stairs into a room filled with metal shelves containing records. She moved to the *C*s and slid an album out for him to look at: *Lauren Wyler Plays Chopin.* "You owe your girlfriend some money," she said triumphantly.

Alec took the record before she could slide it back onto the shelf. The photograph on the cover showed a young woman seated in profile at a grand piano, dressed in an alluring black gown, her arms gracefully arched and her fingers brushing the keys, her head bowed, her lush black hair streaming down her back. Her eyes were closed, her lips slightly parted, her expression implying either deep concentration or rapture—or both.

She was gorgeous.

He stared at the photograph as long as he dared. Sensing the librarian's growing suspicion, he nodded and grinned sheepishly. "That'll teach me to gamble," he conceded.

Long after he left the music library, the photograph of Lauren Wyler remained imbedded in his consciousness. He recalled the pale, graceful line of her throat, the curve of her back, the snug fit of her gown's bodice around her slender waist and up over the gentle swell of her breasts. He recalled the translucent beauty of her complexion, the thick black fringe of her eyelashes, the sculpted delicacy of her cheekbone and chin.

He tried to put the picture together with the bumbling, fumbling piano player he'd heard through the floor of his apartment the past several nights, but he couldn't. The woman in the photograph on the album jacket didn't look like a person who made mistakes.

He willfully shook his head clear. He had more important mysteries to work out: the mystery that shaped the plot of his new novel, and the mystery of what Professor Phelps did or did not do to his law-school-bound student last year. Alec strolled across the campus to Dwight Hall, following the winding paths rather than tramping over the well-kept lawns. He shared the paths with young women, scores of them, some carrying books in their arms and some using backpacks, some coasting slowly along on bicycles, some jogging, some in tattered dungarees and others in high-fashion miniskirts and tights. The sheer concentration of youthful femininity had a disorienting effect on him. He could almost smell the estrogen in the air. He wanted to say something out loud just to hear a low-pitched voice among all those chattering sopranos.

They were young, of course—much too young to appeal to him in anything other than the most superficial way. Not only were they too young but they all seemed innocent, untouched by life as he knew it. There was a universal ingenuousness about them that put him in mind of apple blossoms and green, rolling hills, crystal ponds and clear skies. Even those who affected funky or sophisticated poses appeared chaste underneath their outlandish garb and haughty expressions. The young women he saw strolling the streets of Boston's North End seemed infinitely tougher.

Dwight Hall loomed ahead, a fairly new brick building adjacent to the school's main library. Roger Phelps's office was located on the second floor, and as Alec trudged up the stairs he contemplated various plans of action.

He still hadn't met the good professor, and he was beginning to lean toward Mags's suggestion that he casually get acquainted with the man at her reception the following afternoon. Even if he waited until then to meet Phelps, though, he wanted to get a feel for the professor's milieu. He had hoped to sit in on one of Phelps's classes, but they were all advanced seminars with small enrollments, so he couldn't easily blend into a crowd there. Perhaps he would pick up some vibes from the man's office.

At the second floor, he flexed his knee to ease a cramp, then ambled down the hall until he reached Phelps's door. It was closed; a schedule of student appointments was taped onto it. According to the schedule, Phelps was currently meeting with a student named Emily Spaeth.

Alec loitered discreetly in the hall, scanning the notices tacked to the bulletin board across the way. Someone was going to be lecturing on the Ethiopian famine that evening; some rock group he'd never heard of was going to be performing in Springfield that weekend. Someone had posted a list of used textbooks for sale; someone was looking for a ride to Dartmouth. The campus recycling center needed volunteers.

Alec shifted from one foot to the other to keep his muscles loose. Hearing the click of a door latch behind him, he snapped to attention and glanced with practiced nonchalance over his shoulder. Phelps's office door opened and a pretty blond girl backed out, hugging her books to her amply endowed chest. "Thanks so much, Dr. Phelps," she gushed. "I really, really appreciate this. This is just, like, the best thing that ever happened to me."

A male voice emerged from behind the door. "One hand washes the other, Emily."

"It's just—it's such a terrific opportunity."

"For both of us. Call me Roger, okay?"

"Oh...okay. Roger," she said breathlessly. "Thanks again." She took another step backward, and the door closed. She stared at it for a minute, her arms tightening around her books, then spun around with a skipping step and headed for the stairs.

Alec followed her, maintaining a discreet distance. He couldn't very well question her on what terrific opportunity Professor Phelps had offered her—or what terrific opportunity she'd offered him, for that matter. But Alec could tail her for a while, maybe get a sense of who she was and what she was about. With her sunshine-colored hair, her cheerleader smile and her curvaceous figure, she was certainly attractive enough to turn an older man's head.

Ignoring the slight limp brought on by his trek up and down the stairs, he continued to shadow her out of Dwight Hall and along a path that cut across one of the campus's offensively perfect lawns. A couple of students passing in the opposite direction gave him a blatant once-over, but Emily Spaeth was unaware of him as she bounced along in her classy leather sneakers, her hips packed snugly into her fashionable jeans. Her lilting voice echoed in his head: "It's just a terrific opportunity."

I'll bet, he muttered under his breath. A terrific opportunity to get into some elite law school—and, in exchange, a terrific opportunity for Phelps to get into her undies. Thank goodness Alec had been a cop and not a judge. Impartiality wasn't exactly his strong suit.

Emily sauntered past a dormitory, past the theater building and another dorm to the solid brick building that housed the music department. She entered through a side door and started up the stairs.

Cursing under his breath, Alec followed her, knowing his legs would make him pay for the day's extensive hiking. But he wouldn't stop, wouldn't abandon her yet. There were other ways to find out about her but he kept going, cursing again as she bypassed the exit onto the second-floor hallway and continued her ascent. A student passed him going up. A white-haired man carrying a violin case passed him going down. Alec kept climbing.

Emily bypassed the third-floor exit. It was almost enough to make Alec give up, but he took a deep breath and forged onward, driven by some inexplicable need to find out where the lovely young student would go after her private session with Roger Phelps.

She reached the fourth floor, and Alec took consolation in the discovery that it was the top floor of the building; Emily could lead him no higher. She vanished through the door and, after a reasonable pause, he pushed the door open and followed her into the corridor.

Although it was empty, Emily remained oblivious to him as she approached one of the heavy wooden doors and knocked on it. It swung open—and there stood Lauren Wyler.

Although Alec had never actually seen her up close, he recognized her at once. He knew her heart-shaped face, her creamy complexion, her sleek black hair. He knew the hauntingly beautiful dark eyes above her sculpted cheeks, and the exquisite curve of her lips as she greeted Emily with a smile. He knew her petite build, her narrow waist, her long legs and her left hand. Her right hand was tucked into her pocket, as usual.

"Hello, Emily," she said, stepping aside to let the student in. Her voice was like velvet, soft and rich.

Emily responded with a cheerful hello, then began babbling something about her lesson as she pranced into the room.

As she leaned against her door to shut it, Lauren noticed Alec. She hesitated for a fraction of a second, her eyebrows dipping slightly as her gaze swept over him. A new smile flickered across her lips, vague and uncertain, and then she closed the door with a muted click.

WHO WAS HE? Why wasn't she alarmed by the sight of a strange man—a tall, muscular one at that—skulking about in the usually empty fourth-floor hallway? Why wasn't she locking the door and dialing the number of the campus security office?

She'd seen him before, that was why. She didn't know where or when, but his dirty-blond hair, piercing hazel eyes and harsh jaw struck her as familiar. And the smile he'd sent her way had told her, however illogically, that she had nothing to fear.

Emily was chattering about something, and Lauren felt guilty about not paying closer attention. But for a long, delicious moment she allowed her mind to linger on the stranger in the hallway, on the implicit power in his shoulders, on his lean torso and long denim-clad legs, on his scruffy sneakers and the sinewy shape of his forearms, visible beneath the rolled-up cuffs of his shirt. Her thoughts returned to the ruggedly hewn features of his face—and to his knowing, penetrating eyes that glinted with too many colors to count.

Who was he?

"So anyway, I thought I'd start with the Bach," Emily said, already settled on the piano stool.

"Fine," Lauren agreed, tearing her thoughts from the man she'd glimpsed outside her office and directing them to the piano lesson at hand.

Emily Spaeth was Lauren's most talented student. While Albright College was a liberal-arts college and not a conservatory dedicated to training musicians for performing careers, a few students were as gifted as any of Lauren's classmates back at Juilliard had been, and Emily was clearly one of them.

Lauren was convinced that Emily could have a future in music, if not as a concert artist then at least as a teacher or accompanist. She hadn't yet persuaded Emily to consider a musical career; Emily claimed her choice of a major—political science—was more practical. Practicality, in this instance, meant the likelihood that she would be able to earn money after college. She was attending Albright on a combination of scholarships and loans, the continuation of which depended on her maintaining a high average.

Whenever Emily complained about her shaky finances, Lauren assured her that if she kept her mind focused on her music—and her other studies, of course—the money would take care of itself. The grade Lauren intended to give her would definitely help to boost her average and keep her scholarship money coming in.

It was thanks to students like Emily that Lauren understood the appeal of teaching: not merely working with gifted young people but fighting for them, encouraging them, goading them to excel. Teachers had an enormous power over their students, and Lauren enjoyed using that power to prod people like Emily toward success.

Emily opened her book to the Bach fugue she'd been working on. Lauren felt a twinge of envy as Emily's nimble fingers took over the keyboard, playing with an agility Lauren hadn't had since the accident. Emily's playing wasn't quite right, though. The notes were correct but the mood was wrong.

"Emily," Lauren broke in after a minute, "this isn't a rhapsody."

"Huh?" Emily let her hands fall to her lap and gazed inquisitively up at her teacher. She had a charming, open face, and her expression was so frankly bewildered Lauren chuckled.

"It should be played cooler," Lauren explained. "You're pouring much too much emotion into it."

"Oh." Emily's cheeks flamed with color and she grinned sheepishly. "I guess I'm kind of emotional these days."

"Are you?"

"I think I'm in love," Emily erupted, obviously unable to contain her joyous news.

"That's nice." Lauren gave her a tolerant smile. "Did you meet him at the fall mixer last weekend?"

"No. He isn't a college student. He's..." Emily blushed again. "He's older, and he's so...he's so mature, Ms. Wyler. I mean, it's like...he's so different. He respects me, and he can do things for me because he's older. He can help me with my life. He cares about what happens to me. It's so incredible, having someone who can take care of things for you and make everything easier, just because he's older."

An image of the man in the hallway flashed through Lauren's mind. Was he Emily's new boyfriend? He'd definitely looked older than college age, and he was certainly handsome enough to cause a girl's heart to flutter out of control.

Lauren didn't doubt that Emily was smitten—but she questioned the wisdom of a college girl becoming involved with an older man. More specifically, she questioned the judgment of a full-grown man dallying with a twenty-year-old girl. The situation didn't seem quite right to Lauren.

However, how Emily spent her private time was none of Lauren's business. She would never interfere. "Well, I'm very happy for you," she said, "but what does being in love have to do with the way you're playing the Bach fugue?"

"Well...Bach fathered seventeen children, didn't he? He must have known something about love."

Lauren laughed. "He presumably knew something about sex. But he didn't write music to seduce women. He wrote it to feed those seventeen children, and the people paying his salary were strict Lutheran church-men. So try the fugue again, and this time keep it clean.''

Emily began the piece once more, playing with greater restraint. Lauren listened, but a part of her mind strayed, meditating on Emily's giddy state, on the tu-multuous excitement of being twenty years old and in love. Once upon a time, Lauren herself had been twenty years old and in love. She could understand what Emily was feeling.

Lauren would never stifle her student the way her manager had stifled her. She would never admonish her on the danger of engaging in a relationship with an older man. Nor would she issue an ultimatum, as Ger-ald had, forcing the girl to choose between her art and her heart. Lauren would never say, ''You are married to music. You mustn't let anything get in the way.''

Perhaps her own great love affair would have even-tually died a natural death. But she'd never had the chance to find out. She had obeyed Gerald's edict, ended the romance and devoted herself body and soul to her career.

And where did that get her? she thought, flexing her right hand, exerting herself to straighten her stub-bornly bent fingers. There were enormous hazards in devoting oneself exclusively to one's career. There were automobile accidents, and there were painful regrets.

Positive attitude, she exhorted herself. She wouldn't dwell on what she'd given up, what she lacked, what she'd never really known. She wouldn't think about how no handsome man with dynamic eyes and a sen-sual mouth waited outside a door for her.

What waited for her was her career, as soon as her hand was fully healed. For twenty-nine years that had been enough to sustain her. And when she opened her office door and left the music building, when she finished her year at Albright College and returned to her real life, a life of stages and tours and audiences cheering, it would still be enough.

She had to believe that.

CHAPTER THREE

"WELL, don't you look spiffy."

Alec gave his aunt a tolerant smile. He didn't look the least bit spiffy. In honor of her prissy garden party he'd donned the fanciest apparel he'd brought with him to Albright: a pair of beige jeans, a white oxford shirt and a tan corduroy blazer that was entering its dotage. He simply wasn't cut out for classy clothes. The only suit he owned he'd bought for his father's funeral eight years ago, and he'd worn it maybe three times since then. Neckties he considered the devil's handiwork, stiff collars the invention of a sadist. One of the nicest things about being a writer, he had learned, was that you didn't have to dress up for work.

Mags looked properly elegant in a floral dress and stylish pumps, her hair more subdued than usual and her face polished with a discreet application of makeup. She reigned over the terraced backyard of the president's house, which swarmed with guests, all of whom seemed to be talking at once. On the slate patio abutting the house, a long linen-draped table held crystal punch bowls and fluted goblets full of wine punch; waiters carrying trays of canapés wove among the throngs. Late-blooming mums and marigolds bordered the patio. At the bottom of the slope spread the lake, its motionless surface mirroring the cloudless autumn sky.

"Pretty refined," Alec assessed the gathering.

"I hope you're suitably overwhelmed," Mags joked, handing him a glass.

"No Budweiser?"

"Not today. We're on good behavior today, aren't we." It was a statement, not a question, and Alec gave her one of his docile yes-Auntie-dear nods. He took a taste of the wine, grimaced and set his glass back on the table. If he wanted to drink something that tasted like water, he would just as soon drink the real thing.

Smiling at his predictable reaction to the bland wine punch, Mags slipped her hand through his elbow. "Now tell me, Alec, is there someone in particular you'd like me to introduce you to?"

From his slightly elevated vantage on the patio, he surveyed the flocks of chattering guests. He needed to meet Phelps, but there was a different someone in particular he wanted to be introduced to, a woman with hair the color of midnight and a face as pale and delicate as fine porcelain, a woman whose dark, haunting eyes had locked with his for an instant yesterday and sent his nervous system into orbit.

He had almost rung her doorbell last night. During dinner and afterward, as he'd settled into his armchair with the sports section of the *Boston Globe,* he'd listened for her to come home. She hadn't arrived at the duplex until after seven o'clock, prompting him to wonder whether she'd had dinner, where she'd had it and with whom. He wondered whether she had a boyfriend.

A few minutes after he'd heard her enter her apartment, she'd embarked on her nightly music routine: scales, chords, more scales, more chords, then some florid stuff brought to an ignominious conclusion by a series of bloopers. And then silence.

Why couldn't he just go downstairs and say hello? What was holding him back?

The silence. It was unlike anything he'd known. Growing up in South Boston and currently residing in the North End, he had never had the opportunity to experience true, utter silence. City life always unfurled against a background din of car engines, neighbors shouting at each other through open windows, sirens wailing in the distance. Even here in Albright, he would probably be able to hear some noise if he strained. The town was quiet but it wasn't dead.

Yet the silence filling his apartment seemed total, almost palpable. It rose through the floorboards, through the rugs, through the windows, tainting the air. It was heavy, oppressive, laden with despair.

Maybe he was too caught up in his new career as a fiction writer. Maybe he was reading more than he should into the abrupt halt of his neighbor's brief nightly practice sessions. But he couldn't bring himself to go downstairs and break the silence. He just couldn't do it.

So he'd sat in his chair last night, the sports pages forgotten in his lap, and thought about Lauren Wyler's beautiful hair, her beautiful figure, her stunningly beautiful eyes, her beautiful left hand—and her right hand, the hand he'd never seen.

He hadn't actively thought about meeting Lauren at his aunt's reception, but it had occurred to him, as he'd strolled across the campus to the president's house Friday afternoon, that as a member of the faculty she would be likely to attend. Sure enough, he spotted her beside a decorative stone railing that bordered one of the terraced gardens. Engrossed in an animated discussion with a trio of associates, she wore an ankle-length skirt and a matching scoop-necked blouse of an exotic, brightly woven fabric that set off her creamy complexion. In her left hand she held a glass of wine punch; her right hand was tucked into the skirt's pocket.

He tore his eyes from her and turned to his aunt. "Is Phelps here?"

"Roger Phelps would never pass up an opportunity for a free drink," she said, accompanying Alec off the patio and across the impeccably maintained lawn, down two stone steps to a lower terrace, across it and down two more steps to the next level, pausing intermittently to acknowledge the faculty members who waved and called to her in greeting.

Alec recognized Roger Phelps from twenty paces. He'd seen the man on television once or twice, pontificating on this and that news show, analyzing what the Constitution had to say about executive privilege or the individual's right to privacy. In the flesh Phelps looked very much as he did on the tube—handsome, in a plastic sort of way. His chestnut-brown hair was sprinkled with gray and had been blow-dried to within an inch of its life, and his face sported the kind of character lines that were supposed to set women's hearts aflutter. He was nearly as tall as Alec, trim and compact of build, his attire reeking of fine tailoring and his expression reeking of overweening self-confidence. Beside him stood an attractive fortyish woman in a silk dress, her hair coiffed in a sleek pageboy and her wrist adorned by a glittering diamond tennis bracelet.

"Roger," Mags hailed him as she marched Alec across the lawn. "This is my nephew, Alec Fontana.

He's been dying to meet you. Alec, Roger Phelps and his wife Carol.''

Not exactly a discreet introduction, Alec muttered to himself. "I've caught your act on television a few times," he said, extending his hand. "My aunt's lucky to have you working here."

"How do you do?" Roger said in the deep, silky voice Alec had heard emerging from behind a door in Dwight Hall yesterday. "Have you joined the faculty here at Albright? Margaret—" he eyed Mags reprovingly "—I do believe I detect a whiff of nepotism."

"No, he's not teaching," she assured Roger. "He's working on a book and he needed a change of scenery. So I invited him to spend some time out here in the Berkshires."

"I can answer for myself, Aunt Margaret," Alec murmured, sliding his arm free of her hand. So far she hadn't done any irreparable damage, but she was prattling a bit too much for his comfort.

"A book," Roger echoed with a supercilious smile. "What's the subject?"

"Well, it's a novel."

"Alec is a bestselling author," Mags boasted.

Alec rolled his eyes and gave her a gentle nudge. "Go be a hostess, would you? You're embarrassing me."

"That's what aunts are for," she said blithely, patting him on the arm and taking her leave with a farewell nod.

"You're Alec Fontana!" Roger suddenly exclaimed, wagging a finger at Alec. "You wrote *Street Talk!* Carol, this is Alec Fontana!"

Roger's wife smiled at Alec. He smiled back, feeling almost as embarrassed by Roger's adulation as he'd been by his aunt's bragging. "You hated the book, didn't you," he guessed, grinning at Carol.

To her credit, she didn't flinch. "It was too gritty for my taste."

"Verisimilitude," Roger orated. "The grit was there because that was the world the novel was dealing with. If you're writing about street crime in the ghettos of Boston, you can't escape the grit. I thought it was a splendid novel, Alec. May I call you Alec?"

"Sure."

"A splendid novel," Roger repeated, giving Alec's hand another, heartier shake.

The most splendid thing Alec could think of about his novel was its earnings. The second most splendid thing about it was that its success gave him a new career and a new identity once police work was no longer a viable option. As far as the plot and the writing, the grit and the verisimilitude—a word Alec hated on principle— "splendid" was a serious overstatement. Roger Phelps's enthusiasm seemed wildly out of proportion.

Alec had always figured that highbrow professors wouldn't be caught dead reading popular fiction. He'd assumed that in their spare time, when they weren't watching ballet recitals on public broadcasting or putting together articles on the economic situation in Outer Slobovia for fusty magazines with a circulation of seven, they entertained themselves devouring books by Joseph Conrad and Henry James, all those ponderous tomes Alec was supposed to read in high school but never did, novels filled with words like "verisimilitude."

"Now correct me if I'm wrong," Roger said, his eyes bright with excitement, "but you're a law-enforcement officer, aren't you?"

The publisher had made a big deal about Alec's police background in promoting his book. "Actually," he answered with a wry smile, "those of us in the business prefer the term 'cop.'"

"You're a cop, then?" Roger was evidently unused to relying on such short, simple words.

"An ex-cop."

"I see. Why did you leave that work, Alec? May I ask?"

Alec shrugged. "I found out writing a bestselling novel pays a hell of a lot better—plus you don't have to deal with people threatening to cut off your body parts with a steak knife. At least not on a regular basis. There were a few occasions when my editor might have considered taking a knife to me. . . ."

Roger laughed longer and louder than necessary. His wife Carol smiled faintly. She really was a nice-looking lady, chic and elegant. Alec wondered why Roger would feel the need to cheat on her—if, indeed, he was guilty of seducing his student. Even during his rowdy youth, Alec had never cheated on a woman. He considered such behavior unforgivably dishonorable.

All right, so maybe Roger hadn't deceived his wife, either. Maybe he was innocent of the charge against him. Maybe the student who'd sent the letter had a grudge against him and wanted to bring him down. Maybe *she'd* tried to seduce *him,* and he'd rejected her offer, and she wanted to get even.

Alec really ought to try to be fair about this thing. If Roger Phelps was such a big fan of *Street Talk,* he couldn't be all bad.

"Tell me, Alec, would you be willing to autograph my copy of your novel?"

"For a small fee." At Roger's startled look, Alec quickly added, "Just kidding. Of course I'll autograph it for you."

"When?"

"How's Monday?" Alec suggested, knowing full well that Monday was the lightest day on Roger's schedule.

"Let's do lunch."

"Okay."

"Do you know where my office is?"

Alec pretended he didn't. He pulled his notepad and pen from the inner pocket of his blazer—it was an old habit from his police days always to have a notepad handy—and jotted down Roger's directions to Dwight Hall. As he slipped the pad and pen back into his pocket his gaze drifted toward the stone railing bordering the terrace above him. A pair of gloriously dark almond-shaped eyes met his.

A tingle of heat coursed through his body as his gaze merged with Lauren's. He wanted to laugh, shout a greeting, race up the steps to her. But her expression, a blend of surprise, bewilderment and distrust, stifled that impulse. Instead he sent a cautious smile her way.

She held his gaze for a minute longer, then turned and resumed her conversation with the round-faced gray-haired woman standing next to her.

"If you'll excuse me," Alec said to Roger and his wife, "there's someone I've got to talk to."

"Go right ahead. We're on for Monday," Roger confirmed.

"Mrs. Phelps, nice meeting you," Alec said as he backed toward the stone steps carved into the grassy slope. He ought to use the moment to memorize everything of importance about Roger Phelps: his pricy clothing, his urbane demeanor, his attractive wife, his flagrant hero worship of an erstwhile cop who'd happened to pen an entertaining pulp novel, his irritating language—not just the ten-dollar words but the phrase "let's do lunch," which Alec considered the most nauseating trio of words ever to join forces in a sentence. He ought to have been recording every bit of data in his brain's memory file.

But all he could think of was the raven-haired woman by the stone railing one terrace above him. All he could think of was that he was at long last going to meet her.

SHE HAD SENSED his presence from the moment he'd arrived at the president's house. In the middle of Peter Villard's long-winded story about the years he'd spent touring with a brass ensemble, she'd felt a sudden, inexplicable impulse to look toward the patio—and there he'd been.

Who was he?

Well, he wasn't Emily Spaeth's boyfriend—of that much Lauren was reasonably certain. Just because Emily had announced that she was in love while he happened to be loitering in the hallway outside Lauren's office didn't mean he and Emily had anything to do with each other. His presence at the president's reception confirmed Lauren's suspicion. This party was only for Albright College faculty members and their spouses.

So he was a faculty member—evidently a favorite of President Cudahy's, given the way the president latched on to him, taking his arm and personally escorting him among her guests. When Lauren had first seen him yesterday she'd thought he looked familiar. She realized that if he was teaching at Albright she might well have glimpsed him on campus or at some other faculty affair.

Once she knew he was at the party she couldn't dismiss him from her mind. She laughed at Peter's story and made the appropriate comments at the appropriate times, but one part of her mind remained with the tall, sandy-haired stranger in the appealingly seedy jacket, pale jeans and loafers. She was aware of his lanky build, his bemused smile, the ironic quirk of his eyebrows and the penetrating force of his hazel eyes. She was aware of his curiously lopsided gait as he accompanied Margaret Cudahy among her guests.

A few minutes later, she was aware of him crossing the grass to the steps, ascending, approaching to within a foot of her. Inhaling deeply, she rotated to face him.

Up close he looked even more handsome than he had from a distance. He had a rough, defiant edge about him; nothing in him spoke of sophistication or refinement. His hair was rakishly long, his chin thrust forward, his jaw darkened by a faint shadow of beard. His eyes, gray and green and glittering gold, captured her attention with merciless force. Even the hint of a dimple punctuating the left corner of his mouth as he smiled held a challenge.

She knew at once that he wasn't like the men with whom she usually socialized. She found his nearness vaguely menacing—and extremely interesting.

"Hello, Lauren," he said in a low, gravelly voice.

Her eyes widened at his use of her first name. "Do I know you?"

"I'm your neighbor."

The man upstairs. No wonder he'd looked familiar to her—although she couldn't truly recall any specific instance when she might have seen him on Hancock

Street. Perhaps she'd noticed him without realizing it. She recognized his uneven walk, at least—she'd been listening to the syncopated pattern of his footsteps above her head for the past five days.

A confusion of emotions assailed her. She had been annoyed to the point of fury by his invasion of the upstairs apartment. She'd been mortified by the understanding that someone could hear her fouling up every piece she attempted—and in turn she'd been silenced by him, too chagrined to continue the practice she desperately needed. She'd spent the past week vilifying him in her mind, resenting him, loathing him, wishing him a speedy departure. If only she'd known he was such an outright sexy man.

For heaven's sake, she had no time for men, sexy or otherwise. She had to focus all her energy on healing her hand, regaining her proficiency and emerging from her one-year contract at the college fully prepared to resume her performing career. She couldn't become involved with a neighbor, no matter how virile his physique, no matter how mesmerizing his gaze.

Then again, he hadn't shown any particular inclination to become involved with her. He lived upstairs, that was all. Neighbors were supposed to be neighborly, and his coming over to her at this gathering was simply an act of neighborliness.

He offered his hand. "Alec Fontana," he introduced himself.

Sending a message to her fingers to stay straight, she pulled her right hand from her pocket and placed it in his. His grip was firm, his palm warm and leather-smooth, his bones thick. As soon as he released her hand she plunged it back into her pocket, before her fourth and fifth fingers had a chance to relax into their crooked curl.

"How did you know my name?" she asked, her voice emerging softer than she'd expected.

He opened his mouth and then closed it, looking as uncertain as she felt. Then he smiled again, an easy, surprisingly contagious smile. "I could say I recognized you from your picture on a record album, or I could say I peeked inside your mailbox. Your choice."

He didn't look like the sort of man who would own Chopin records. "My mailbox, huh?"

"Be grateful I didn't steam open the envelopes."

She wasn't grateful. She wasn't sure what she was. The thought of this good-looking stranger pawing through her mailbox unnerved her.

"I'm safe," he said, as if he'd read her mind. That he would say such a thing convinced her that he wasn't the least bit safe.

"Lauren? Are you going to introduce us?" Bella intervened.

The man bailed her out by addressing her music-department colleagues. "I'm Alec Fontana," he said, shaking hands with Peter and Harold and then Bella.

"He lives on top of me," Lauren explained, then felt her cheeks burn with color at her inept choice of words. "In the upstairs apartment," she clarified. "This is Bella Bronowitz, Peter Villard, Harold Stemsky—"

"It's a pleasure," Alec said with a certain brusque finality. "If you'll excuse us . . ."

Before Lauren had a chance to object, he slid his hand around her arm and led her away. She glanced helplessly over her shoulder at Bella, who winked. So much for expecting her friends to rescue her.

Alec ushered her down from terrace to terrace until they reached the edge of the lake. The cocktail chatter blurred into a dull hum behind her; before her spread the broad oval of water, silver and still.

Alec removed his hand from her arm and she took a safe step back from him. She wasn't exactly frightened by his arrogance in dragging her away from her friends. Bemused, perhaps, and startled, but not really alarmed. After all, she was within screaming distance of the entire faculty of Albright College if he tried anything.

What would he try, anyway? He was her neighbor. If he had any nefarious designs on her he would have put them into action at the duplex on Hancock Street, not here at a well-attended party.

Her confidence returning, she gave him a look of benign disapproval. "That was rude, pulling me away from my friends like that."

He experimented with a sheepish smile, then abandoned it. His gaze fell to her right hand, safely tucked inside her pocket, and then to her left, which she held in a loose fist at her side. His focus traveled further down, to her tiny feet in black leather flats, and then back up to her face. He opened his mouth again, closed it without speaking, shrugged, and pulled a wooden toothpick from a pocket of his blazer. He bit down onto the toothpick and shrugged again. "All right. I'm rude," he agreed.

She was fascinated by the way the toothpick moved as he spoke. She didn't want to be fascinated by him, though, and she exerted herself to hang on to her anger. "I was talking to my friends—"

"I'm sorry," he cut her off.

That was as good a cue as any to say goodbye to him and return to Bella and the others. Yet she sensed he was apologizing for something more than merely having hauled her away from the reception. She didn't know what—and she couldn't leave him until she did.

She stood with him on the flagstone path rimming the lake, ignoring the tinges of bright color in the leaves of the maples and sycamores shading the ground, the motionless beauty of the water, the lively party in full swing behind her—everything but the toothpick clenched in his teeth and the fierce tenacity of his gaze.

"I listen," he said after a long minute. "When you play every evening, I listen. And then it becomes silent, and I—look, maybe I'm crazy, but I think it's my fault that you stop playing. I don't know why, or what I'm supposed to do. But if it's my fault, I'm sorry."

It was her turn to be at a loss for words. She scarcely knew this man. Yet the subject he'd raised was extremely personal. She couldn't begin to discuss it with him. She couldn't talk to a total stranger about her frustrations, her impatience, her inchoate fear that maybe, no matter what she did or how hard she tried, her hand wasn't going to get any better.

It *was* his fault that she stopped playing—but it was her own fault even more. He couldn't be blamed for having taken up residence in the upper half of her building, or for the fact that his presence upstairs inhibited her. He had as much right to live in the Hancock Street duplex as she did.

"Don't apologize," she said, her voice once again sounding softer and less confident than usual. "I get plenty of practice time on campus."

His eyes strayed to the pocket of her skirt, the colorful fabric stretched around her right hand. "You could play all you want, even if I'm home. I don't mind."

"No—that's all right. I'd rather not disturb you."

"What disturbs me is that you always stop."

Why should it disturb him that she was sensitive about exposing him to her awful playing? He ought to be grateful not to have to listen to her mangling the various pieces she attempted. If she'd been too loud he would have a legitimate gripe. But why in the world should he complain about having too quiet a neighbor?

"Look, Mr. Fontana," she said in an artificially polite tone, "I think we ought to go back to the party."

"Alec," he corrected her, reaching out and touching her shoulder. Despite the near weightlessness of his fingers on her, his caress seemed to freeze her in place. She felt the understated strength of his hand not just in her shoulder but down her back, through her flesh, deep inside. "*I* think we should work this out," he said. "We're neighbors, after all."

"So, we're neighbors." Lauren didn't know the names of most of her neighbors in New York City. Just because fate forced her to share an address with this man didn't mean they had to become bosom buddies.

"The truth is, I don't even like classical music. So whether or not you're playing it right doesn't matter to me. I wish you'd just go ahead and do it. If you blow it, big deal. I'm not some snooty critic putting a little black mark next to your name every time you hit a wrong note."

"Who *are* you?" she blurted out.

A smile teased the corners of his mouth, and he let his arm drop, apparently certain she was no longer on the verge of fleeing. "I'm Margaret Cudahy's nephew," he said.

President Cudahy's nephew? Well, that was something, Lauren supposed. "What are you doing in Albright? Are you teaching at the college?"

He shook his head. "I'm working on a novel. Mags suggested it might do the old muse some good if I got away from Boston for a while."

"Mags?"

"Oops." Grinning, Alec shifted the toothpick in his teeth and peered up the sloping lawns toward the patio, where his aunt was chatting with several of her guests. "That's her family nickname," he told Lauren. "Don't tell her I let it slip out, or she'll boil me in oil."

"It will be our secret," Lauren promised, smiling in spite of herself. Her smile faded as she realized the implications of her remark. She didn't want to get close enough to Alec Fontana to be entrusted with his secrets.

Anxious to restore her distance from him, she said, "So, you don't like classical music?"

"I don't *not* like it, either," he claimed. "It's just—it's boring, you know?"

"No, I don't know."

"It has no words."

"Operas have words."

He rolled his eyes and laughed. "Oh, of course. Operas. They're all in Italian."

"Not all. Although in most cases it's just as well if you can't understand the lyrics," Lauren conceded with a laugh. "They're really silly, some of them. All that overheated passion, all that melodrama. It can be a bit much."

"There's nothing wrong with a little overheated passion," Alec observed. His tone was mild, in contrast to the searing intensity of his gaze.

Lauren once more felt the need to put some distance between him and herself. She wasn't sure why he made her so edgy. He was just a man who lived upstairs from her, trying to be friendly. Yet the way he looked at her wasn't friendly at all. The way his eyes glittered when he mentioned overheated passion...

She focused on his toothpick to avoid meeting his gaze. As if he could sense her disapproval, he removed the sliver of wood. "It's a substitute for cigarettes," he explained.

"Oh."

"Less obnoxious than gum chewing or nail biting, right?"

"I don't know...." She drifted off. Once again she and Alec seemed to have stumbled onto an intimate topic. She didn't feel the least bit comfortable discussing oral habits with him.

"So tell me, Lauren, what's a world-famous piano player like you doing in a place like this?"

He didn't waste much time, did he? From passion to vice, from rudeness to her uneasiness about practicing the piano when he was home, he had galloped through quite an assortment of difficult subjects. "I decided to take a little time off from performing," she said evasively. "It's nice and quiet here in Albright. I enjoy it."

Angling his head, he scrutinized her. His gaze lost its sharp edge and his smile grew warm. "There's a bench over there," he said, pointing toward a decorative wooden bench alongside the path, overlooking the water. "Would you like to sit down?"

Sitting on the bench would still place her within screaming distance of the party—and, her misgivings to the contrary, she had to admit she found Alec Fontana too intriguing to walk away from. Nodding, she started down the path, and he fell into step beside her.

Again she noticed his slightly uneven stride, his right leg extending further in front of him than his left. If she was as tactless as he was, she might have asked him about it—but she was an extremely tactful person, so she kept her questions to herself. Oddly enough, the subtle limp didn't detract from his inherent grace. His body was lean and rangy, his posture relaxed, his arms swinging freely from wide shoulders.

She was used to men with courteous manners, men who dressed in neat suits and adored classical music, men as tactful as herself. Alec was the kind of man she'd left behind when she'd left home, the kind of man she might have married if she hadn't been blessed with exceptional talent. If she'd stayed with her family through her adolescence, she probably would have fallen in love with an unpretentious, salt-of-the-earth fellow with an ethnic name, married him and lived a happy, mundane life.

Not that there was anything particularly mundane about Alec. He was Margaret Cudahy's nephew—and a novelist. "Have any of your books been published?" she asked as she lowered herself onto the bench.

"Just one," he said, hovering above her. "Do you want me to get you some wine before I sit?"

Recalling the half glass she'd left on the stone railing, she smiled at his belated attempt at etiquette. "No, thanks," she said. "It wasn't that good."

He grinned and settled himself comfortably on the bench next to her, leaving several feet of space between them. "It tasted like bilge water," he concurred.

"Tell me about your novel. What's it called?"

"*Street Talk.*"

The title struck her as vaguely familiar. On the rare occasions when she had time to read for pleasure, though, she usually selected historical romances. *Street Talk* didn't sound the least bit historical—or romantic. "I'm afraid I haven't read it," she admitted.

"That's all right. You wouldn't like it."

"What makes you say that?"

"It's full of blood and gore."

She crossed her legs demurely at the ankle and gazed out at the lake. True, she didn't like reading novels brimming with violence, but it bothered her to think she was so transparent that a stranger like Alec could figure out her taste in literature within minutes of meeting her. People were always jumping to conclusions about her: because she was small and dainty-looking and a musician, they assumed she was fragile, her emotions delicate. They always wanted to protect her.

If there was anything good about her forced exile from performing, it was that she'd escaped from Gerald's patronizing protectiveness. She certainly wasn't going to tolerate having Alec protect her from a lurid work of fiction. "If we're neighbors," she said, "I ought to read your book. Is it still available?"

"It's still in print, if that's what you mean," he said. "Only in hardcover, though—the paperback won't be released for another year. But forget about buying it, I'll give you a copy."

"You don't have to do that," she insisted.

"They priced it at twenty-two-ninety-five. Borrow my copy."

She eyed him speculatively, unable to shake the comprehension that his generosity stemmed from something more than simple neighborliness. Yet he didn't seem to expect anything in return. Nothing crass or obvious, at least. He carefully maintained the space between them on the bench; he made no effort to flirt with her.

She almost wished he *would* flirt. She knew how to parry a man's advances. She didn't know how to parry Alec, though. She couldn't begin to guess what he was after, let alone how to defend herself against him.

It would have been easier if she was living her usual life of performances and tours. She knew the rules and limits there, and even if she hadn't known them Gerald would have been at her side, hovering over her, mother-henning her, reminding her again and again of what was important and where her attention needed to be. Ever since the accident, though—ever since the nerve damage that had forced her to take an unwanted sabbatical from that life—Gerald had made himself scarce.

She didn't condemn him for steering clear of her. She suspected he felt guilty—he'd been driving the car the day of the accident. And as long as she didn't have a career for him to manage, he had no business playing the role of her manager. "All you have to do is keep me apprised," he'd said the last time she'd spoken to him, just before she'd moved up to Albright. "As soon as you're ready I'll get your career back in gear for you."

It was strange not having Gerald peering over her shoulder, warning her away from late nights and too-rich foods, advising her on her wardrobe and her friends. It was strange finding herself seated beside Alec Fontana on a bench by a lake without Gerald breathing down her neck, without his constant voice whispering in her ear: "Back off, Lauren. This guy lacks class. If you're looking for someone to squire you about town he isn't the one, and if you're looking for something more basic I'll set it up for you discreetly."

She wasn't looking for anything from Alec, either as a gentlemanly escort or as a sexual service. Gerald often made his slimy little offers to "set up something for her," and she invariably found them unworthy of a response. "Just so long as you don't fall in love," he would add, and she wouldn't respond to that, either. "Your heart belongs to your career. Sex has its place, I won't deny that. If that's what you want I'll take care of it. But *love,* Lauren . . . that's too important. That's something you've got to save for your music."

Why was she even thinking about sex and love? Alec Fontana was her neighbor, and he would lend her a copy of his novel, and there was really nothing more to it than that. His long legs and blunt-tipped fingers, his tawny hair and piercing eyes and dangerous smile— none of it had anything to do with her in any but the most superficial way. She was going to teach at Albright College for a year, and continue her therapy, and maintain a good attitude as Dr. Hayes insisted she must, and next June this would all be a memory.

"Thank you, Alec," she said with a smile. "I would love to borrow your book."

CHAPTER FOUR

WHEN HE CAME downstairs, he was carrying two chilled bottles of beer and a copy of *Street Talk*. That Lauren didn't own his book didn't bother him one way or the other, but when she'd told him she had no beer in her apartment he realized that drastic action was called for. One sip of the wine punch Mags had been serving at her presidential wingding had left a metallic taste in his mouth; he could think of nothing better than an icy beer to wash it away.

Lauren had invited him to have dinner with her. "I'll stir-fry some chicken and vegetables," she'd said, making him even more positive he'd need a beer. Stir-fry wasn't his idea of real food. He'd suggested they go out for dinner, but she'd said that since he was her new neighbor she wanted him to be her guest for a home-cooked meal.

Which would have been fine, if she'd been serious about home cooking. To Alec's way of thinking, anything that came out of a wok didn't qualify as cooked. Sure, his father had died of a heart attack, and Alec had dutifully given up whole milk for low-fat and reduced his salt consumption by half—and finally quit smoking, too. But just because his old man had passed away didn't mean Alec had to spend the rest of his life eating green things that crunched.

On the other hand, he conceded as he rang her doorbell, he could put up even with health food for the pleasure of gazing across the table at a face like Lauren Wyler's.

She answered the door carrying a wooden spatula and wearing an apron over her colorful dress. "Come in," she said with a shy smile.

"I brought some beer," he said unnecessarily—she could see the bottles in his hand.

Her smile expanding, she beckoned him through her tidy living room, past the piano and the shelves of teacups, past the round dining table draped with linen and adorned with a cut-crystal vase of yellow roses. Although her living room was directly below his, exactly the same size, with the same placement of windows and the same dull, serviceable furniture, her decor seemed much brighter than his. In addition to the roses, she had a trailing philodendron on a plant stand near one window and a purple-leafed coleus on her coffee table, which was otherwise devoid of clutter. Her rug looked thicker than his and bore the shadowy traces of a recent vacuuming. Her chairs and sofa were decorated with cheerful throw pillows. Her fireplace was swept—Alec's still held a residue of ashes from the previous winter—and she had replaced the standard-issue black fireplace screen with an ornamental brass one. Large framed posters from recent exhibits at New York's Museum of Modern Art hung on the walls.

If he was a sexist, he'd ascribe the room's agreeable ambience to the fact that its tenant was a woman. Trying to be open-minded, however, he decided to chalk it up to the fact that she was an artiste with a highly developed sense of aesthetics. She knew how to prettify her surroundings, how to turn an apartment into a home.

He followed her into her spotless kitchen, where a lidded pot steamed on a back burner of her stove and a formidable aluminum wok occupied a front burner. She balanced the spatula on the edge of the sink, dried her hands on her apron, and then turned to him. He started to hand her a beer, but she reached for the book instead. "Let me see your novel," she said, her lovely smile softening the blunt demand.

After passing her the book, he twisted off the caps of the two bottles and took a swig from one. She was nodding at the dust jacket of the novel, her smile widening. Then she flipped over the book to study the photograph of Alec on the back. "Of course," she murmured to herself.

Alec had never cared for the dust-jacket photo. When his publisher had requested a picture, he'd had Rosie's husband Mike shoot a roll of black-and-white film with his Nikon, and he'd sent the publisher what he considered the three best prints from the roll. To Alec's great irritation, the publisher had rejected all three and hired a professional photographer to shoot another batch. The publisher wanted a darker, more sinister portrait to grace the cover: Alec sporting a day's growth of beard, wearing his old denim jacket with the collar turned up, posing against the graffiti-marred wall of a crumbling tenement in Dorchester and staring insolently at the camera, his arms folded and a toothpick protruding from his lips.

Verisimilitude, he thought with a quiet snort as Lauren scrutinized the photograph.

She nodded again and placed the book carefully on the breakfast table. "You looked so familiar to me," she said, "but I didn't think I'd ever seen you here on Hancock Street or over at the campus. Where I'd seen you was on this book cover."

"Oh." But she hadn't known he was an author. How could she not know if she'd seen his picture on his book?

He handed her the beer he'd brought for her, and she accepted it with a quiet thank-you. "Would you like a glass?' she asked, noticing that he had already taken a few swallows straight from the bottle.

He shook his head, and she pulled a glass for herself from one of the cabinets. She poured in a couple of inches of beer, sipped it thoughtfully as if it were a vintage wine, and then busied herself selecting an ominous assortment of vegetables from her refrigerator. "Last spring my manager was reading your book," she answered his unvoiced question. "He works out of an office in his apartment, and whenever I was over there, I saw your book lying around. I guess your name never registered, but I did remember your picture from the back cover."

"I take it your manager didn't like the book," Alec said pleasantly, leaning against the counter and watching as she washed the vegetables in the sink.

"Oh, no—he loved it."

"Not enough to insist that you read it."

She glanced over her shoulder, as if to make sure Alec wasn't offended by her manager's refusal to recommend the book. Her smile became pensive. "He told me I wouldn't like it," she said, pulling a knife from a drawer and lining up several stalks of celery on a cutting board. "Just like you, Alec—he thought it was too violent for a delicate little lady like me." She proceeded to hack at the vegetables with a determined lack of delicacy.

Alec watched the brisk motions of her right hand wielding the knife. She clamped the wooden handle tightly between her thumb and her index and middle fingers; her ring finger and pinkie remained curled snugly into her palm. It was an odd way to hold a knife, he thought. Maybe professional pianists held knives differently than just plain folks. Or maybe she was so mad about his having jumped to the wrong conclusion regarding her taste in fiction that she had to hold the knife strangely to keep from plunging it into his chest.

Now there was a violent thought. "Are you a delicate little lady?" he asked.

"I'm not as delicate as I look."

Even with her back to him, she looked damned delicate. She had a slender build, and her pale complexion implied that she spent little time exposed to the elements. Perhaps if she cut her hair into a short, chic style she'd look more sophisticated. But Alec thought the long black cascade down her back was glorious.

"Is there anything I can do to help?" he asked, eager to defuse the undercurrent of anger he discerned in her.

His offer worked; she peered over her shoulder and sent him a winsome smile. "No, thanks. Just keep me company."

She returned to the refrigerator and pulled out a package of chicken fillets. From another cabinet she removed a bottle of soy sauce and a bottle of sherry. Alec ran a mental inventory of the junk food he had upstairs. He estimated that by approximately nine o'clock that night he was going to get walloped with hunger pangs.

The silence in the kitchen wasn't like the usual silence emanating from her apartment. This silence was warm and companionable. He couldn't imagine why he should feel warm toward Lauren Wyler. She wasn't like any of his women friends in Boston. Those women wore jeans and sneakers or short, smart dresses and high heels, not colorful peasant-style dresses with long, billowing skirts that somehow looked sexier because of what they hid rather than what they revealed.

Lauren looked sexy, no doubt about it. But lounging against a counter in her kitchen, Alec felt surprisingly relaxed. He knew hardly anything about her, except that she was famous and gifted and—according to his aunt—not in the market for a social life. That knowledge freed him, somehow. He didn't have to knock himself out trying to get close to her. If she was truly unreceptive to anything of a romantic nature, he didn't have to do more than be a good neighbor.

"So you came to Albright because your aunt is the president of the college?" Lauren asked as she adjusted the heat under the wok.

"That's right."

"And you're from Boston?"

"Right again."

"It's a nice city. Symphony Hall is marvelous."

"Have you played there?"

"A few times."

A few times. But of course. This was the world-famous pianist he was talking to. He wondered what she would say if he told her the closest he'd ever come to the Symphony Hall was meeting an informant outside the Christian Science Church across the street one evening a few years back. While they'd stood on the paved plaza outside the church building discussing the personnel of a newly formed crack dealership the informant happened to know a great deal about, they'd watched a battalion of smug-looking suburbanites in mink and cashmere climb out of Cadillacs and enter the concert hall. For all Alec knew, they might have been going to see Lauren Wyler perform.

"Well," he said with a touch of aggressiveness, "I grew up in Southie—"

"What?"

"South Boston. A working-class neighborhood. You wouldn't exactly pass through it on your way to Symphony Hall."

She poured some sherry and soy sauce into the wok, added the chicken, stirred it with the spatula, and then turned to Alec. "I grew up in a working-class neighborhood, too," she said, once again tempering her brusqueness with a smile. "I come from Allentown, Pennsylvania. A steel town."

"No kidding?" He understood that she was trying to combat his reverse snobbery, but far from feeling put in his place he was elated to think he and Lauren shared a similar background.

"No kidding. My father works in a refinery when he's not laid off, and when he is laid off my mother works as a typist through a temporary-employment service. So yes, Alec, I know more about life than just the fastest route to Symphony Hall." She rotated back to the stove, added the vegetables to the wok and gave them a stir. Opening a drawer, she counted out knives, forks and linen napkins. Then she took two dinner plates down from a shelf. "Would you mind setting the table? I've got to keep an eye on the vegetables so they don't get overcooked."

Maybe in Allentown, Pennsylvania, people were in the habit of using cloth napkins, he thought as he left the kitchen for the dining area in the living room. In his family, a formal dinner generally meant laying out the expensive paper napkins instead of the cheap ones, matching plates and no forks with crooked tines. If he and Lauren happened to share a similar background, Lauren had learned a few more Emily Post maneuvers than he had over the years.

Lauren carried out the food on a tray—the wok's contents in an attractive serving bowl, steamed rice in another bowl, sliced French bread in a basket and butter in a crockery butter dish. "It isn't much," she apologized, returning to the kitchen for their beers.

"It's fine," he said. "I'm in awe of people who can whip up a well-balanced meal in no time." He waited until she'd taken her chair before sitting, then added, "You know what I really miss about Boston? If you don't feel like fixing dinner you can take a walk and find at least five delicatessens on any given block."

"I miss that about Manhattan, too," she agreed. "More than that, I miss all the places that make home deliveries. You don't even have to put on your shoes—they deliver right to your apartment. There's only one pizza place in Albright that delivers, and their pizza is pretty mediocre."

"You live in Manhattan?"

"When I'm not in Albright," she said with a smile. "But I like it here, too. I like the slower pace. And the air is so clean."

He nodded and tasted a sliver of chicken. It wasn't awful.

"So, you grew up in South Boston," she said. "Do you live there now?"

"No, I live in the North End. Little Italy."

"You're Italian?"

"Half Italian, half Irish. I'm a mutt."

"You've obviously inherited the best of each," she observed.

He wasn't sure that was true—let alone obvious—but he basked in the compliment, anyway.

"I don't really know much about Boston—other than Symphony Hall," she confessed.

"It's an interesting city. The North End is great, very close-knit, very ethnic. It's got lots of narrow cobble-stone streets, street fairs, the best restaurants this side of Naples and some major Colonial landmarks. You know the Old North Church, where Paul Revere got the signal about whether the British were coming by land or by sea? It's about two blocks from my apartment."

Lauren's eyes sparkled. "That's exciting."

"Boston is like that—full of history."

"Being a policeman there must have been like work-ing as a museum guard," she said. She'd spent enough time staring at the back of his book's dust jacket to have read the brief author's bio—including the part about his experience as a city cop.

"Not quite," he corrected her. "Most of Boston is a typical urban mess. I was assigned to a precinct across town in an area called Mission Hill. They had their share of street crime, but it was an integrated residen-tial neighborhood, trying its best. I liked it. A lot of good people lived there."

"But you quit the force," she half asked, offering the breadbasket to him.

He helped himself to a slice and buttered it. "Writ-ing pays better," he said, resorting to his usual pat an-swer.

He watched as she buttered a slice of bread for herself. Once again the two outer fingers of her right hand remained tucked tightly into her palm as she manipulated the knife. When she lifted the bread to her lips and took a bite, her expression was dubious.

"You don't believe me?" he challenged.

She swallowed and smiled hesitantly. "Well...you just said you liked the work and the people. I would hate to think you gave up something you liked so much just because something else paid better."

Maybe he wasn't as adept at hiding the truth as he used to be. Or maybe Lauren was more perceptive than most people. "I had to quit," he told her. "I've got a bum leg." He rarely discussed his injuries with strangers, but she didn't really seem like a stranger to him. She was his neighbor, and at the moment he was eating dinner in her home. He felt comfortable enough to talk about it with her.

Lauren clicked her tongue. "That's terrible. How did you hurt it?"

"Line of duty," he said vaguely. It wasn't a pretty story, and as relaxed as he felt in Lauren's company, he wasn't about to go into the gruesome details over dinner. "To be a street cop, you need to be able to run fast and stand around without getting tired. My leg tends to give out on me. I can't keep up with the physical demands of the job anymore."

"Do you mean to tell me you got hurt on the job, and they fired you?" She bristled with indignation. "How could they do that? It's unfair!"

"I could have stayed on the force if I wanted to," he explained. "I was offered a desk job. They would have been happy if I stayed. It would have saved them money. I'm sure they'd rather pay me to push papers than fork over my disability pension and get no work out of me." He shrugged and ate some rice. "A desk job didn't interest me, though," he continued. "If I was going to be a cop I wanted to be out on the streets, doing things, dealing with the community."

"Nailing the bad guys," she guessed, smiling.

"I *did* deal with the community," he asserted. "The Boston police department has a reputation for being kind of overzealous at times, skirting a little too close to the edge. But a lot of us were trying to change that, trying to build a positive relationship with the people we served. I made it my business to get acquainted with as many teenagers as I could in Mission Hill, just to be there for them when they needed someone to talk to. I thought that kind of thing was important." He took a swig of beer, then lowered the bottle and reluctantly mirrored her smile. "That's not to say I didn't also get a kick out of nailing the bad guys."

"Perhaps you can nail the bad guys vicariously in your books," she suggested.

"If you're looking for a happy ending, don't read *Street Talk*," he warned. "I went for realism in that book—which, in the police biz, means most of the bad guys avoid getting nailed."

She sipped her drink, her eyes still on him, glittering enigmatically. "Your work must have been awfully dangerous."

His consciousness centered for a minute on his knee, the crunched cartilage and disfigured bone. From there it shifted upward, pausing to visit each scar along the way: the vertebrae, the ribs, the torn and mended lung, the shoulder, the skull. All his wounds and flaws, all the broken pieces stitched and pinned, all the souvenir aches and pains reminded him of precisely how dangerous his work had been and why he wasn't doing it anymore, why he could never do it again. "There were a few dangerous moments," he said impassively.

"Some people seem to enjoy danger," Lauren remarked. "My brother is like that—he loves taking risks. He recently traded in his motorcycle for a used Corvette, which he drives much too fast. He wants to take skydiving lessons, too, but his girlfriend won't let him. He thrives on that kind of high-risk activity. He and my father go hunting. They love tramping through the woods and firing their rifles." She wrinkled her nose, obviously repulsed.

Alec suppressed a frown. He was astounded to think that Lauren Wyler had a brother, let alone one who drove a muscle car and enjoyed hunting. That all seemed so normal, so regular. Alec wasn't into hunting—his police work had bred in him a strong aversion to guns—but he could understand the appeal of fast cars a hell of a lot more easily than he could understand the appeal of classical music. "Is your brother a musician?" he asked, hoping he didn't sound as surprised as he felt.

Lauren shook her head. "There was a time he wanted to be a rock and roll star, but..."

That, too, Alec could understand. Just about everyone in his generation had wanted to be a rock star at some point. "Was he any good?"

She shrugged. "I wouldn't know. I don't know anything about rock and roll."

This time he frowned openly. "What do you mean, you don't know anything rock and roll? How could you grow up in America and not know anything about rock and roll?"

She smiled diffidently and shrugged again. "That kind of music never caught my fancy. Besides, Gerald always warned me not to listen to it because it's usually played so loudly it can damage your eardrums."

"Gerald?" Her brother? he wondered. Her boyfriend?

"My manager. He's always been protective of me. His theory was that if you blast your ears with amplified music, after a while you dull the outer ranges of your hearing, and then you can't hear the nuances when you're playing the piano. And I *do* have sensitive hearing, so I don't suppose it's done me any harm to avoid rock music."

"Maybe not physically," Alec argued. "But spiritually, Lauren—rock music is a spiritual thing. It's got beat and pulse and power...." He realized he was waxing a bit too poetic, and he laughed at his overblown enthusiasm. "You need an education, Lauren. You're lucky you met me."

She laughed, too.

"So, given your brother's failure to become the next Elvis, is he envious of your success?"

Her laughter faded. "No," she answered too quickly. She lowered her gaze to her plate and toyed with her food for a moment. Then she lifted her eyes to Alec again, staring at him with a directness that contradicted her earlier evasiveness. "Maybe he is. I don't know. I never asked."

Once again Alec scowled in surprise. How could Lauren have turned into a superstar pianist and not figured out how her brother felt about it? Alec remembered with utter clarity the way his family had reacted to the publication of *Street Talk*. Mary-Beth had chewed him out for a full half hour on the filthy language in the book. Rosie had organized a series of autographing sessions at her local bookstore. Mary-Beth had telephoned everyone she knew to brag about him, then telephoned him and yelled at him for not doing his own bragging. Rosie had asked him for a loan to help finance the extension on her house. His mother had had an announcement printed in her church newsletter. Grandma Fontana had plastered the walls of the rec center at her retirement community with promotional posters from the publisher, and she'd circled Alec's last name with a red pen so everyone would realize he was related to her. Grandma Cudahy had critiqued him on the sex scenes. "If your grampa were alive today I would've made him read those parts. Maybe they would've given him some ideas."

Not every family was as open as his, though. Some families hid their resentments and their jealousies—and their pride. Some families simply didn't talk about things.

As if she could guess his thoughts, Lauren said, "I'm not terribly close to my family."

"That's too bad."

She put down her fork and lifted her glass. "I don't have a bad relationship with them," she explained. "I correspond with them. I try to see them when I can, and send money when they need it. I paid my brother's and sister's college expenses." She sipped her beer, then lowered her glass and mulled over her words. "It's just—my life has been so different from theirs since I left home. I love my family, and I'm incredibly grateful for all they've done for me, but we really..." She sighed. "We really don't speak the same language anymore."

That *was* too bad. Alec might not have achieved the sort of acclaim Lauren was accustomed to, but he still spoke the same language as his family. Professional success hadn't changed who he was inside or how he felt about his loved ones.

"But you grew up with them," he persisted, driven by curiosity to probe deeper into Lauren, to make sense of her. "It doesn't matter what you've done as an adult—you've got a shared history with your family."

Lauren gave him a poignant smile. "When I was fourteen," she said, "my parents sent me to New York City to study. I had outgrown every music teacher I'd worked with in Allentown. I was invited to audition for a teacher in Manhattan, and when she said she wanted to take me on, my parents shipped me off to New York."

"Just like that? Just so you could study with this teacher?"

"That sort of arrangement isn't so unusual," she said. "Lots of young people live with foster families in order to study with a special teacher or coach. Gymnasts and tennis champs, and musicians, too. If you can't find the teachers you need where you live, sometimes you have to pick up and move to where the teachers are."

"Maybe it's not that unusual," Alec conceded. "But still, to get sent away when you're just a kid . . ."

"I'm very grateful," she claimed with enough vehemence to arouse Alec's suspicions. "My family made a huge sacrifice to give me my chance. I owe them everything in the world."

Well, maybe, Alec conceded. Maybe if he had a child who was blessed with extraordinary talent, he would send the child away to receive the best training possible. It seemed like a pretty extreme option—for the child as well as the parents. But who was Alec to say it wasn't worth it? Here was Lauren, world-famous and prosperous, sending her parents money and putting her siblings through college. Maybe her family had viewed the whole thing as an investment—and it had paid off handsomely. Who was he to say they were wrong?

"How do they feel about your abandoning the spotlight and burying yourself in Albright?" he asked.

"I haven't abandoned performing," she said, her smile regaining its earlier glow. "I'm just taking a little time off."

"Why?"

She leaned back in her chair, regarding him speculatively. He noticed the way her smile emphasized her cheekbones and the luscious curve of her lower lip. "Believe it or not," she said, "I've got a bum hand."

His gaze zeroed in on the two bent fingers of her right hand. "Bad news," he muttered sympathetically.

"It's healing," she assured him.

"Don't tell me you did it in the line of duty. Piano playing can't be as hazardous as police work."

"It happened in an automobile accident," she said. "A minor one. There were four of us in the car, but I'm the only one who was injured, lucky me."

"What kind of injury?" He wasn't asking to be nosy. But as someone who'd spent a pretty intense portion of his recent past contending with the medical profession and the limitations of his own body, he tended to take an interest in the subject.

"I cracked a bone in my wrist. Unfortunately there was also some nerve damage. But I've been getting all sorts of therapy for it, and my neurologist said it's only a matter of time before my hand is back to normal."

"And in the meantime, you're teaching."

"Yes."

"And making mistakes when you play the piano."

Her cheeks colored slightly. "I'm sorry you've had to hear—"

"Hey, we already worked that out. I don't mind. If you want to play, go ahead. The mistakes don't bother me."

Still blushing, she examined his face as if looking for a hint that he was lying. "The mistakes bother *me,*" she admitted. "But if you're sure you don't mind, I'll try to pretend I don't mind, either."

He eyed her hand for a moment longer. Tracing the slope of his gaze, she saw what he was focusing on and dropped her hand to her lap. "Your fingers were straight when we shook hands at Mags's party," he remarked.

"If I concentrate I can get them to straighten out. They just don't stay straight, especially if I let my concentration slip."

"You don't have to hide them," he said. It occurred to him that he wasn't exercising tact—that, in fact, he hadn't been tactful with Lauren for some time. But she hadn't asked him to shut up, so he kept on pushing. "Your hand looks okay, Lauren. Why do you hide it?"

Again her cheeks darkened, and her eyes flashed with an emotion too stark for Alec to interpret. "It doesn't look okay to me," she answered with a touch of bitterness. She lifted her hand back onto the table and studied the bent fingers grimly. "When I look at my hand, Alec, what I see is a life on hold, a career sidetracked. I see how close I came to losing everything. Nobody else sees what I do."

"I'm sorry," he said belatedly. "It's none of my business."

"That's all right." Despite her apparent discomfort, she managed a crooked smile. "You've been through something worse with your leg, Alec. You *did* lose your career as a policeman. I've only been forced to take a little time off from my career. I have no right to complain."

He gave a benevolent wave of his hand. "Oh, please, complain all you want. I happen to think complaining is one of life's great pleasures."

She laughed, then glanced at his plate. He'd polished off his rice and bread and done a creditable job on the rest. "Would you like me to make some coffee?"

His gaze drifted automatically toward the teacup collection on the wall. "You must drink a lot of coffee," he observed.

She twisted in her chair to see what he was looking at. "Oh," she said with another laugh. "I drink my coffee in mugs. Those are teacups."

"I noticed." He rose and crossed the room to the shelves. She had at least thirty cups with matching saucers, most of them white, many decorated with patterned borders or distinctive imprints.

"They're from hotels that I've stayed at," she said, moving to his side.

"You filched them?"

"Of course not. I paid for them—except for a few, when the hotel management refused to accept any money from me." She lifted one. "This is one I didn't pay for. It's from the Shinjuku Prince Hotel in Tokyo."

Alec knew she was famous in her field, but he was impressed anyway. "You've been to Tokyo?"

"A couple of times. And this one—" she set down the first cup and lifted another "—is from Sydney, Australia."

"Wow."

She picked up a thicker-edged cup. "This one's from the Royal Garden, in London."

He stared at the cup. "England, huh? Have you ever been to Ireland?"

"Not yet. I'd like to perform there, though."

"I'd love to go there, not just to Dublin but to the whole countryside. Rumor has it I've got a bunch of distant Cudahy cousins living in County Cork."

She sighed and set the cup back in its place on the shelf. "When I was in London I wanted to see the countryside, too. I wanted to take a trip to Stonehenge. But there just wasn't time. I did three concerts at Albert Hall, and the next day we were off to Amsterdam for two concerts, and then Paris and then back to New York again."

"You mean, you went all the way to England and never got out of London?"

"I barely got out of the hotel. I ate, I practiced, I performed, I slept. International touring is grueling, Alec. It sounds exciting, but really it's a lot of hard work. Rewarding work," she hastened to add. "I can't wait to get back to it. But as far as being a tourist and seeing the sights, well, that will have to wait until I retire."

Alec surveyed the cups and steeled himself against a reflexive grimace. He'd had scant opportunity in his life to travel, but if he had he sure wouldn't have wasted the opportunity. Even if he'd had to remain within London's city limits, he wouldn't have restricted himself to the Royal Garden Hotel and Albert Hall. Lauren probably hadn't had much choice; her trips hadn't been geared toward recreation. But it struck Alec as sad that she could have been so many places and seen so little.

The cups depressed him. If she'd been to Tokyo, she should have brought back a silk kimono, not a cup. If she'd been to Amsterdam she should have brought back a pair of wooden shoes. Not a cup. Not a souvenir from a hotel dining room.

"So, now you're touring western Massachusetts," he said, forcing lightness into his tone. "Have you checked out the picturesque splendor of Springfield, yet?"

She grinned. "I've heard Springfield is a fairly ordinary city."

"I've heard it's got a few decent rock clubs," he countered. "It seems to me, Lauren, that for all your traveling you've lived a sheltered life. It may be too late for you to develop an appreciation of *real* music, but I think it's time you were exposed to it." At her stunned silence, he said, "Seriously, how about it? We could head down to the big town tomorrow night, take a look around, maybe find a decent rhythm and blues band playing at a club somewhere. It could be fun."

She regarded him solemnly for several seconds, then turned away and stuffed her right hand into the pocket of her skirt. Her gaze roamed the shelves lined with cups; her mind seemed to churn furiously. "Look, Alec...I..." She struggled with her words. "I'm kind of in limbo at the moment. Not just socially, but my entire life—it's very unsettled, and I've got to pull all my energies into, well, my work." She closed her eyes and took a deep breath. Then she opened her eyes again and attempted a faint smile. "I don't mean to be presumptuous, but...exactly what are you talking about?"

Whatever her agenda was, it clearly had no room in it for any sort of outing that might even superficially resemble a date. She actually appeared threatened by the prospect of spending a Saturday night in Springfield with him.

He tucked his thumb under her chin, trying not to respond to the satiny texture of her skin or the swanlike grace of her throat, and urged her to face him. As soon as her eyes aligned with his he dropped his hand. "We're talking about two neighbors enjoying some good music on a Saturday night," he said quietly. "Nothing more."

Her dark eyes searched his face, questioning.

"Nothing more," he repeated. She seemed so anxious for reassurance.

A mysterious smile hovered on her lips. "What about my ears? Will the music damage them?"

"I've been listening to rock music for more than twenty years and I'm not deaf yet."

"Well . . ." She wavered, apparently torn in half by what Alec thought was a reasonably simple proposition.

"Hey, you're teaching music at Albright College," he argued with a grin. "You owe it to your students to be informed."

"All right," she relented. "I'll go, for the sake of research. But if it hurts my ears . . ."

"You can blame me," he offered generously. He peered down into her face, trying to decipher the emotions that danced in her expressive eyes, excitement mingling with apprehension, curiosity mixing with an undefined panic. He couldn't guess how much her acceptance of his invitation had cost her—and he wouldn't dare to ask. In fact, he wouldn't dare to stick around in her apartment—not only because his presence would give her the chance to change her mind and say no to tomorrow, but because if he gazed into her magnificent brown eyes for a split second longer he might be unable to keep himself from kissing her.

"I'd better go," he murmured, taking a step backward. "The dinner was great. Thanks."

"Are you sure you don't want coffee?"

Did she know the effect she was having on him? Did she know that he was less aware of the scent of roses and cooking wine than the scent of her, the herbal fragrance of her hair, the whisper of lilac in her perfume? Did she have any inkling that standing next to her awakened in him an absurd longing to find out if her waist was as tiny as it looked, and that the fragile shape of her collarbone above the scooped neckline of her blouse issued an invitation he could scarcely resist?

If he left her apartment right now, he would probably recover, come to his senses, remember his aunt's warnings as well as Lauren's. If he left now they would both be safe.

"I'll take a rain check on the coffee," he said. "But thanks again for dinner. I'll see you tomorrow—seven-thirty."

He started for the door. Gracious hostess that she was, she accompanied him and held open the door. "Thank you for letting me borrow your book," she said.

He stared into her eyes for a tantalizing moment longer, then lowered his gaze to her lips. "I hope it doesn't give you nightmares," he murmured, knowing too well that, thanks to her beauty, her intelligence and her disturbingly wistful smile, he himself was going to suffer an exceptionally restless night.

CHAPTER FIVE

THE BOOK BEGAN with a murder. Not a particularly gruesome one, just an everyday run-of-the-mill killing, all the more shocking because of its prosaic depiction. By the time Lauren had reached the end of the first chapter, she realized, even more chillingly, that the opening murder wasn't the focus of the story. It was simply a scene, something to establish the world of *Street Talk*.

She adjusted the pillows behind her shoulders and sank comfortably into them, then smoothed the blanket over her lap. As soon as she'd finished cleaning up from dinner, she had taken an early shower, donned her nightgown and climbed into bed with Alec's book. It was much too early to retire for the night, but she didn't care. To her, bed was the perfect location for pleasure reading, and sleepwear the perfect attire.

She'd met authors before, at receptions and fundraisers and galas. She'd met authors who dressed like dandies, who carried log-size chips on their shoulders, who spoke in perfectly crafted sentences and well-shaped paragraphs as if they expected their cocktail chatter to be reviewed in *Publishers Weekly*. She'd met female authors who smoked too much, male authors who leered too much, authors of both sexes who drank as if they believed alcoholism was a requirement for the Pulitzer Prize.

But Alec Fontana was nothing like any author she'd ever met before. There was no pretense about him; he put on no airs. He acted as if he considered writing a novel far less important than helping inner-city teenagers in Boston.

It dawned on Lauren that perhaps she'd been hanging around with the wrong crowd. She wasn't exactly a social butterfly, but Gerald had always made it his business to select the affairs she would be seen at: fundraisers for noble causes, opening-night receptions, private parties certain to be covered in the right newspaper columns. She'd been alternately bored and benumbed by those parties, but she'd gamely attended them, convinced that her career hung in the balance—and along with her career, her brother's and sister's college expenses and maybe a new pickup truck for her father, if she could spare him a few thousand dollars. She'd gone to the parties, shown her face and engaged in the smallest of small talk.

And all the while there'd been a writer in Boston's North End, an ex-cop, a man who could smile so disarmingly that before she knew what had hit her, he had her agreeing to cruise the rock clubs of Springfield with him on Saturday night.

She recalled the first time she'd seen a copy of Alec's book, lying on a mahogany end table in the living room of Gerald's Fifth Avenue apartment last spring. She'd just had the cast removed from her wrist, but instead of rejoicing she was in a state of panic. Almost as soon as the plaster had come off, her fingers had started to cramp and contort. "It's a kind of dystrophy related to nerve damage," the orthopedist had explained.

She'd telephoned Gerald in hysteria. He had told Lauren not to worry, he would take care of everything.

She'd gone to his apartment to talk about insurance and neurologists and postponing her fall tour, and when he'd been on the phone in his office, his housekeeper had served Lauren a cup of coffee in the living room.

She'd sat on the stiff sofa, trying not to judge Gerald's fussy taste in decor too harshly, and sipped the coffee. Anxious for distraction, she'd picked up the novel lying on the table at her elbow. She'd flipped the book over.

The photograph had had an almost visceral impact on her. More than merely handsome, the author had exuded power and provocative boldness. Lauren had absorbed every detail: the macho bristle of beard darkening his rugged jaw, the rebellious length of his tawny hair, the snug fit of the shirt under his open jacket, the stubbornness of his folded arms, the toothpick poking from his mouth, and most of all his eyes, pale in the black-and-white photograph, set deep beneath slightly disheveled brows and fringed with short, dark lashes— eyes that seemed to leap out of the photo and snag her, sinking into her like barbed hooks and refusing to let go.

"I want to borrow this book" was the first thing she'd said to Gerald when he'd emerged from his office.

Compared to the rough-hewn appeal of the man on the book cover, Gerald had looked excessively refined. Small in stature and impeccably groomed, Gerald favored tailored suits and monogrammed shirts, stylish red-rimmed spectacles and Bally loafers. While the man in the photograph was merely unshaved, Gerald had a genuine beard, but it was neatly trimmed and groomed, as was his reddish-blond hair.

"I'm sorry you had to wait," he'd said as he'd swept out of his office, moving silently across the Aubusson rug to Lauren.

"Can I borrow this novel when you're done with it?"

"No," he'd said swiftly, removing the book from her lap and setting it aside. "You'd hate it."

She'd entertained the illogical thought that she couldn't possibly hate anything written by such a gorgeous man. "Why would I hate it?"

"It's very violent. It begins with a murder on page one, and it's all downhill from there."

"But you've read over half of it," she'd remarked, pointing at the bookmark protruding midway through the text. "If it's that awful, why are you reading it?"

Gerald had given her a patronizing smile. "Compulsion, I suppose. Trust me, Lauren—you'd hate it. There's enough blood in it to supply the Red Cross for a year. It's really not your kind of book."

Trust me, Lauren. She'd been trusting him with so much for so long, it had seemed natural to trust him with her leisure reading, as well. Gerald was right; she didn't like crime stories. No matter how good-looking the author was, she'd probably hate the book.

Especially then, when she'd been suffering so much stress concerning her hand. Gerald had soothed her, calmed her, told her about Dr. Hayes, who was reputed to be a brilliant neurologist and also happened to be a Chopin aficionado. "You'll relate well to him," Gerald had cheerfully predicted. He'd told her he had taken care of her concert bookings for the remainder of the year, and insurance would cover all her medical expenses, and she really had nothing to worry about.

"What am I supposed to do for income?" she'd asked, unpersuaded by his optimism. "I'm self-employed. I can't qualify for workmen's compensation."

"Lauren, you've got tons of money saved for situations like this. Remember that stock fund you invested in? You can draw an income from that."

True enough. But no matter how high she'd risen from her humble beginnings, she hadn't fully escaped their influence. Living off dividends wasn't the sort of thing done by the daughter of a steelworker from Allentown. Besides, she'd tapped into the stock fund a number of times in order to send money to her family. At this point, her income from the fund would barely cover her daily living expenses.

"I haven't worked for five months," she'd groaned. "I'm going crazy."

"Don't go crazy. Go home and relax. Read something uplifting—not this hard-core police trash," he'd said, gesturing toward the novel. "I'll set up an appointment for you with Dr. Hayes, and he'll get those fingers of yours back in working order. You just let me take care of everything."

She'd gone home, but she hadn't read "something uplifting." Instead she'd gotten on the phone with some of her friends and asked them if they knew where she might secure a temporary teaching position. She couldn't bear the thought of remaining idle. More than the income, she'd needed to keep busy to preserve her mental health.

Gerald had not been pleased when, two weeks later, she'd told him she'd accepted a one-year faculty position at Albright College. "You should have consulted me first," he'd scolded.

"You would have told me not to accept the job."

He'd fidgeted with his Christian Dior tie. "Not necessarily. I happen to think you'd be better off taking it easy."

"I've been taking it easy for too long," she'd argued. "I need to be working, Gerald. I can't just sit around doing nothing any longer. I can't stand feeling useless."

"You aren't useless. What did Dr. Hayes say? You had your first appointment with him, didn't you?"

Lauren had nodded. "He said he saw no reason to think I wouldn't get back most of what I lost. He measured my strength on some machines, and he gave me a bunch of exercises, and he gave me this pacemaker-type thing that sends electrical pulses into the muscles in my forearm. He also talked about an operation he'd had some success with. But that doesn't mean I can't teach for a year."

"All right, all right," Gerald had snapped. "You want to teach, go ahead and teach. It probably won't tarnish your image any. I just wish you'd trusted me with this."

"Of course I trust you," she'd insisted, although in retrospect she wondered whether that had been a completely honest statement. If she'd trusted him she would have checked with him before taking the teaching job at Albright.

She had trusted him the frigid day last January when he'd driven onto a patch of ice and skidded into the car in front of him, damaging his fender and her wrist. Ever since that fateful day, she'd found it increasingly harder to give him her full trust.

"Are you done with that book?" she'd asked. She'd spotted *Street Talk* on the credenza in Gerald's office, lying facedown, with the brooding countenance of the author staring up at Lauren.

"No. Not yet. And don't ask to borrow it, Lauren—it's a brutal novel. Addictive but brutal."

She'd considered strolling down Fifth Avenue to a bookstore and buying her own copy, if only to spite Gerald. Yet it had seemed silly to buy a book just because she'd developed a schoolgirl crush on the author's photograph. She'd had no desire to read a brutal novel.

On a Friday evening in early October, however, in the bedroom of a first-floor apartment on Hancock Street in Albright, Massachusetts, she did have that desire. She devoured Alec's book, swallowing hard at every grotesquery but refusing to turn away, refusing to put it down. She read it as the sky outside her window darkened from blue to black, as the alarm clock at her bedside ticked through the hours. She read about a hard-bitten street cop who'd gone crooked, and another hard-bitten street cop who faced the dilemma of whether to rat on his best buddy, and a female detective who was close to uncovering the first cop's venality and even closer to sleeping with the second cop. She read about how the second cop—the book's embattled hero—wound up seducing the detective one night to keep her from shadowing his friend.

It was after eleven o'clock when Lauren reached that passage. She was tired, she ought to call it a night—but she kept on reading, not only because the story was addictive, as Gerald had warned, but because she wanted to find out what sort of seduction scene Alec Fontana would write.

It wasn't soft and dreamy like the love scenes in the historical romances she usually read. Alec used no eu-

phemisms, no gentle adjectives. The hero and heroine
got tangled up in the sheets and each other, sweating
and groping and fighting for dominance. Lauren's only
sexual experiences—with Bryan, back at Juilliard—had
been nothing like the heated, steamy encounter in Alec's
book.

A dark tremor spun through her flesh as she read. She
swallowed again, this time not to suppress her queasi-
ness over the book's violence but to stifle a sigh as the
hero and heroine thrashed about, groaning and gasping and climaxing all over the place. Sex wasn't really
like that, she was sure. Sex was quiet and civilized and
pleasant. At least that was the way it had been with
Bryan.

With Alec, though . . . it was bound to be different.

Wait a minute. This wasn't about Alec; it was about
a fictitious character named Jack Fallowes. He was
burly and muscular, not lean and lanky. He had black
hair, not a sandy shade between light brown and dark
blond, and he had blue, not hazel, eyes. He was pure
Irish, not a "mutt," and he believed in intimidating
neighborhood youths, not communicating with them.
He drank hard liquor, not beer, and in his free time he
listened to jazz, not rock music.

It didn't matter how many times Lauren told herself
that Jack Fallowes was a fictional creation. When she
reread the section, and then read it a third time, she
pictured Alec as the hero, Alec tearing off his shirt and
stripping off his slacks, Alec overpowering and being
overpowered by the woman he'd taken to bed. She pictured Alec, and her body trembled again, her muscles
tensing, her hips shifting uncomfortably, her toes curl-
ing.

She pictured Alec, and when at last she forced herself to put the book down and turn off the light, she found herself nearly as breathless and overheated as the characters she'd been reading about. Readjusting her pillows for sleep, she smiled wryly at the thought of how tepid her usual reading was going to seem after *Street Talk*.

"TELL ME THE TRUTH, NOW," he said, shooting her a quick glance and then directing his gaze back to the road. "You really haven't ever been to a rock club?"

"I really haven't," she swore with a laugh.

Shaking his head, Alec shifted gears and steered onto the highway ramp. Lauren didn't know much about sports cars, other than the fact that her brother still owed her eighteen hundred dollars on an interest-free loan she'd extended to him when he'd bought his Corvette. But she could feel the power in the engine of Alec's sleek silver coupe. He didn't have to rev the motor or leave skid marks on the pavement for her to understand the car's capabilities.

It was rather like Alec himself. Even when he was seated sedately in his leather bucket seat, maneuvering the steering wheel and the gear stick, she could sense his innate power, the dynamic force of his personality, restrained but scarcely tamed.

He was wearing a pair of formfitting black jeans, a white shirt and a denim jacket—she wondered if it was the same jacket he'd worn in the photograph on his book. Unlike the photograph, though, he was clean-shaved and toothpick-less, and his sneakers seemed unthreatening. Lauren tried to concentrate on them. If she didn't, she might get to thinking about his book and superimposing the character of Jack Fallowes on him, and then she might get to reminiscing about the way Jack Fallowes had performed in bed ... and that was definitely a dangerous thing to do.

"How old are you?" Alec asked. "Almost thirty?"

"Don't rub it in," she joked, dusting a speck of lint from her pleated wool slacks. She should have worn jeans, too, but Gerald had always impressed on her the importance of appearing properly attired in public. Jeans were for doing housework in. For even an informal night on the town, tailored trousers and an angora sweater were required.

"And you live in New York City. It seems to me," Alec remarked, his eyes twinkling with laughter, "that you must have to go out of your way to avoid rock and roll. I mean, it must take a major effort to remain so ignorant."

"I'm not ignorant," she retorted, although she accepted his needling good-naturedly. "You can't walk down a street in Manhattan without hearing the stuff blasting out of a boom-box or an open car window. I'm familiar with Bruce Springsteen, and the Beatles...."

"No kidding! I guess I don't have to check and see if you've got a pulse, then," he teased.

Her smiled faded. She knew his taunting was meant strictly in fun, but his comments touched a tender spot in her soul. She had lived an unusual life, burdened with restrictions other young people hadn't had to endure. She'd been amply rewarded for her sacrifices, but still... She'd been denied the chance to fall in love as girls like Emily Spaeth did, to dance the night away, to swoon and moon over the latest rock and roll stars. She'd never joined a fan club, or memorized the lyrics of a popular hit, or belted out songs in the shower and imagined herself dressed in a gold lamé jumpsuit, standing at the center of an arena stage with twenty-five thousand exurberant fans waving their hands at her and screaming for more.

Instead she'd dressed in black velvet and played Chopin and had twenty-five hundred decorous fans calling with polite enthusiasm for an encore. Had that been her own dream, though? Had her wildest fantasies been of taking Carnegie Hall by storm? She'd never actually thought about it before, and now that she *was* thinking about it she wasn't terribly pleased with the conclusion she kept reaching.

With a sigh, she stared out at the gray expanse of road before them, stretching south to Springfield. She hoped her spirits would improve before they got to wherever it was Alec was taking her.

"What do you do on dates?" he asked.

"I beg your pardon?"

"What do you do when you go on a date? Visit a museum?"

"You mean, as opposed to a rock and roll show?"

He glanced at her and nodded.

His question implied that tonight *wasn't* a date. Which was as it should be, she reminded herself. It didn't matter that Alec was handsome, raffishly charming, outlandishly sexy. She'd made it clear yesterday that she wasn't interested in dating him, and he was obviously willing to respect that decision. For all Lauren knew, he had no desire to date her, anyway.

"Actually, I don't date much," she confessed.

He shot her another look, this one incredulous. "Why not?"

"Too busy," she said automatically.

He clearly didn't believe her. "Come on, Lauren. I don't care how busy you are—a woman's got to get out and party sometimes."

"Does she?" Lauren smiled faintly. "Well, I do go out on dates on occasion—if you could call them that. Mostly I'll go to receptions or opening nights at the Met or something. The kind of party where you wear elegant clothes and stand around drinking ghastly wine punch."

"Yawn," Alec groaned. "I'll bet your boyfriends really enjoy that."

"I don't have—" She clamped her mouth shut.

Alec didn't have to look at her this time. "You don't have boyfriends?" he guessed, a hint of arrogance coloring his smile.

"It isn't that I haven't had the opportunity," she said, feeling the need to defend herself. "But when you're a concert pianist, you've got to invest all your emotion into your performance. You can't dissipate it on love."

"I wasn't talking about love. I was talking about boyfriends. And partying."

So why did it sound as if he were talking about sex? Why was Lauren suddenly visited with a memory of the scene she'd read in his book last night, a vision of naked, sweaty bodies, of intertwined limbs and passionate groans? Why did she feel even more defensive?

"Don't be insulted," Alec said, evidently detecting her discomfort. "All I'm saying is, you're one hell of a good-looking lady. I'd think you would have to fight men off."

"Am I going to have to fight you off?" she asked warily.

He sent her what was supposed to be an innocent smile. "Me? I thought you set out the limits very clearly last night. This trip is strictly educational."

Educational, she pondered. Alec could undoubtedly educate her on many subjects. Merely thinking about them made her blush.

"Whose theory is it that you have to put all your emotion into your playing?" he asked, his tone altered. He sounded nothing more than curious.

"Gerald's."

Alec frowned, trying to place the name. "Your agent?"

"My manager," she said. "He oversees a bit more of my life than an agent would."

Alec eyed her quizzically. "How much more?"

"Well . . . when I first left home and moved to New York City, he more or less took over where my foster family left off, acting in loco parentis. He made sure I practiced, entered the right competitions, auditioned for the right teachers. He made sure I kept in good health— believe it or not, piano playing can be quite taxing physically. He counseled me on my clothing. I knew absolutely nothing about how to dress when I first got to New York, but he showed me what sorts of clothing looked good on me and projected the right image. And then, when I got older, he also performed a lot of the more professional chores—organizing my concert schedules, negotiating my recording contracts, that sort of thing."

"He must be a very busy man."

"He's well paid for his services."

"And when he's not picking out your clothing and organizing your schedule, he's locking you away so potential boyfriends can't get at you."

"You make it sound silly."

"It *is* silly," Alec asserted, downshifting as he neared the highway exit. "Rapunzel, let down your hair. I'm here to rescue you."

"Save it for the crime victims of Boston," she muttered, trying without success to ignore the glint of mischief in his eyes. His low chuckle ignited an echoing chuckle inside her. It bubbled up and out, filling the car with her soft, lilting laughter.

He steered down the ramp and into the heart of Springfield. "Do you know where we're going?" Lauren asked as he cruised confidently to a traffic light.

"Yeah."

"You've been to this place before?"

"No, but I asked Mags to find out what was the best no-glitz joint in the area. She said there was a decent place right down...here," he said after reading the street sign at the intersection. He turned left and coasted past a restaurant and a few dark shops until he found the entry to a parking lot. After parking the car, he chivalrously circled it to help Lauren out.

"Is there anything you want to warn me about before we go in?" she asked, glancing toward the door that stood open at the bottom of a short concrete flight of stairs at the rear of the building.

He peered down at her, his eyes glittering like gemstones, emerald flecked with silver and gold. "Don't take your shoes off. If the band takes requests, don't ask them to play 'Moonlight Sonata.' And if anyone else asks you to dance, tell them you're with me."

"Yes, sir," she said with mock obedience. Through the open door emerged a cacophony of electric guitar twangs and human voices. The nightclub's interior appeared dark and crowded, and Lauren slipped her hand around Alec's elbow so she wouldn't lose him.

He escorted her across the potholed parking lot to the steps and down. A husky young man in stylishly tattered jeans sat on a stool by the door; Alec handed him ten dollars and he nodded them into the room.

It was indeed dark and loud, the air thick with amplified music and cigarette smoke. Alec deftly led Lauren through a forest of tables to the edge of a parquet dance floor dense with people. They skirted the dance area, then meandered through another grove of tables to a vacant one in a remote corner of the room. A dim candle flickered inside a tinted glass at the center of the small table. Alec helped Lauren into one of the wooden chairs, then moved around the table and sat facing her. He shrugged out of his jacket and draped it over the back of his chair.

The candle shed little light, but Alec's face was partially illuminated by the blue neon lights above the dance floor. The bluish glow threw his profile into high relief, emphasizing the sharp lines of his nose, jaw and brow. Before Lauren could speak, a waitress materialized out of the shadows.

"What would you like to drink?" Alec asked Lauren.

Even if she'd wanted wine, she wouldn't dare to ask for it. "A beer, I guess," she said, figuring that was an appropriate choice.

Alec asked the waitress to list the available brands before he ordered two Budweisers. "Another warning—if you get thirsty from dancing, don't chugalug the beer. I'll get you some water."

"Who said anything about dancing?" Lauren countered with a smile. "I thought we were just going to sit here and listen, and you were going to explain the finer points of this drum solo."

"Drum solos," Alec said definitively, "are for the birds. Let's wait till they get a little livelier and then we'll hit the floor."

"I'm not a very good dancer," Lauren demurred. She recalled dancing with her girlfriends back in Allentown during a few preteen pajama parties, but that had been so long ago, and they'd only been practicing.

"All you have to do to be a good dancer," Alec explained, "is relax and not worry about making a fool of yourself."

"You make it sound easy," Lauren mumbled.

He threw back his head and laughed. "Loosen up, Lauren. No one's going to complain if you miss a note here. This is supposed to be fun."

The waitress arrived with their drinks, and Lauren waited until she and Alec were alone again before she spoke. "Who taught you how to dance?"

"My sisters."

"How many sisters do you have?"

"Two, both older than me. They used to drag me into their bedroom and teach me the steps so I wouldn't bring shame upon the family at the school dances." He poured Lauren's beer into a glass for her, then poured his own. "I used to kick up a fuss, but secretly I was glad. I mean, who wants to look like a jerk at a school dance?"

Lauren sighed again. Once she'd moved to New York she'd never attended a school dance at all.

"Do you have any brothers?" she asked.

He shook his head. "I was really outnumbered, growing up. I'm even more outnumbered now that my father's passed away. I've got two widowed grandmothers, a widowed mother, and two sisters. At least my sisters are married, so I've got a couple of brothers-in-law.''

"You must feel right at home at Albright," Lauren commented with a smile. "You're used to being surrounded by women." As soon as the words slipped out she realized they could be taken more than one way. A man with Alec's striking good looks was undoubtedly used to being surrounded by women, countless adoring women who bore absolutely no resemblance to his two widowed grandmothers. She glanced toward the dance floor and sipped her beer, relieved that the room was dark enough to hide her blush.

The band embarked on a buoyant tune. "This one's for you," Alec said. "Pay attention to the words."

She strained to decipher the lyrics above the din of voices and the distorting buzz of the band's amplifiers. As best she could tell, the song made the claim that rock and roll was going to conquer classical music.

"Roll Over, Beethoven," Alec informed her. "By Chuck Berry. It's a classic."

"It has no melody."

"It doesn't need a melody."

"That's your opinion," Lauren argued, although when her gaze met Alec's she couldn't suppress her smile.

He motioned with his head toward the dance floor. "Come on. Let's give it a try."

She didn't want to humiliate herself by attempting to dance in front of witnesses. But the beat was catchy and inviting. Without realizing it, she'd been tapping her feet against the rung of her chair in time with the song. "Promise you won't laugh at me?" she asked as Alec circled the table to her.

"Promise." He closed his hand around hers, as if to prevent her from escaping, and tugged her toward the crowded square at the center of the room.

The music sounded louder there, and the light from the blue neon tubes above Alec glinted along the fair streaks in his hair. All around her people gyrated and bounced. More than a few of them seemed totally out of sync with the music; more than a few of them, she acknowledged, looked extremely foolish. Yet they appeared to be having fun.

Mustering her courage, Lauren decided to have fun, too. The heck with presenting the proper image; the heck with being seen with the right sort of man in the right sort of gathering. The heck with all of Gerald's rules and regulations. Right now, Lauren wasn't a concert pianist playing egghead music for the intelligentsia; she was a college teacher out on the town with an ex-cop in denim, and if she made a fool of herself, so be it. *Roll over, Beethoven,* she thought—and Chopin and Bach and Mendelssohn and Ravel and all the others.

The next song the band played also featured a fast, driving tempo. She moved her feet uncertainly, then glanced nervously at Alec. Instead of letting go of her, he clasped both her hands in his and began an easy, shuffling step. His smile heartened her, and she did her best to follow his moves.

"What's a mojo?" she asked, nearly shouting to be heard over the music. The lead singer, of whom she caught occasional glimpses through the crowd, was sweating profusely and moaning that his "mojo" wasn't working.

Alec chuckled and drew her closer so he wouldn't have to holler. "Sexual charm," he said.

"Oh." She immediately danced back a step.

Alec refused to let go of her. Sometimes he would drop one hand or the other from her—and then he'd slip his free hand around her waist or onto her shoulder. "The big thing rock music has over classical," he said, pulling her back to him, "is that rock music is about sex."

"Classical music is about love," she countered piously.

"Well, I guess it's a matter of opinion which is better," he said with a sly smile. He let her swing away, then drew her toward him again, unexpectedly launching her into a spin that left her dizzy.

She staggered a step and he caught her. "Why does it feel like my feet are sticking to the floor?" she asked once her equilibrium returned.

"Because they are. When beer dries it gets sticky, and I'm sure the equivalent of a keg has spilled onto this floor. That's why I told you to keep your shoes on."

She nodded, then braced herself as Alec set up to spin her again. This time she didn't lose her balance. "The room has gotten awfully warm, hasn't it?"

"It's crowded and you're dancing." He swung her around once more. "Do you want to sit and cool off?"

"No," she answered honestly. Her initial awkwardness faded as the band segued from one song into the next. More than feeling warm, she was feeling warmed-up, less inhibited and more accustomed to the music. She stopped worrying about how she looked and simply moved to the rhythm, moved with Alec. Later, when the band stopped playing, she would sit and have a drink and swab her damp cheeks with a handkerchief. Right now, when she was finally beginning to get the hang of it, was no time to stop.

Apparently aware of her growing confidence, Alec smiled. Unlike some of the other men on the dance floor, he didn't flail his arms or wag his head; he didn't show off. His motions had an unselfconscious grace to them, and throughout every dance he maintained physical contact with her. There was nothing particularly forward in the way he brushed his fingers over her shoulder or ran his hand across her back as he twirled her around. Rather, he seemed friendly and attentive, his motivation to keep track of her amid the seething swarm of dancers.

"Okay, boys and girls," the band's lead singer bellowed into the microphone. "Time to catch your breaths. We're gonna do a blues number now and bring it on down." The deep-pitched drum thumped out a slow pulse, a guitar whined, and all around Lauren the dancers began teaming up, fusing into pairs and rocking slowly to the music.

Lauren didn't resist when Alec drew her to himself. Like the other people on the dance floor, she was too tired to keep dancing so energetically, but she was enjoying herself too much to stop. Alec placed his left hand on her waist and folded his right hand around her left, leaving a narrow space between them as the singer began to wail about how he'd put a spell on someone.

"I needed this," Lauren confessed, grateful for the song's restful beat.

"So did I," Alec agreed, sliding his hand further around her waist and pulling her fractionally closer to himself. "That fast stuff can be murder on my leg."

"We can sit if you'd like." As soon as she spoke she admitted to herself that she truly didn't want to go back to the table. She wanted to stay right where she was, in the ever-tightening circle of Alec's arms, her head less than an inch from his shoulder and her right hand pinned between his chest and hers.

"Not a chance," he whispered, pulling her even closer. Through lowered lids she gazed at the harsh angle of his jaw and the strength of his neck. His skin smelled of soap and warmth; his palm felt smooth around her fingers. His other hand traveled the width of her waist in back, then centered on her spine, roaming up under her hair to the nape of her neck, brushing tantalizingly over the skin there and then descending to her waist again, and lower, to the flare of her hip.

Her legs felt weak as he pressed against her, so gradually, so subtly, she couldn't find it in her to object. Her feet became motionless, stuck in place not because of the spilled beer but because of Alec's uncanny ability to sap her of strength. He insinuated one of his knees between hers and flexed it in a way that brought her hips to his, moving in an instinctive rhythm, approaching and retreating and approaching again.

Heat pooled below her belly and her pulse fluttered wildly in her temples. *We're only dancing,* she told herself, knowing that it was a lie, that something much more was going on between her and Alec. Knowing she ought to stop it—and knowing she wouldn't. Knowing she didn't want to.

Sensing her acquiescence, he guided her right hand up onto his shoulder, then let go of it and brought his other hand to her back so he could hold her even more firmly to himself. A small protest formed on her lips, but it emerged as a gasp of mindless delight as he molded his hands to her hips and moved them languorously back and forth.

"My father always used to say dancing was the vertical sublimation of a horizontal desire," he murmured, his breath brushing over her cheek.

"I thought..." Her voice sounded foreign to her, low and thick. This dance felt much too good. Her head was swimming, her spine melting, her knees sliding against his again and again. She really had to say something before she lost control of the situation. "I thought this was just supposed to be an educational outing. I thought we came here to enjoy the music."

He didn't withdraw, didn't loosen his hold on her. "I'm enjoying it," he insisted, a laugh underlining his words. "Aren't you?"

Oh, yes—more than she should. More than was safe. "It's just, I'm not very experienced at this. Dancing, I mean," she hastened to add.

"If anyone should understand the importance of practice, it's you." He wedged his leg further between hers. Through the wool of her slacks and the denim of his jeans she could feel the sleek, tempered muscle of his thigh. A hot shiver racked her spine.

"This isn't exactly the same thing as keyboard drills," she argued weakly.

"If it was, I wouldn't be enjoying it so much."

An exasperated laugh escaped her. "Alec, we're neighbors."

"And you're in limbo, and you want to put your energies into your work," he added in a calm recitation. "I heard what you said last night. That's why we're sticking with the vertical sublimation."

She was hardly assured. "I think we should go back to the table."

He bent his knee and used his hands to guide her hips down so she was straddling his thigh. The sensual motion of his leg against her caused her breath to catch, then emerge in a helpless moan. This was worse than reading the sex scene in Alec's novel. It was real, and it felt so good, so dangerously, devilishly good.

"Do you really want to?" he whispered, then touched his lips to the crown of her head.

Really want to what? Let him continue to arouse her this way? Let him make love to her? She could scarcely think, let alone comprehend what he was talking about.

He refreshed her memory. "Do you want to go back to the table?"

No. But the song was reaching an end, the singer growling his last mournful syllable into the smoky air. Lauren tried to convince herself she was relieved, but even as the drummer clattered to a halt Alec didn't loosen his hold on her, nor she on him. They simply stood where they were, their legs entwined, her breasts flattened against the muscled wall of his chest and her head nestled into the hollow at the base of his neck. Not until the band launched into a loud, sprightly song did Alec lift his hands from her hips and withdraw his leg from between hers. Reluctantly she raised her head and drew back.

He stiffened, twisted his head away and grabbed her shoulders. His fingers bit into her flesh and his body went strangely rigid, teetering slightly. He struggled to right himself by tightening his hands on her. A muscle twitched in his jaw and he closed his eyes.

Perplexed, she tried to shrug out of his bruising grip. "Alec?"

"Don't move," he mouthed, his face still averted and his fingers pinching. A quiet curse escaped him, and when he turned back to her she was shocked by his pallor, which was magnified by the atmospheric blue lights overhead. "Let's go," he said tautly.

He rotated her and hooked one arm around her shoulders, holding on to her with near desperation as she took a step toward the table. Then she realized one of his legs wasn't working. The leg he'd slid between hers, the leg he'd moved so sensually against her, the leg with which he'd turned a simple dance into an interlude of astonishing intimacy. His bum leg.

His knee was locked, his ankle limp and his foot dragging as he and Lauren moved laboriously back to their table. When they were within reach of it, he let go of her and pitched forward, grabbing the tabletop and swinging himself into his chair. Then he slumped forward, resting his head in his hands, his eyes once again closed, his breath ominously slow and steady.

"What can I do?" she asked.

"Do you know how to drive a manual transmission?"

"Yes."

"Okay." He took another deep, unnaturally steady breath. "Order me a double whiskey." Another breath. "In my jacket—toothpicks in the pocket."

"Right." She found a box of mint-flavored toothpicks, pulled one out and tapped his hand.

He opened his eyes and gazed up at her, his beautiful multicolored irises glassy with pain. Nodding his thanks, he took the toothpick and bit down on it.

She took her own seat, searched the room for their waitress, spotted her and waved. The waitress held up a finger, then finished taking an order at another able.

Lauren turned back to Alec. His eyes were closed again, his clenched teeth causing the tip of the toothpick to twitch.

She was overwhelmed by guilt. She should have insisted that they stop dancing as soon as the band had ended its set of fast songs. If she'd listened to her common sense this wouldn't have happened. If she hadn't succumbed to the bluesy music and the blue lights—and to the magic of Alec's embrace—he would have been fine.

"I'm sorry," she said.

His eyes fluttered open and a bittersweet smile crossed his lips. "I'm not," he whispered, then shut his eyes once more.

CHAPTER SIX

DAMN. Damn, damn, damn.

He hadn't had one of these episodes in nearly a year. He'd thought they were behind him for good. Sure, there were things he couldn't do, activities he knew would knock his jerry-built knee out of alignment, but dancing hadn't been on the list.

Then again, he and Lauren hadn't quite been dancing.

With one deep swallow he consumed half the double shot of rye whiskey the waitress had delivered. Alcohol was supposed to be a muscle relaxant—and if it didn't work on his muscles, maybe it would work on Pain Central in his brain. The throbbing in his knee was excruciating, his foot numb, his ankle nonfunctional—and his too alert mind was dutifully recording every twinge, every fiery convulsion.

Less than ten minutes ago another part of him had been on fire—definitely not the sort of fire he would want to extinguish with booze. In retrospect, it occurred to him that that erotic fire might have been far more hazardous than what he was experiencing now. But he had reveled in it. He'd wanted to feed it, stoke it, keep adding fuel until it blazed out of control.

So had Lauren.

Man, but she'd felt good. Despite her petite build, he'd sensed enormous strength in her, energy and yearning. The way her breasts had felt, pressed so firmly against him he could feel the hardness of her nipples through her sweater and his shirt, the way her hands had clung to his shoulders, and her breath had skimmed the underside of his jaw, and her legs had all but wrapped around him....

Even if his knee hadn't gone screwy on him he would have had a difficult time walking back to the table. Thank goodness for jeans, he thought, a trace of humor glimmering through the oppressive haze of pain that clouded his skull. Thick, sturdy, metal-and-denim flies had undoubtedly kept more than a few men from embarrassing themselves in public.

His amusement faded as another agonizing spasm jolted him. Maybe he ought to have agreed to undergo one more operation. But they'd cut and patched and rearranged his leg so many times already. They'd opened him up to pull out the splinters of bone, and then they'd opened him up again to reattach some tendons and fuse a prosthetic cap onto his thigh bone where it had been shattered, and then they'd opened him up again to remove the prosthetic cap when his body had rejected it. Then they'd attempted microsurgery to clear away some calcium chips, and then they'd discovered a keloid on what was left of his kneecap and broached the subject of further surgery.

He'd said no. Enough was enough. The ordeal had taught him something he prayed Lauren would never have to learn: that when doctors said, "We can make it as good as new," the odds were they couldn't. Alec's doctors had done a marvelous job repairing his body, considering the shape it had been in when he'd been wheeled into the emergency room at Deaconess Hospital. He didn't blame them for the fact that every now and then his knee dislocated and sent him to the brink of hell. He was eternally grateful to the medical experts who had labored so hard to put him back together. But he wasn't a guinea pig. Enough was enough.

The whiskey wasn't kicking in as fast as he would have liked. He took another drink and lowered the glass. Instead of smelling the liquor he smelled coffee. He forced his gaze across the table and saw Lauren stirring packet after packet of sugar into a mug.

She sipped, then lowered the mug and studied him. He tried to get a handle on what she was thinking, but her face gave nothing away. Her eyes were too dark, too inscrutable, and her lips, those full, lush, magnificent lips, were pursed in such a way that even in his semi-delirious state he wanted to kiss her.

"Is the drink helping?" she asked.

"Yeah," he lied, then reconsidered and decided it wasn't a lie, after all. The pain was beginning to lose its razor edge. He figured the liquor would dull it completely or it would knock him out cold—either outcome was all right with him. He drained his glass. "Are you sure you can drive my car?"

"Don't worry about it."

"You drive a Volvo."

"It's a standard transmission."

She said something more, but he missed it as a fresh wave of pain surged through him. It shot up his leg to his hip, up his spine to his brain, scrambling every lucid thought. Closing his eyes, he heard himself groan.

He felt her hands on his arms, guiding them into the sleeves of his jacket and then adjusting it on his shoulders. She lifted his arm around her neck, slipped her own arm around his ribs and levered him out of his chair. His consciousness regained some clarity as the most recent spasm waned, and they began their torturous journey toward the door.

He wanted to lighten the dismal mood. He wanted to reassure her. He wanted to tell her that her hair felt like silk on the exposed skin of his wrist, and that she vertically sublimated better than any other woman he'd ever danced with.

Speech seemed too much of an exertion, though, so he didn't bother. He stockpiled his energy for the concrete stairs he was going to have to scale outside the door to the parking lot. There were only three steps, but as he and Lauren hobbled to a halt in the doorway, Alec felt as if he were gearing up for an assault on Mount Everest.

"What do you want me to do?" Lauren asked.

Kiss me, he thought. *Anesthetize me with a kiss*.

"You need some help, miss?" asked the fellow who'd collected their cover charge when they'd arrived at the club. He rose from his stool. Without having to look at him, Alec could sense his burly size.

"He's not drunk," Lauren said in a touching display of discretion. "He has a bad leg, and he can't bend his knee."

The doorman sized Alec up. In a swift move, he took Lauren's place, arched a muscle-bound arm around Alec's back, hooked his beefy fingers around Alec's belt and lifted him off his feet. "Which car?" he asked once he'd heaved Alec up the steps.

Closing his eyes against a rush of vertigo, Alec felt the man half haul, half drag him across the lot. The doorman propped him up against the aerodynamic curve of the car's passenger side. Alec grabbed hold of the side mirror to keep himself from collapsing onto the ground when the doorman released him. Somewhere, either inches or miles behind him, he heard Lauren thank the man.

His dizziness transformed into nausea. He felt limp. Wretched. And suddenly aroused, as he felt her hand probing the depths of his pocket. "I need your keys," she explained.

A small, hoarse sigh escaped him. "Other pocket," he mumbled.

She dug into his hip pocket and his buttocks clenched, not in pain but in pleasure. Cripes. At another time, in another life, he would love having this woman's hands on his buttocks, on his naked skin, all over his body, searching, exploring, touching him wherever she wanted.

"Other pocket," he whispered brokenly. "In front."

She had apparently been avoiding the deep front pocket above his left leg. If he'd had the strength he would have explained that moving her hand along that thigh wasn't going to make a damned bit of difference in how awful it felt. As it was, when she inserted her hand he didn't feel it at all. All he felt was constant, grinding pain.

He heard a metallic jingle as she pulled out his key ring, and then the click of the door opening. "Adjust the seat," he mumbled. "There's a lever..."

She groped under the front of the seat for the lever, gave it a tug and slid the bucket seat as far back as it would go. Then she guided him down into the leather upholstery. Rigidly extended as it was, his leg didn't fit in the space beneath the dashboard. He had to angle his body and jam his deadened foot into the corner. The pressure on his knee was all but unbearable, and he tore loose with a few choice expletives.

Ignoring his foul language, she leaned across him to fasten his seat belt. Her delicate fragrance soothed him. She smelled like coffee and autumn, like mercy itself. "Thank you," he said as she straightened up. He was thanking her not only for buckling him in but for putting up with him, with this entire disaster.

Her eyes met his for an instant, and she smiled enigmatically. "You're welcome."

She closed his door, circled the car and got in on the driver's side. It would have taken too much effort to watch her as she took the controls of his beloved vehicle, so he only listened and hoped to heaven she wouldn't strip the gears.

The engine ignited smoothly. She took a minute to find the headlight switch, then released the parking brake and coasted slowly over the pitted asphalt to the street. He wondered whether she would be able to find her way back to the highway. He certainly wasn't in any condition to navigate for her.

She remembered the route. She drove cautiously, demanding little of the car and nothing of Alec. A few miles north of Springfield a fine mist began to form, and after a few fumbles she located the switch for the windshield wipers and turned them on. She obeyed the speed limit, remained in the right lane and kept the tachometer needle steady.

Not only was she gorgeous, he thought, but she could be trusted not to destroy his car. Not only that, but she had enough sense not to attempt a conversation. She remained blessedly silent, allowing him to conserve what little strength and sanity he had left. If she weren't in limbo, her life at a critical juncture and her dreams completely at odds with anything Alec might ever want in his life, he would probably fall in love with her.

Then again, he'd fallen in love with just about every nurse who had ministered to him during his hospital stays—old nurses, young ones, middle-aged married ones carrying twenty extra pounds on their hips, black nurses, white nurses, Asian and Hispanic nurses. He'd loved them all. Sex aside, the one thing men really wanted from women was to be taken care of—the way Lauren was taking care of him.

He closed his eyes and exhaled. The car purred; his knee raged; the whiskey entered his bloodstream with a fierce kick. His mind concentrated on the way Lauren had felt in his arms during their final dance, the way the warm center of her had rubbed against his thigh. The way she'd sighed and clutched at him and told him, probably without meaning to, how much she wanted him.

Maybe she was lucky his leg had gone out on him. If it hadn't, he might well have been driving the car right now, exceeding the speed limit, eating up the miles until they could get back to Hancock Street, to their building, to her bed.

And maybe he, too, was lucky his leg hurt so much. It kept him from seducing a woman he knew he ought to leave alone.

They reached the Albright exit and she steered unerringly through town, around the campus to Burke Street and then onto Hancock. Alec heard her downshifting, rolling to a halt along the grassy edge of the road, yanking up the parking brake and turning off the car. "Don't move," she ordered him as she climbed out of the car. "I'll help you."

He doubted he could have moved without her help, even if he'd wanted to. He was able to unlatch his seat belt, and then the interior light came on as she opened the door. Her hands were steady on him, easing his right leg out, reaching over his lap and trying to unwedge his left leg. Taking in a deep breath and gritting his teeth, he let her swing the leg around.

Before the pain could register fully he was out of the car, standing shakily and using Lauren as a crutch. They hobbled up the short path to the porch, and he stared at the two front doors. Behind his was a long flight of stairs.

Lauren seemed to share his thoughts. She lugged him up the porch steps and directly to her door. He didn't question her. He knew she wasn't inviting him into her home out of choice.

They entered the living room and she headed toward the couch. He broke from her and dropped onto the rug. The couch might be too soft, too lumpy. At least with the floor he knew he'd be level.

Lauren turned on a lamp and knelt beside him. "Are you comfortable?" she asked.

He smiled feebly. "Relatively speaking."

Returning his smile, she rose and gathered the loose cushions from the couch. Once she'd arranged a few of them under his head, she pulled off his jacket and draped it over the arm of a chair. "Should I take off your shoes?"

"No." He reached for her hand, clasping it just as another pulse of pain blazed up from his knee. When it began to ebb he let out his breath and relaxed his clasp. "Have you got anything to drink?"

She freed her hand from his and instinctively slid it into her pocket. "Coffee, tea, juice, milk, wine..."

"I've got some hard stuff upstairs." He started to reach for his keys, then remembered she'd taken them from him. He thought about their abrupt departure from the club, about her picking his pockets, about the whiskey he'd consumed there, her coffee, their beers—and another curse slipped out. "I forgot to pay for our drinks."

"Don't worry about it," she said. "I paid."

"Jeez. Some date."

"It wasn't supposed to be a date, remember? It was an educational trip."

"Let me pay you back." He lifted his hips to pull out his wallet, but Lauren pushed him back down.

"You seem to be recovering," she observed, rising to her feet. "Are you sure you want another drink?"

"I won't get drunk," he insisted.

She smiled down at him from what appeared to be a towering height. Her right hand was hidden, her left cupped around his keys. "Where do you keep your liquor?"

He told her and she left the room. He lay motionless on the floor, staring up at the ceiling and listening for her footsteps above him. He tried to imagine ascending the stairs himself. His leg did feel, if not exactly better, then marginally less horrendous. It was still stiff and aching, though, his foot still numb, dragging on his ankle like a free weight.

He reached for his wallet and pulled out a ten-dollar bill and a few singles, which he left on the coffee table. Steadying himself with a deep breath, he shoved his wallet back into his hip pocket. Date or no date, he'd be damned if he was going to let Lauren pay for their drinks.

A few minutes later he heard the sound of her front door opening and closing, and then footsteps as she headed directly into the kitchen. He heard a cabinet open and close. More footsteps, muffled as she stepped from the hardwood floor of the hall to the plush rug of the living room. When she reached him she knelt down again, poured some whiskey into a glass and handed it to him as he raised himself into a semi-sitting position.

He took a sip, then lowered the glass. She stared at him with a mixture of concern and disapproval.

"You think I'm drinking too much," he guessed.

"I didn't say that." Lounging next to him, propping herself up with a couple of the cushions, she removed her loafers and wiggled her stockinged toes.

"I tried a variety of painkillers," he told her. "Morphine is addictive, so I didn't want to get messed up with that class of drugs. I used one painkiller that had no effect. The one after that worked, but it did weird things to my head. I hallucinated a door where there wasn't one, and wound up walking into a bookshelf and knocking a bunch of my mother's knickknacks onto the floor. My doctor finally told me if the pain got bad I should have a few stiff drinks."

"Some doctor," Lauren reproached, though she was grinning. Her smile faded as she peered into his face. "You must have been hurt dreadfully."

"On the dance floor?"

She shook her head. "When you injured your leg. You told me it happened in the line of duty, Alec, and I keep thinking..." She glanced away, her gaze alighting on the flowery pattern of the rug. "I keep thinking about what being a policeman meant to you, and how you felt about your job, and I wonder how you could have liked such a job if it caused you so much suffering.''

He took another sip of his drink. It warmed his throat and chest and spread downward, eroding the pain, blunting it. ''The job didn't do this to me,'' he said, setting his glass down on the coffee table. ''One jerk did it—with a little help from his friends.''

Lauren continued to scrutinize the rug's pattern, tracing a vining brown stem from one faded flower to another. ''But he ended your career,'' she persisted, her voice low and thoughtful. ''One day you were a cop and the next day you weren't. Just like that.'' She lifted her eyes to his face. ''I don't think I could survive something like that.''

You might have to, Alec thought, although he didn't say it. Maybe things would go better for Lauren. Just because he'd been forced to rearrange his entire professional life didn't mean she wouldn't be lucky enough to be able to pick up where she'd left off, to resume her journey down the same glorious path she'd set out on so many years ago.

Then again, maybe her hand wouldn't heal—and maybe that would be lucky, too. When Alec gazed back at the convoluted course his life had taken, he could see major dips and rises, major peaks and valleys, disappointments, fear and anguish—but an immeasurable quantity of good fortune, as well. He hadn't just survived. He'd found something else, something many people would consider an improvement over what he'd lost.

''Tell me about it,'' Lauren implored him, her eyes as dark as the night sky.

''About my leg?''

She nodded solemnly.

He sighed. He didn't like to talk about it, but with Lauren he didn't mind. He wanted her to know. He wanted to offer her whatever he could, so she could draw strength from his experience when it was her turn to face the truth.

"We were trying to break up a fencing operation," he told her. "There'd been a rash of thefts in the neighborhood, private homes and shops. So we went undercover, rented a storefront and put out word that folks could bring their hot items to us for cash. My backup and I took turns, one of us out front serving the clientele and the other in a back room running a hidden camera and getting everything on videotape."

He took a final sip of his drink and rearranged the pillows under his shoulders so he could see Lauren better. She watched him, her left hand resting on her knee, curiosity mixing with dread in her expression.

"We were doing well," he continued. "Putting together an impressive video library and beginning to round up the suspects. And then one day, when I was out front, this guy came in and recognized me as a cop. I'd arrested his brother a year earlier on an assault charge—he'd broken his girlfriend's jaw. Sometimes those domestic assault cases slip through the cracks because the woman won't testify, but I convinced her to and we nailed the creep. And his brother didn't like it. So a year later—what's the old Bogart line?—of all the pawn shops in Mission Hill, he had to walk into mine."

"And recognize you," Lauren murmured sadly.

"Too bad I didn't recognize him. If I did I wouldn't have left the shop with him. But he gave me this song and dance about how he had a whole load of VCRs in the back of his van, which was parked just up the street. He wanted me to help him carry the VCRs back to the shop. It sounded plausible, and when I looked out the door I could see the van halfway down the block, with the back doors open and two of his buddies sitting there, waving at me. So I said sure and left the shop with him.''

Lauren shuddered, as if she knew what was coming next.

"When we reached the van," he continued, "the guy told his buddies I was the cop who'd busted his brother and they were going to bust me. I had a gun on me, but before I could get it one of them whacked me on the head with something hard, some sort of metal pipe.'' He sent her a crooked smile. "I woke up three days later in intensive care, with a lot to tubes sticking out of me."

"Oh, God..."

"Hey, it wasn't so bad," he assured her. "I *did* wake up. And to tell you the truth, once I began to figure out what they'd done to me I was just as glad I'd been unconscious through it all.''

"What had they done?"

"Besides totalling my knee? They broke my other leg down along the shin. That was a simple fracture. And they broke two vertebrae and three ribs—one of which punctured my lung—and bruised a bunch of other organs and cracked my skull. Oh, and they stole my watch and my gun and the ten bucks they found in my pocket, and they dumped me in an alley and left me for dead.''

"Alec..." Her voice trembled; she looked grief-stricken.

He hadn't told her about the incident to upset or depress her. He'd told her to reassure her that if he could triumph over such a ghastly collection of wounds she could triumph over her hand injury. He'd told her so she would understand that surviving was everything, that as long as you were alive there were possibilities.

But she didn't seem to be getting that message. Her eyes filled with tears as she scanned his healthy-looking body stretched out on her living room floor.

"You know what the worst part was?" he asked, desperate to cheer her up.

"That you couldn't be a policeman anymore?"

"Those damned doctors wouldn't give me a cigarette. There I was, immobile, hooked up to a dozen monitors and getting poked and squeezed and cut and stitched. I could have died any minute—and they were nagging me about how bad smoking was for my health."

To his great relief, she permitted herself a tenuous smile. "With a punctured lung, smoking would not have been a great idea." Her gaze trailed along his body again, as potent as a touch. She paused at his bad leg, where the pain had mellowed into a deep ache, and then drew her attention back to his face. Her smile was gone. "I'm glad you quit smoking, Alec. It's a terrible way to have to quit, but I'm glad you did."

"Why?"

"Because you're a good man," she declared. "After everything you've been through, it would be a shame for you to wind up with some smoker's disease."

"I haven't been through that much," he said modestly. "I didn't even have any brain damage." Her eyes glowed with such abundant admiration that it made him uncomfortable. "Lauren, cops have died on the job. I was lucky."

"You were more than lucky. You were strong and brave—"

"I was stupid. I shouldn't have left the storefront."

She pressed her fingertips against his lips to silence him. "I'm talking about afterward, Alec. When you woke up in that hospital room and realized you were going to have to invent a whole new life for yourself, a whole new identity. If I thought for one minute that I would have to stop playing the piano and do something else with the rest of my life... I would go crazy. I wouldn't be able to adapt. You've got so much—" she groped for the right word "—courage, to keep going forward, to refuse to let it defeat you or make you bitter. I know, this is a really corny speech...." Her cheeks colored, and she lifted her hand from his mouth.

He grasped it before she could pull it completely away. Her wrist was so narrow his fingers closed easily around it. "I like corny speeches," he murmured, daring to draw her hand back to his lips. Her fingers felt seductive on his mouth, turning him on with their gentle pressure. He kissed the beautifully tapered fingertips, causing her eyes to widen in surprise. "Give me your other hand," he demanded quietly.

Refusing to tear her gaze from him, she pulled her right hand from her pocket and presented it to him.

He circled that wrist with his other hand and kissed her knuckles. With his thumb he straightened out the two curled outer fingers and guided them to his lips. He nibbled, moving his mouth lightly over the smooth oval nails, over the top joints and the soft pads of flesh. He continued to watch Lauren, to wait for her to shut him down, to slap his cheek or make another, less corny speech about how she was in limbo and they were neighbors and this wasn't a date.

Her eyes grew infinitely darker, luminous with a desire that superceded fear. As if of their volition, her fingers came to life, playing against the inside of his lip and allowing his tongue to lure them between his teeth.

A low groan filled his throat as arousal shot through him. He wanted to taste more of her—her lips, her throat, her body. He wanted to devour her.

"Alec . . ." She issued a quivering sigh.

"Tell me to stop," he whispered, his eyes locked with hers as she drew her hand away. Without breaking her gaze from him, without saying a word, she stroked her fingers along the hard ridge of his jaw and down to his neck, to his shoulder. She didn't say a word.

He looped his arms around her and pulled her down. He sensed no resistance in her as his lips moved against hers. They were as soft as they looked, as pliant and welcoming as he could have dreamed. He sipped and savored, nipped and tasted, restraining himself when every nerve in his body clamored for him to take her, to invade and possess her, to conquer first her mouth and then the rest of her.

Her hair spilled over his palm and through his fingers as he cupped his hand at the back of her head, seeking the warm, sensitive skin at the nape of her neck. His caress provoked a gasp from her, and the parting of her lips undermined his self-control. He slid his tongue past the dainty ridge of her teeth—deep, teasing, testing, reveling in pleasure when her tongue engaged his in erotic play.

He urged her higher onto him, arranging her carefully so she wouldn't bump his bad leg. The angle of her upper body enabled him to stroke her shoulders and back, following her spine down to her waist. He slipped his hands under the edge of her sweater and let them roam across her smooth warm skin.

He heard her gasp again—whether in objection or delight he couldn't tell. "Tell me to stop," he repeated as his hands traveled upward, discovering the delicate curve of her rib cage, the strip of lacy fabric where her bra spanned her back, the clasp at its center. He fingered the fastening and waited for her to speak.

She arched against him, her body fluid and graceful, her hair tumbling down around her face and his, her hands trembling on his shoulders as she braced herself above him. She peered down at him, and he saw the dewy moisture his kisses had left on her lips, the astonishment and panic they'd left in her eyes. She opened her mouth and sighed, sinking onto him, unable to refuse the pleasure he offered.

He plucked open her bra, then drew his hands around her sides and forward to circle the fullness of her breasts. She murmured something unintelligible; he swallowed her words with a deep kiss. His thumbs found her nipples and she moaned again. "Alec..."

Her voice faded as he rubbed her nipples, chafed them, felt them tighten into stiff points. He kissed her chin, the underside of her jaw. He wanted to yank her sweater off, to press his mouth to her sweet, hot flesh, to swirl his tongue over the rosy tips. He wanted her naked, around him, taking him into her, and the thought of how good it would be increased the tension in his groin to an agonizing level.

He wriggled one hand out from under her sweater and clamped it over her hip, attempting to pull her fully onto him.

"No," she murmured, burrowing her head into the crook of his neck. "I don't want to hurt you."

He almost argued that the only way she could hurt him was to stop now, when he was so hard and hungry.

But he understood she was talking about his leg. It still ached, and as insanely as he wanted Lauren, he knew his leg would hurt a lot worse if he placed any real strain on it.

He could please her, though. Without moving his leg, he could still accomplish a lot. He ran his hand from her hip to her thigh and forward. "Let me," he murmured, stroking between her legs and smiling as her body arched again, as another helpless moan escaped her. Shifting onto his side, gnashing his teeth as his knee sent a furious protest up his spinal cord, he eased her onto her back. He lifted his hand to the button on the waistband of her slacks and bent to kiss her. "Let me do this for you," he implored.

"No." She covered his hand with hers and held it immobile.

Their eyes met. She looked so vulnerable all of a sudden, so worried. "I won't hurt my leg," he assured her. "I'll just—" His voice was raw, his pulse racing. "I'll make it good for you, Lauren, just like this."

"Alec . . ." She struggled with her breath, and he noticed the rise and fall of her breasts beneath her sweater. It took all his willpower to hear her out before he tore off her clothes and kissed her senseless.

More than vulnerable, more than worried, she looked frightened. "I'm not going to hurt you," he promised.

"I told you . . . my life is too unsettled right now."

"That's all right—"

"It's not all right." She sounded sad, and sublimely frustrated. "Please, Alec . . . I can't get involved with you."

Involved? Who said anything about getting involved? He wanted to make love to her, that was all. He wanted to touch and taste and stroke her until she climaxed. And then afterward he wanted to hold her and hug her and find his own fulfillment in knowing he'd satisfied her. His leg might have put him out of commission, but he could take enormous pleasure in giving pleasure.

Involvement had nothing to do with anything.

To her it did, though. To her this was more complicated than a friendly encounter between neighbors. For Alec to go any further would imply commitments and emotions and all sorts of ponderous things, as she saw it.

He should have known better. Lauren wasn't only unsettled in her life; she was also grossly inexperienced. Just that evening she'd told him she'd had very few boyfriends, and the dates she described to him sounded more like business appointments—and boring ones at that. He'd talked about partying and she'd talked about love. It was probably nothing short of a miracle that she'd spent the evening with Alec without first getting written permission from her manager.

He gazed down at her, at her lovely face, her creamy skin, her heart-stopping eyes. She was so beautiful, so tantalizing—and so unlike any other woman he'd ever known. The difference between Alec and Lauren was more than just their agendas. It was their perspectives.

Exhaling, he removed his hand from her and dropped back onto the cushion beneath his head. He tactfully looked away as she fumbled under her sweater to refasten her bra. "I'm sorry," she mumbled.

"Don't be."

"I should have stopped you right away. It was my fault."

He gathered her hand in his and pulled on it, forcing her to look at him. "This is a no-fault situation," he said with a rueful smile. "We're two adults who happen to be attracted to each other, that's all." That sounded like an understatement to him, but it would have to do. To tell her the truth—that his attraction to her was something on the order of nuclear fusion, and just as explosive—would only alarm her. "So we got a little carried away," he continued with a mildness he didn't quite feel. "It isn't a crime."

"You don't hate me?" she asked, then bit her lower lip and searched his face nervously.

Lord. If she kept worrying her lip with her teeth like that, and sending him such soulful looks, he might wind up doing something she'd definitely hate him for—or love him for. He didn't want her love any more than he wanted her hate. Love meant involvement—and Alec agreed wholeheartedly with her that involvement was out of the question.

"I don't hate you," he swore, pulling himself up to sit. Shaking his head, he allowed himself a wry laugh. He ought to have been frustrated by her innocence, but he found it appealing in an archaic sort of way. "You're one of a kind, Lauren Wyler."

She averted her gaze, and when he slid his hand under her chin and tipped her face up, he realized that the unnatural sheen in her eyes was caused by tears. "I'm not handling this well," she lamented.

"Don't be so hard on yourself."

"Name one thing I did right this evening."

You kissed me, he almost said. *You responded. You held me and moved against me—and moved me.*

"You drove my car really well," he said, giving her what he hoped was a comforting smile.

He scanned the room, taking in the yellow roses on her table, the plants, the framed wall prints and the brass fireplace screen. For some reason, he wanted to stay right there in her apartment, even if they never kissed again, even if his leg stopped hurting and Lauren stopped looking at him with such undisguised longing. He didn't want to leave.

But he had to. "I think I can manage the stairs," he said, propping himself with one hand on the coffee table and one on the arm of the easy chair.

Lauren swiftly rose to assist him, positioning herself in the bend of his arm so he could transfer his weight from the coffee table to her. "I'll walk you up," she offered.

He permitted himself another ironic smile at her failure to insist that he stay downstairs. She seemed to know as well as he did that as long as they remained in the same room they were likely to lose control again, to give in to their attraction.

"I think I can make it up the stairs myself," he said. He put on his jacket so he wouldn't have to carry it, then slipped his key ring around his index finger. He lifted the bottle of whiskey from her coffee table, released her shoulders, waited until he was certain he had his balance, and attempted a lurching step toward the door. When his leg didn't collapse under him, he took another, more confident step.

"Are you sure you don't need any help?"

"Positive." They paused at the door, Lauren gazing up at him, her expression troubled. "I had a good time tonight," he said.

"You must be a masochist," she joked.

He grinned, reassured by her humor. "Promise me something, Lauren."

"What?"

"I want you to play. The piano, I mean," he said, gesturing with the bottle toward the console piano against the wall. "I want you to practice. I don't care how many mistakes you make."

She bit her lip again, momentarily reigniting his hunger for her. "I'd hate for you to have to hear," she said.

"The silence is worse. Please, Lauren—just play. You're not doing anyone any good by not playing." When she didn't immediately acquiesce, he said, "If not for yourself, for me."

"Okay."

"Thank you." He reached for the doorknob and pulled her front door open.

"Alec?" she called out as he stepped cautiously onto the porch. He gripped the door frame and raised his eyes to hers. "Can I keep your book until I'm done with it?"

"You can keep it forever," he said, feeling the dark power of her gaze deep inside him, not only in his muscles and nerves but somewhere deeper, some undefined place in his soul. What he felt was more than simple arousal. If he analyzed it, he might suspect it had something to do with involvement.

But that was too scary a thought, so he only smiled, nodded and limped across the porch to his own door, then embarked on what was to be an arduous, extremely sobering hike up the stairs.

CHAPTER SEVEN

SHE WOULD NEVER SEE him again.

Well, of course she would see him. She would bump into him on the porch or at the grassy edge of the street, where his snazzy sports car was parked behind her clunky old Volvo. Or she would come upon him at some gathering on campus, at one of his aunt's faculty luncheons or some such thing. They would exchange pleasantries, make observations about the weather and wish each other a good day.

But she would never *see* him, not the way she'd seen him that night. Not in a way that would leave her lying restlessly in her bed for hour after moonlit hour, her body smoldering and her eyes staring up into the darkness, knowing that he was directly above her in his bed. She wondered if he slept curled up or sprawled out, his limbs hanging over the edge of the mattress. She wondered if he slept in pajamas or underwear—or in the nude. She wondered whether right now he was awake like her, punching his pillow and kicking the sheets, his body tense with unspent passion and his thoughts spinning in maddening circles: longing chasing regret chasing lust chasing conscience chasing longing.

Perhaps he was fast asleep. Perhaps he'd dropped off at once. For all she knew, what had happened between them in her living room had had no real impact on him. He'd tried to score, he'd failed, and that was that.

No. She couldn't believe he was that shallow. He'd done nothing deceptive or duplicitous; he hadn't forced himself upon her. In fact, he had invited her several times to stop him, and when she finally had he'd immediately backed off.

Thinking about how much she trusted him only made her wish she *hadn't* stopped him. She lay under the blanket, one pillow beneath her head and the other hugged to her stomach, and relived his kisses, each brush of his lips, each searing thrust of his tongue. She relived the feel of his fingers on her skin, on her breasts, the devastatingly sensual way he'd kneaded and stroked them, the thrill of his hand rounding her hip and sliding between her legs.

She heard the low rasp of his voice: *Let me do this for you....* She understood what he'd been suggesting, what he'd been willing to do for her, what he'd been prepared to deny himself. In spite of his pain and its disabling effect on him, he had wanted to bring her satisfaction.

How could she not trust him?

A silent sob filled her throat. As wonderful a man as Alec Fontana was, she'd been right to halt him. She already liked him too much; she couldn't afford the emotional expense of becoming attached to him. She had to preserve her soul for her music, for her healing. There was no room for love—and she couldn't imagine making love without being in love, particularly when the man in question was Alec.

So she lay alone in her bed, in the dark, and wished everything was different. She wished her wrist was all better; she wished her career didn't mean so much to her; she wished she wasn't so indebted to her family. She wished she could indulge herself in a lighthearted sexual escapade without attaching all sorts of emotional significance to it. She wished she could forget about love and concentrate on partying.

She wished she could close her eyes without remembering the sensation of Alec's hands and lips on her, his leg pressing into her, his body hard and potent against hers.

She wished she could stop wishing.

AT A FEW MINUTES past noon on Monday, Alec arrived at the faculty club, a squat stucco building on the western shore of the lake. Earlier that morning Roger Phelps had telephoned him and suggested that they meet for lunch at the faculty club rather than Roger's office. It occurred to Alec that Phelps might have some sleazy reason for not wanting Alec to come to his office—maybe he was negotiating a law-school recommendation with a student. But Alec had readily agreed to the revised plan, because it meant he wouldn't have to hike up the stairs to Roger's second-floor office in Dwight Hall. By Monday the pain in his knee had pretty much subsided, but he didn't want to exert his leg unnecessarily.

He'd spent Sunday relaxing in his apartment. He'd phoned his mother to say hello when he knew she would be home from church, plowed through the Sunday edition of the *Boston Globe* that Mags was kind enough to have delivered to his address, watched the New England Patriots get their butts kicked on television and feasted on a cold roast beef sandwich, a sliced pickle and half a bag of potato chips. He'd drunk iced tea instead of beer. The whiskey he'd consumed the night before hadn't left him with a hangover, but he'd decided not to push his luck.

He'd had no hangover from the whiskey, but from Lauren ... The aftereffects of his evening with her had reverberated through his mind and body all day long. Distracting himself with the newspaper and TV had offered only temporary relief; the instant his concentration lapsed, his thoughts had drifted back to her, to her lustrous hair and her luminous eyes, to the surprising fullness of her breasts, to her vibrant response to his touch. To the way she'd purred and arched her back like a kitten when he'd massaged her back, the way she'd writhed when his hand had found the warmth between her thighs. To the crazy way he'd wanted her, wanted to hear her cry out as she peaked in his arms.

Why had she spoiled everything by talking about involvement?

Because she was who she was, that was why. Alec had to admire her principles, even if they'd gotten in the way of her own gratification. He had to respect her honesty. It wasn't often he met women as up-front about what they needed and expected as Lauren Wyler was.

He could accept it. That was the way she was.

Sunday evening, she'd faced off with her piano—the worst practice he'd ever been privy to, but he'd been pleased to hear her go at it. He'd listened to her plod through exercises, runs, scales, tedious patterns of notes played much too slowly. Then she'd performed a piece, fumbled it with all the ineptitude of the Patriots wide receivers, performed it again and fumbled it again.

All right, so he couldn't get close to her. At least he had this: her botched piano playing. In an odd way, listening through the floor of his apartment as she mangled her practice pieces was as special as kissing her had been. Not as much fun, granted, but it was a shared intimacy, something that existed between him and her, something real and deeply personal.

He'd watched from his window as she left the duplex Monday morning. He'd tried not to react to the natural sway of her hips as she ambled up Hancock Street, and he swallowed his disappointment when she didn't turn and glance up at his windows. Once she was out of sight he'd poured himself a cup of coffee, limped to the den and set to work on his manuscript, typing and crossing out, pounding on the keys and spewing out sentences and all in all discovering that writing was another way to sublimate a horizontal desire.

By a quarter to twelve he'd covered three complete pages with type. A preliminary reading informed him they weren't worth saving, but everything he ever wrote seemed lousy to him on the first reading, so he seldom bothered to evaluate what he'd written until a day or two passed.

After sliding the pages into a folder and draping the dustcover over his typewriter, he donned his sneakers and denim jacket and left for his lunch appointment with Phelps. The day was clear and crisp; the rounded hills visible north of the lake blazed with autumn color. This little corner of the world seemed too pristine a setting for the garbage Roger Phelps was alleged to have engaged in.

A pretty girl barely out of her teens greeted Alec at the entry to the faculty club's main dining room. "Are you a member?" she asked politely.

"No, I'm supposed to meet someone for lunch. Roger Phelps."

"He's already here. Please come this way."

Alec followed her through the cozy dining room. Roger Phelps sat at a table next to a wall of glass overlooking the lake. Spotting Alec, he beamed a smile. The girl left a menu for Alec as he settled into the armchair across from Roger.

Alec stared after her. "Is she old enough to be working here?" he asked once she'd returned to her post near the entry.

Roger shrugged. "She's a student."

"An Albright College student?" Alec had trouble believing that an upper-class girl of the sort who attended Albright would take a job as a dining room hostess.

"Work-study, no doubt," Roger exclaimed. "A scholarship kid. These students do all sorts of things to pay their way through school. Now, before you get engrossed in the menu..." He pulled a copy of *Street Talk* from his leather briefcase and passed it across the table, along with a fountain pen.

Alec had always considered fountain pens the ultimate in pretentiousness, way up there above crew teams and cloth napkins. He knew of no statistical correlation between fountain pens and sexual harassment, but the fact that Roger owned a pen like this—not just a fountain pen, but a sterling silver and gold-plated one— was a definite strike against him.

Alec signed the title page and handed the book back to Roger. Then he scanned the room. Over half the tables were filled; Alec recognized a few of the faces from Mags's reception. "This place is open only to faculty members?" he asked.

"And their guests. It's one of the few places on campus where we can escape from our students."

"Do you like to escape from the students?" Alec asked.

"Every now and then," Roger replied with an oily smile. "Don't get me wrong, I love the students. But... they have their place, as it were."

"Where's their place?" Alec asked.

Roger chuckled and exchanged a meaningful look with Alec. "Why, in the classroom, of course."

Of course, Alec thought wryly, lifting his menu and scanning the listings. There wasn't much to choose from: sandwiches, salads, a couple of entrées. He decided on a cheeseburger.

A waitress came to the table. Like the girl who'd seated Alec, she appeared to be not much older than twenty, with a fresh-scrubbed face and neatly braided brown hair. Once she'd filled their water glasses and taken their orders, she left. "Another work-study student?" Alec asked.

"Presumably."

"Seems like you can't even escape the students here."

"Well..." Roger sent him another meaningful look, although once again Alec couldn't be sure what meaning he was trying to convey. "It's one thing to have students waiting on you," Roger clarified, "and quite another to have them badgering you about their term papers and their grades. Having attractive young ladies pouring my water and serving my lunch is not the sort of experience I need to escape."

It was all said in a ha-ha, wink-wink tone. Alec knew he couldn't condemn the man for simply engaging in an elite version of locker-room lechery. The waitresses *were* attractive young ladies; Alec wasn't about to argue the point.

He gazed out the window at the scenery, the surface of the lake reflecting the fire-hued leaves of the trees surrounding it. As he surveyed the view, he mulled over possible lines of questioning. If elite locker-room talk was what Roger was in the mood for, Alec would play along. "I could never work at a place like Albright," he said, turning back to Roger and returning the professor's slick smile. "Being surrounded by so many cute girls... the temptation would drive me crazy."

"There are ways to deal with temptation," Roger pointed out. "I would think that as a police officer you had to deal with plenty of temptation, too."

Alec's eyes narrowed on Roger. He tended to get defensive whenever anyone implied that cops were unscrupulous. Sure, some were, and when they were caught they paid the price—with their jobs if they were lucky, with more if they weren't. Alec knew a guy from the force who'd wound up in jail, another guy who'd wound up in an alcohol treatment center, and two guys who'd been dismissed for accepting payoffs. But given the risks cops took and the perils they faced, Alec believed that succumbing to a few temptations was, if wrong, at least understandable. He himself had never succumbed, but he could forgive a cop for crossing the line a hell of a lot more easily then he could forgive a smug, arrogant college professor.

Before he could redirect the conversation, Roger said, "I imagine you faced all sorts of temptations in your work. I mean, the controlled substances, the bribes, the prostitutes—stolen goods, women willing to do *anything* to beat a ticket—"

"You've been watching too much TV," Alec said dryly. "Police work is nothing like that."

Roger leaned back in his chair and grinned. "Go ahead, then, disillusion me."

"The only cops who wind up on the take are people who would have wound up in hot water no matter what they did,'' Alec declared. ''I'll bet more secretaries commit on-the-job theft than cops do. More doctors have drug problems than cops. More priests have drinking problems. More college professors—'' he kept his tone light ''—have had affairs with their students.''

Roger didn't even flinch. Quite the opposite, he threw back his head and let out a rousing laugh. ''Now, that's a bet I wouldn't take. You've made your point, Alec.''

Their lunches arrived. ''Imagine the power you've got over these girls,'' Alec persevered, pretending to be busy with the ketchup bottle so his attack wouldn't seem obvious. ''The grade you give them determines their future—whether they'll get into grad school, whether they'll get their scholarship renewed. I mean, it's one thing to beat a parking ticket, and quite another to get into Harvard Law School.''

Roger didn't look at all concerned. ''There is a fair degree of power involved in being a professor—I won't deny it. Let's face it, we don't go into college teaching to get rich. We do it for the intellectual stimulation and the power.'' He salted his roast chicken, then gave Alec a direct, unapologetic stare. ''I'd be the first to admit what a supreme thrill it is to gaze out at a classroom full of bright young girls and know they're all looking at me with reverence, hanging on my every word, wanting to do their best to please me.''

''Sounds like a major turn-on,'' Alec commented.

Roger chuckled. ''With an attitude like that, Alec, you might have a future in academe. Have you ever thought about teaching?''

Alec bit into his cheeseburger, chewed and swallowed, all the while eyeing Roger impassively. Not only did the man show no signs of guilt, he seemed downright amused by the exploitive aspects of his job. ''I don't know," Alec mumbled. "I'd think, particularly at a place like Albright, where it's all-girl..." He shook his head. "I don't know if I'd be able to keep my hands to myself."

"The girls here are of legal majority, you know."

"Yeah ... but they're students."

"Some are more mature than others," Roger noted. "Back at Columbia University, where I taught before coming here, one of my colleagues married a graduate student of his. They wound up coauthoring some marvelous papers. These associations can prove beneficial—to say nothing of delightful on a personal level." He ate for a moment, then said, "You aren't married, are you?"

A picture of Roger's attractive wife flashed through Alec's brain. "No. I guess your wife keeps you on the straight and narrow, huh?"

"Carol is an exceptional woman," Roger said cryptically. Their waitress came over to refill their water glasses. Alec stared after her as she walked away, her neat brown braid swinging like a pendulum between her shoulder blades. She was cute, all right, but he couldn't imagine how a grown man could find a kid like her sexier than a real woman like Carol Phelps.

He'd expected to picture Roger's wife again, but the image that loomed up in his imagination was of a slim, intense woman with ebony hair and ivory skin, with fathomless brown eyes and exquisite lips and a body warm and yearning in his arms. All of a sudden he found himself praying that Roger Phelps and Lauren Wyler never crossed paths. If Roger ever touched Lauren, if he so much as leered at her, Alec would tear the good professor's head off.

"Now, here's an idea," Roger broke into his thoughts. "Maybe it's just the proposition of an avid fan, but do give it some thought—how would you like to present a guest lecture in one of my seminars?"

"Me? Teach a seminar?" Alec snorted.

"I'm serious."

"What could I possibly give a lecture on?"

"Police law. I teach an honors seminar on the Constitution. You could offer some valuable insights into the concrete application of the law, the way law-enforcement officers translate our nation's noble philosophy into pragmatic action."

There he went with the law-enforcement-officer talk again. Alec had been a *cop,* pure and simple. He'd attended a huge public university, graduated with a B-minus average and become a *cop.* His understanding of the United States Constitution was no better than the typical citizen's. What he knew were local ordinances, state laws, Supreme Court rulings about obtaining warrants and notifying suspects of their rights, and that was pretty much it.

He shook his head. "I'm no scholar. The students here haven't coughed up thousands of dollars in tuition to hear a lecture from an ex-cop from Boston."

"You're more than an ex-cop, Alec. You're a best-selling author."

"Of a commercial novel. I wouldn't feel competent to teach an English course, either."

"Well, how about sitting in on one of my seminars, then? I'd love to have you as a guest."

"That I'll do," Alec promised. He welcomed the opportunity to watch Roger Phelps in action, to see how he related to his students in a classroom setting.

"I have a seminar that meets at two o'clock this afternoon. Consider yourself formally invited."

"Thanks. I'll come."

They talked mostly about the weekend football games during the rest of lunch. Roger bemoaned the fact that at an all-women's college like Albright he couldn't assume his students would understand the sports allusions and analogies he used in his seminars. Alec mentioned that his sisters were as up on sports as any man he knew—in particular, baseball, although they were no slouches when it came to basketball or hockey. Roger seemed to regard this as proof that Alec was from some other, more highly evolved race. "Sisters who understand sports! I'd love to meet them!"

Not in my lifetime, Alec retorted silently. Although he was younger than Rosie and Mary-Beth, he'd always been protective of them—particularly after his fifteenth birthday, when he'd suddenly found himself nearing six feet in height and physically capable of defending them against any creep who dared to give them a hard time. Once he'd split the lip of a guy Rosie was dating because the guy had pawed her against her wishes. And if the same thing happened today he'd split the guy's lip again, even though Rosie was a happily married thirty-three-year-old mother of two.

Alec declined Roger's offer of dessert and coffee, and waited as Roger signed the bill to his account. Then they left the building.

The air had warmed slightly since Alec had arrived at the faculty club. The mild breeze lifting off the lake tugged the browner leaves from their branches, but the campus walkways were clear, as always. The way Alec figured, either the grounds keepers maintained constant vigilance, raking up every stray leaf the instant it hit the pavement, or else the trees of Albright College, like the students, were of a superior quality, somehow capable of missing the paths when they shed their foliage.

He and Roger strolled across the campus at a relaxed pace, Roger dapper in his tweed blazer, tailored trousers and moccasin-stitched loafers, Alec dressed down in his denim jacket and jeans. They attracted more than a few stares from the lively students swarming across campus, journeying to their afternoon classes. "You've got to admit," Roger whispered conspiratorially, "it does a man's ego a world of good to have all these cute young things giving him the eye."

Alec grinned, but Roger's words reverberated sourly inside him. *Cute young things.* Alec might have his share of macho reflexes—the time he'd punched Rosie's boyfriend in the mouth, she'd been as disgusted with Alec's violence as she'd been with her boyfriend's pushiness. But macho reflexes notwithstanding, his sisters had done a good job of indoctrinating him in the ways of feminism. He could see how dehumanizing it was for a woman to be called a "thing." Particularly a "cute thing."

At the entry to Dwight Hall, Roger said, "Come on upstairs to my office. I need to pick up my lecture notes and drop off your book. It's heavy. I'd rather not lug it around."

With a sigh, Alec accompanied Roger up the stairs, his knee cramping only slightly from the strain. Down the hall, a tall, voluptuous blond girl hovered near Roger's office door. Alec recognized her at once as the girl he'd tailed from Roger's office to Lauren's last week.

Spotting Roger, the girl's face brightened. She appeared about to wave, then obviously realized she couldn't. Her arms were burdened with books and folders of paper.

"A student of yours?" Alec asked as he fell into step with Roger.

"Student, assistant and all-around charmer," Roger whispered out the corner of his mouth. He sent Emily a silky smile, then increased his pace. As soon as he reached her he lifted some of the bulky folders out of her arms. "You're quite loaded down there, Emily," he said, oozing compassion.

Her eyes darted between him and Alec, and her cheeks turned pink. "It's all stuff for you, Ro—Dr. Phelps. The research materials you asked me to get."

"You look as if you've been working overtime," he noted cheerfully, pulling a set of keys from a pocket in his blazer and unlocking the office door. "Emily," he informed Alec, "has been helping me to amass some documents for a series of articles I'm putting together. So far she's proven herself indispensable."

Emily appeared embarrassed by Roger's praise. She shot Alec another look, this one uncertain. Alec kept his face blank.

"I don't mean to take up your time," she said, following Roger into his office and dropping the remaining books and folders on his desk. Alec stepped inside and cased the room with a quick glance. Wall bookshelves held the requisite overabundance of books. Two polished-wood file cabinets stood near the door. Roger's desk was also wood-lacquered walnut, not the standard-issue steel furniture Alec would have expected. A thick rug covered the linoleum floor, drapes framed the windows, and in front of the windows stood a couch.

Alec tried not to laugh out loud. It wasn't that he was startled to find a couch in a professor's office—even professors deserved comfortable seating. But this couch had wide, nicely rounded cushions, curved mahogany legs and red velvet upholstery. It looked like an updated version of the divans that furnished Wild West brothels in grade-B Westerns.

Emily had her back to Alec as she spread her folders over the top of the desk. "I photocopied every article you needed," she explained, her voice as sweet and ripe as her body. "I had a lot of trouble finding a few of the pieces. There was a whole year of *The Public Interest* misplaced in the periodicals storage room, and it took the librarian almost an hour to find them."

"I'm sorry it was a problem," Roger said, although he didn't sound even remotely sorry. Practically ignoring the girl, he thumbed through one folder after another, nodding and smiling as he scanned their contents.

"Oh, it wasn't a problem. I mean, I don't mind. It's an honor to be doing this kind of research."

She seemed to be waiting for him to look at her. When he didn't, she drummed her fingers nervously against the surface of his desk. "Is there anything else you want me to get for you?"

At last he lifted his eyes to her. "No, not right now."

"So...everything's all right?" Her voice was hesitant, as if she were desperately eager for his approval.

"Everything's fine, Emily. I'm sure I'll be needing more from you, but we can discuss it some other time."

"Well, I mean . . ." She shifted her weight from one foot to the other, clearly anxious. Roger had returned to scanning the folders. "I mean, I'd be happy to do more."

He glanced up again, and gave her a surprisingly wolfish smile. "I'd be happy to have you do more, Emily. We'll discuss it later. Now, be a good girl and run along. We'll work it all out on..." He flipped through a leather-bound appointment book on his desk. "How's Thursday for you?"

She looked crestfallen. "I can't. I have a piano lesson late Thursday afternoon."

"What time does it end?"

"Five o'clock," she said. "Dinnertime. But you know what?" Her expression brightened. "I could skip dinner and come here straight from the music building. Or I could cancel the lesson if you want."

Alec almost intervened. How dare she cancel her music lesson with Lauren to spend time with a dirtball like Roger Phelps?

"No need to cancel your lesson," Roger assured her. "You just come here afterward. We can catch a snack somewhere along the line." Roger peered past her, catching Alec's eye and sending him a smarmy smile.

Alec labored hard not to grimace. He still had no proof that Roger had seduced his student last year. But judging from his behavior toward Emily Spaeth, Alec could certainly believe it of him.

And when Emily waltzed out of the office, all blond youth and effervescence, thanking Roger and batting her big blue eyes at him, Alec had the sinking feeling that he'd just witnessed an exchange between Distinguished Professor Roger Phelps and his latest victim.

For the first time since Rosie and Mary-Beth got married, Alec felt the nearly irrepressible urge to split someone's lip.

HER PRACTICE went dreadfully that night—as usual. She floundered through a series of exercises, then trudged through a Bach three-part invention, taking it at about one-quarter the proper speed. The outer half of her right hand collapsed on her more than once. Her forearm ached.

Still, she persevered. It was bad enough knowing Alec was upstairs listening to her. If he heard her stop before she'd reached the final chord it would be even worse. So she continued until the last resonant chord, then let her hands drop to her lap and groaned.

She ought to be feeling heartened. That morning she had made an appointment for Friday afternoon with the hand specialist Bella Bronowitz had recommended. Lauren had telephoned Dr. Hayes in New York and asked him to fax her files up to Dr. Nylander in Boston, and although he'd repeated several times that he thought she was making excellent progress with him and shouldn't waste her money seeing someone else who couldn't do more for her than he was doing, he had complied with her request to send along the appropriate records.

Merely thinking about seeing this wonderful doctor of Bella's cheered Lauren. She turned the page in her Bach book and began a new piece—just as sluggishly. She toiled over each note, gnashed her teeth at each mistake, and at one point pinched her pinkie to restore sensation to it. But she kept at it, one beat at a time, note after ponderous note until she reached the final measure.

She tried to convince herself she was enduring this torture for herself, for her hand, for her future. But deep in her heart she knew she was doing it for Alec upstairs.

Later, after a long, soothing bath, a glass of milk and a review of her lecture notes for the following day's classes, she climbed into bed and reached for the lamp. Next to it on the night table lay Alec's book—faceup. She hadn't read any of it since Friday night.

She turned it over, indulging herself in a slow, pensive examination of it. She contemplated Alec's rebellious posture, his pugnacious expression, the toothpick, the chin, the hypnotic eyes. She was astonished at how strongly a two-dimensional black-and-white photograph could affect her.

It wasn't the photograph affecting her so much as her memory. She had never desired a man the way she'd desired Alec Saturday night. Not even when she'd been in love.

With a tiny sigh, she opened to the page where she'd left her bookmark Friday night—the first sex scene. She exercised what little willpower she had not to reread that torrid passage and instead plowed onward, picking up the tangled strands of the mystery plot. She read about the crooked cop and the hero's attempts to straighten him out before the heroine could catch him. She read about the deteriorating tenements and the surly thugs on the street corners, the casual shootings, the wasted lives and the struggle of the hero and heroine to stay clean and honest amid such squalor.

It was violent, as Gerald had warned. It was gruesome. It was also addictive. Two hours passed before Lauren gave in to exhaustion and reached for the lamp switch. This time, when she closed the book she placed it facedown, so Alec's face would be the first thing she saw when she woke.

She was feeling hopeful. Objectively she knew her appointment with the doctor in Boston was the cause of her optimism, but intuitively she understood that Alec was also a part of it. It was his doing that she'd stuck with her piano practice all the way to the end. It was because of him that she'd kept playing, kept going, refused to cave in and give up.

In the morning, when the early light of the sun filtered into her room and roused her, she wanted to see his photograph when she opened her eyes. She wanted to look at it and think of him. She wanted to view his fine, strong features and his proud stance and think of what he'd given her: not passion, not exposure to rock and roll, not the book he'd written, but courage.

The courage to keep going, to keep hoping.

CHAPTER EIGHT

FOUR DAYS, and the closest he'd gotten to her had been her stumbling, error-riddled piano practices. Four mornings he caught fleeting glimpses of her as she headed up the street toward the campus, her black hair billowing down her back and her right hand tucked into the pocket of her cardigan. Four evenings he heard her muffled footsteps as she moved about her apartment beneath him. Four hour-long interludes, one each night, he listened to her duke it out with her piano.

She played terribly, but that didn't stop her. He almost believed the music was her private message to him: *I'm tough. I'll keep playing. The hell with being embarrassed or frightened. I'll just keep on playing, because you asked me to.*

It connected them: her playing, his listening. What he wanted from Lauren—her kisses, her body, the smoldering heat of her surrounding him—he couldn't have. But he could have her music. In a way, it was almost enough.

THURSDAY MORNING, half-asleep, he dragged himself out of bed and cursed his shortsightedness in leaving his automatic coffeemaker behind in Boston when he'd come to Albright. He'd been up late last night, chomping on toothpicks and pounding out typewritten pages of his new novel until two a.m. When he awakened at a few minutes after eight that morning his head ached and his vision refused to focus. He was desperate for coffee but bleary enough to question his ability to brew a pot of the stuff.

He rubbed his eyes, yawned and staggered to the chair where he'd tossed his jeans the night before. Pulling them on, he almost didn't hear her voice. It sounded incongruously deep, a low, indistinct rumbling.

It wasn't her voice at all. It was a man's voice.

He heard her say, "Please listen to me. This is what I want."

Then the unfamiliar voice again, the words indistinct but the range definitely male.

Alec frowned as the truth dawned on him. Lauren had a man with her, directly beneath him, in her bedroom. At ten minutes after eight in the morning, she had a man in her bedroom.

He swore, then issued a short, dry laugh. So she had a man in her bedroom—and it wasn't Alec. So someone else had won her favor, someone else had been granted admission into her bed. Maybe the guy had agreed to become *involved* with Lauren. If so, Alec couldn't be jealous. Involvement was the last thing he wanted.

He stalked out of his bedroom and into the bathroom, trying to convince himself he didn't care about what was going on in the apartment below. As he washed and shaved and brushed his hair, he told himself over and over that Lauren Wyler meant nothing to him, that the knowledge that she'd spent the night with a man wasn't eating at his gut like acid, that by the time he finished his mission for Mags at the college and returned to his home in the North End Lauren would be nothing more significant than a dust mote on his memory. That she could do whatever the hell she wanted with whoever the hell she wanted, and Alec ought to count his blessings that he wasn't a part of it.

Damn it all. He *did* care. She had said she was saving her heart for her music, and that was fine—he didn't want her heart. What he wanted was what she'd given to the man who was with her right now. Alec could tell himself he wasn't jealous, but he was—so jealous he could scarcely see straight.

Fuming, he went back to his bedroom for a shirt and his sneakers. Once he was dressed he stormed down the hall to the kitchen. He banged the cabinet doors, slammed the coffeepot onto the stove, wrenched the faucet so violently he was lucky it didn't snap off in his hand. Then he slumped into a chair and let his anger percolate in tandem with the coffee.

He heard more voices below, first Lauren's and then the man's, rising and falling in a bickering counterpoint. He tried to recall whether he'd heard the man at her place last night, but he'd been so caught up in his writing he hadn't paid attention to anything beyond the clatter of his typewriter and the flow of his words. There probably hadn't been any loud arguing last night, anyway. Lauren and her guest had undoubtedly been getting along just fine.

This morning they weren't getting along at all. "Don't do this," Lauren demanded. With Alec she'd always been cordial and reserved. With her current guest, however, she was letting it all hang out. "It's my life, all right?"

"Lauren, honey... come on. Don't be this way."

Eavesdropping was wrong, but Alec couldn't help himself. If they hadn't wanted him to hear them, they should have kept their voices down. He turned off the heat under the coffeepot, filled a mug and resumed his seat, listening.

"You don't own me."

"We had an agreement," the man countered.

"An agreement. It's not like I belong to you. I never signed my soul over to you."

"Listen to me." The man's voice had grown tight, threatening. "You just listen to me, Lauren. I've been good to you, you know I have. You need me. We're a team. You have no right to see this man behind my back—"

Alec flinched. What man? Who was she seeing behind her boyfriend's back?

Alec. That was who.

He cursed again, his jealousy transforming into a slowly swelling rage. Despite the fact that he and Lauren had parted ways last Saturday night, neither of them satisfied, neither of them fulfilled, he'd still wound up involved with her. Some clown who'd had the privilege of waking up in Lauren's bed had just involved him.

"Now, listen to me," the man growled, sounding even more menacing, "and listen carefully."

"I won't listen," Lauren protested. "I don't have to listen to you. The whole thing is your fault, anyway. You hurt me—"

"That's a lie."

"Look at me! Why do you think I'm here? You hurt me."

"Shut up!" the man snapped, followed by the sound of something heavy crashing, and then a scream.

Lauren. Screaming.

Setting his mug onto the table, Alec bolted for the door. He'd broken up enough domestic disturbances in his days on the police force to recognize what he was hearing through the floorboards. Whoever Lauren's pal was, whatever he meant to her, however pleasantly he'd spent the night with her, Alec simply could not sit idly by while the man threw furniture at her.

Ignoring the twinge in his left knee, he sprinted down the stairs, out his door and across the porch to Lauren's door. He punched her doorbell several times with his fist, then waited, feeling the adrenaline funneling through his body.

After a moment Lauren opened the door. She was dressed neatly, in conservative woolen slacks and a cowl-neck sweater, her hair combed and her right hand exposed, her two outer fingers rolled tight against her palm. Alec scanned her face for bruises or blood, but he saw no sign of injury. All he saw was her beauty, overlaid with surprise. "Alec!"

Without a word he stepped into her apartment. He surveyed the living room and discovered everything tidy. The roses on her dining table had been replaced with a bouquet of asters. The couch was in order, unlike the last time he'd been in her home, when she'd strewn the cushions across the floor for Alec's comfort and her own.

His gaze continued its journey around the room, ultimately alighting on the man who stood in the kitchen doorway. He was also dressed neatly, in a meticulously casual outfit that reeked of expensiveness. He was several inches shorter than Alec, with reddish-brown hair and a manicured beard. Despite his diminutive build, the man could easily have bullied and beaten Lauren. But his attire was too unwrinkled, his breathing too even, his eyes too rational behind a pair of stylish redframed spectacles.

A spat, that was all it was. No fistfight, no partner-bashing. What Alec had broken in on was nothing more than a noisy lovers' quarrel.

He turned back to Lauren, unsure of whether he should apologize for the intrusion and make a hasty retreat. Staring into those fathomless brown eyes of hers affected him strangely, though. He didn't want to leave her. He wanted to kiss her.

"I—uh—I was wondering if you were finished with my book," he said, snatching at the first excuse he could think of.

Not a good one. She looked puzzled. "I thought... I'm sorry, Alec. I thought you said I could keep it. Of course, I'll go get it."

"Oh, no—no, that's all right. You're right, I told you to keep it." He could tell he was making a jackass of himself. A quick exit was called for. "I'll be seeing you, then," he mumbled, backing up a step and reaching behind him for the doorknob.

Before he found it Lauren had her left hand curved around his arm. She drew him back into the room, presenting him to the bearded stranger. "Alec, I'd like you to meet Gerald Honan, my manager. I've told you about him. Gerald, this is Alec Fontana. A friend of mine."

She could have introduced Alec as her neighbor, or as the author of a bestselling novel. Or even as the man she had dared to see behind Gerald's back. Instead she'd identified him as her friend. Alec liked that.

He shook Gerald's hand. "Alec Fontana," Gerald enunciated, his brows dipping into a frown as he ruminated. "Why does that name sound familiar to me?"

Alec was tempted to come up with a sarcastic answer. But given the tension in the room, he held his temper. "I wrote a novel, *Street Talk*. Lauren told me you read it last spring."

"Ah. Yes. You wrote that?" Gerald peered up at Alec, who nodded in confirmation. Gerald's eyeglasses gave him an owlish appearance. "That was quite a book," he commented. "It was savage. Well done, though."

"Thank you," Alec said stiffly.

"And you live in Albright?"

"Right here on Hancock Street."

"How interesting. I was afraid Lauren would be bored to tears in the sticks. I'm glad to see there are other artists in the community."

"I'm not an artist," Alec retorted. He simply couldn't find it in himself to behave politely toward this guy—the idiot responsible for convincing Lauren that dating guys and listening to rock and roll would destroy her career.

"Maybe that *is* too strong a word," Gerald said, so archly Alec couldn't tell whether or not he was joking. "I imagine anyone who would write a novel like yours must have a rather nasty view of the world."

"The book was fiction, Gerald," Lauren reminded him.

"Don't tell me you've read it." Gerald gave her a reproachful look.

"Yes," Lauren shot back. "As you can see, it's completely corrupted me."

"Exactly what I was thinking."

Alec shifted his weight onto his right leg, but it didn't help. His discomfort arose not from his knee but from his soul. Whatever Lauren and her manager were fighting about, they were probably better off fighting without Alec getting in their way. He'd done his knight-in-shining-armor bit and discovered that the damsel in distress didn't need rescuing, after all. A final glance persuaded him that Gerald Honan wasn't physically dangerous—emotionally dangerous, maybe, but that was a hazard Alec couldn't really help her with.

He turned back to her. "If... if everything's okay, then, I guess I'll just—"

She gave his arm a squeeze, and he realized then that she had never let go of it. Gripping him tightly, she presented her manager with an artificial smile. "Gerald, you're welcome to join Alec and me for lunch today. But you'll have to occupy yourself for the morning. I've got work to do."

Comprehending the tacit message in her clasp, Alec played along, curious to see what Lauren was up to. Not that he had any desire to have lunch with Gerald Honan, but hell, he'd agree to have lunch with Idi Amin if it meant Lauren's hand remained on him for a minute longer.

"I'm afraid I can't," said Gerald. "I'm due back in New York at two o'clock. I'd best leave now."

"I'm sorry you can't stay," Lauren said evenly. Her fingers continued to work out on Alec's wrist. If he were a piano, trills would be pouring from him.

"Thank you for the invitation." There was something painfully stilted about his parting dialogue. "Mr. Fontana, it's been a pleasure meeting you," Gerald said, then let his gaze drift to Alec's right arm, with Lauren's left hand wrapped around it. Pursing his lips, he lifted his eyes to Lauren. "You will keep me apprised," he half asked.

"I will."

"I'm sorry we crossed swords, Lauren."

An enigmatic smile whispered across Lauren's lips. "Then don't let it happen again," she said, offering her cheek for a farewell kiss.

. Gerald obliged, then straightened up and shot Alec a distrustful look. "I'll call you," he said to Lauren before striding out the door.

Lauren released Alec's arm, closed the door and twisted the lock. Then she folded her arms and glowered at Alec. "Would you care to explain what in God's name you're doing here?"

I'm here because you wouldn't let me leave, he almost said. Warmth lingered in his forearm where she'd held it. He wanted that warmth to remain, to spread throughout him. He wanted to gather her to himself and kiss her until the warmth blazed into flames. Four days he'd gone without seeing her, speaking to her, feeling her. Four agonizing days.

He realized she was talking about his barging in on her and then concocting that flimsy lie about his book to explain his rash intrusion. He wasn't going to apologize for meddling, though. If he'd had that morning to live over again, he would have done everything exactly as he had.

"I heard you fighting with him," he said. "I heard you scream."

"Scream?" She scowled. "You mean, when the chair fell over?"

"I don't know. From upstairs, it sounded like he might have hit you with it."

"He didn't. I knocked it over. My fingers went numb when I was leaning on it, and I lost my balance." She took a breath. "You had no right to come down here, Alec."

"I thought you were in trouble. I heard you say he hurt you. When I was upstairs, I mean. You said he hurt you."

Her mouth fell open as the implications of his statement became clear. "What were you doing, pressing your ear to the floor?" she asked furiously.

"You were both yelling," Alec pointed out. "I could hear you just fine without pressing my ear to the floor."

"Great." Her eyes grew cold and her jaw hardened with indignation. "I was yelling. The next time I'm going to have a personal argument with someone I'll whisper."

He took a step toward her and she backed up. He sighed. "Lauren . . . when I was a cop I heard fights between men and women. I heard fights through closed doors, and usually when I charged in I found someone bleeding from the nose or nursing a black eye—or worse. I've witnessed some bad scenes, and they taught me not to hesitate if I thought someone might be beating up on someone else. Even if the door was closed, even if it was a personal argument . . . I learned it was best to go on in." He took another step toward her, and this time she didn't shrink from him, although her expression was far from welcoming. "I'm sorry I misjudged the situation here," he continued. "But it was loud and angry and I heard that chair crashing and you screaming. I didn't know who you were fighting with and I didn't care. I only wanted to make sure he didn't hurt you."

Lauren lowered her head. "All right. Your motives were decent. But Alec—" she raised her eyes, bright and unwavering, to his "—I'm an adult. I can take care of myself. I've had fourteen years of Gerald intervening in my life, making decisions for me, swooping down and taking over. I hate it. I'm trying to get out from under his wing. I don't want you doing the same thing he did. Can you understand that?''

She looked small across the room from him, but steely. The sheen of tears in her eyes didn't detract from their fierce power. She didn't hide her lame hand. She stood stalwart and unafraid, and all Alec could think was that as brave and tough as she was, she didn't need anyone protecting her at all.

''I understand,'' he said.

Several long seconds stretched in silence between them, their eyes locked, a myriad of emotions passing between them. Then Lauren's mouth softened into a diffident smile and she started toward the hallway. ''If you'd like, I'll get you your book.''

''Forget it,'' he said quickly. ''It's yours. I want you to have it.'' He measured her with his gaze before adding, ''And we can forget lunch, too, if you want. I know you were just winging it.''

''I'd like to have lunch with you,'' she said, so quietly he wasn't certain he'd heard her correctly.

''Today?''

''Yes.'' She sent him a brief look, then turned and moved toward the kitchen door. ''I've missed you,'' she murmured.

Her voice was soft, hesitant, as if she wasn't sure she wanted him to hear, as if she wasn't sure she wanted to say it. As if she wasn't sure she believed it.

But she *had* said it, and even if she didn't believe it, Alec did. ''I've missed you, too,'' he called after her as she vanished through the doorway.

To HER GREAT RELIEF, he didn't follow her into the kitchen. She needed some time alone to collect her wits, to recover from the morning's intensity. She needed to come to terms with it all.

When she'd spoken to Gerald a couple of days ago, he'd mentioned he was planning to drive up to the Berkshires to shop for a summer house. It had been his dream for years to buy a vacation house near Tanglewood. During his ill-fated marriage a decade ago, he and his wife had owned a cottage in Lenox, but his wife had gotten custody of it in the divorce settlement. Now, he claimed, with real estate prices soft and his ex-wife no longer a thorn in his side, Gerald was ready to invest in a new summer home.

Lauren had cordially invited him to drop by and visit if he wished; Albright was less than an hour's drive from Lenox. Then she'd made the mistake of telling him about her upcoming appointment with Dr. Nylander, the hand specialist in Boston.

And there Gerald had been, Thursday morning at eight o'clock, pounding on her door. Fortunately she'd arisen early and gotten dressed; all he'd interrupted was a breakfast of grapefruit and toast. She'd graciously fixed a cup of coffee for him and grilled him on his house-hunting expedition. "Did you see anything nice?" she'd asked excitedly. "Something with a big porch, Gerald, and lots of guest rooms so I can stay there when I'm performing at the Summer Music Festival. And lots of trees, and flower beds, and—"

"How dare you arrange to see a doctor without asking me?" he'd exploded.

They'd quarreled. Too loudly, apparently, if Alec had thought what he'd been overhearing was a brawl. Gerald had accused Lauren of being untrustworthy, excluding him from the most significant decisions in her life, sneaking around behind his back.... He'd acted like a spurned lover, for heaven's sake.

In the past, Lauren would have knuckled under to him. She would have done whatever he told her to do, because she was the musician and he was the manager—she made the musical decisions and he made every other decision. That was the way it had always been.

Until now. Until she'd discovered that she could find a job by herself and move to a town and settle in, make her own friends and live her own life. Until she'd found out for herself that rock music was fun and ex-cops were sexy. Until she'd faced the truth that the mastermind of her career was also the cause of its current suspension, and that if he couldn't save her with his handpicked doctor, she could save herself with her own.

The amazing thing was not that she'd thought all those things but that she'd had the gall to verbalize them to Gerald. In all the years they'd worked together, she had never stood up to him. She'd never had a reason to. She had been inexperienced and immature, and he had done everything necessary to make her a star.

But at the moment she wasn't a star. She was a teacher, living on her own, following her own mind and listening to her own heart. She believed Dr. Nylander could help her, and she was going to see him, and Gerald had nothing to do with it.

She heard the uneven pattern of Alec's footsteps on the uncarpeted hallway. Taking a deep breath, she turned to face him as he entered the kitchen. He gazed warily at her, awaiting a cue.

"I'm sorry, Alec," she said. "I shouldn't have chewed you out. I'm just—I want to fight my own battles. I don't want you defending me."

"I was wrong, too," he confessed. "I should have realized you could handle the situation without my help." He looked rather grim. "Lauren, I—" He sighed. "I didn't come downstairs only to break up the fight."

"You want your book back, after all," she joked, hoping a little levity would erase his frown.

He regarded her thoughtfully, his eyes shadowy with an emotion she couldn't decipher. "I came because I thought he was your lover. I was envious."

His candor stunned her into silence. She knew there were loose ends between her and Alec, unresolved desires and unquenched thirsts. But acting on those desires and thirsts was impossible—she'd been honest with him about that.

She supposed he had as much right as she did to speak honestly, even if his honesty led them into treacherous waters. "Gerald and I have never been lovers," she told him.

"Okay."

"That doesn't change anything between you and me."

"I understand." He trailed his fingers along the molded edge of the doorway. She remembered the way they had felt on her skin, slightly rough yet sensitive, teasing and arousing. A shiver of yearning passed through her at the memory. She couldn't get involved with him, but she couldn't seem to stop wanting him, either.

"I can't get caught up in a relationship right now," she said, anxious to convince herself as much as him.

"You've told me."

"It isn't you, Alec. I mean . . . I've got to stay focused. I can't get sidetracked."

"I know." A wry smile twisted his lips. "Are you sure you want to sidetrack yourself enough to have lunch with me?"

She nodded. When she'd said she missed him, she'd spoken the truth. Alec was the only person she knew well in a nonprofessional context. He wasn't a musician, a student, a manager or a medical expert. He was a representative from the vast world beyond her own hermetic existence. He offered a different slant on things, a fresh perspective. She'd missed that even more than she'd missed his passion.

"We could meet at the faculty club," she suggested. She wasn't foolish enough to think they would be safe having lunch alone together in her apartment.

"Noon?" he asked.

"Noon."

His smile widened. "I'll see you there," he said, then left the kitchen. She listened to his lopsided footsteps heading back down the hall, past the living room and out the front door. The glow of his smile remained with her, though, filling her, soothing her after her tumultuous confrontation with Gerald.

She needed a friend a lot more than she needed a lover. She was immeasurably grateful to have Alec as her friend.

HE WAS WAITING on the front steps of the faculty-club building when she arrived, a few minutes late. Her morning her been more hectic than usual, not only because Gerald's visit had thrown things out of kilter but because she'd had to reschedule her Friday appointments in order to free up the day for her trip to Boston. When Alec spotted her hurrying along the path, kicking a few unraked leaves out of her way, his face broke into a broad grin.

"Hi," he said, holding open the door for her and following her inside.

A work-study undergraduate greeted them at the arched entry to the dining room. Before Alec could speak, Lauren presented the hostess with her faculty ID and recited: "Lauren Wyler, music department, account number 0584." While the girl looked up her account in the membership ledger, Lauren turned to Alec. "You're going to be my guest for lunch, and I don't want to hear a word about it."

"Lauren..."

"And while I'm at it, there was no need for you to leave that money for me the other night."

The hostess looked up, wearing a funny expression. Alec chuckled. "I underpaid," he teased. "You were definitely worth more."

It took her a moment to catch on to his insinuation. She blushed. "You're embarrassing me," she whispered.

"I embarrassed myself on Saturday. Now we're even."

"I don't think so," she argued, her eyes glinting mischievously. "For us to be even, *I* have to embarrass you."

"If you do, you'll have to embarrass yourself, too," Alec pointed out. "Fair is fair."

Lauren wasn't sure she followed his logic, but she was spared from further analysis by the hostess, who lifted two menus from her table and led Lauren and Alec to a table with a view of the lake. Alec gave the menu a cursory glance, then shut it and surveyed the room. His gaze narrowed on a table somewhere behind her, and his smile grew dim.

Lauren twisted in her chair to see whom he was looking at. A tall, leanly handsome man in a pompous-looking blazer with leather patches on the elbows was rising from his chair and grinning at Alec. She couldn't recall his name, but she knew who he was. She'd met him at several faculty functions and found him insufferable.

To her great annoyance, he strolled over to their table. "Alec!" he said in a smooth baritone. "Don't tell me you've wrangled a faculty-club membership from your aunt!"

"No," Alec replied, returning the man's exuberant smile. "I'm here as Lauren's guest. Lauren, do you know Roger Phelps?"

Lauren shaped a perfunctory smile and placed her right hand in Roger's outstretched palm. "We've met on numerous occasions," Roger said smoothly. "How lucky you are, Alec, to be having lunch with Lauren Wyler, the brightest star in the music department's constellation."

Lauren did her best not to gag on his overblown flattery. "Hello, Roger," she mumbled, slipping her hand from his and tucking it safely under the napkin in her lap.

"I didn't know you two knew each other." Roger seemed to be addressing Alec, but his eyes remained on Lauren.

"Well, we do," Alec said laconically.

With apparent reluctance, Roger turned to Alec. "If your lunch doesn't run past three, you might be able to catch my lecture on political-action committees in my contemporary political-ethics course this afternoon."

"I'd like that," Alec replied. "Where is it, Dwight Hall?"

"The same room as yesterday's seminar. I'll see you there. And now—" he included Lauren in his smile "—I'll leave you two folks to each other. It was good seeing you again, Lauren. Alec, we'll talk later." He sauntered back to his table.

Lauren gaped after him, astonished. How could a man like Alec have become friendly with a creep like Roger Phelps? The details of her previous encounters with Phelps began to clarify in her mind: the Faculty Sherry, a sit-down dinner at Dean Hettington's home and a reception after Peter Villard's recital. On each occasion Phelps had slithered up to her, fawned over her and communicated, with just enough subtlety to keep her from slapping his face, that if she were ever interested in "pursuing our discussion privately," he would be most accommodating. Even with his wife standing at the other end of the room, he'd come on to Lauren with shameless enthusiasm. He'd never been specific about what he would do if Lauren agreed to meet privately with him, but he'd layered every word, every look, every cocky smile with cloying innuendo.

The arrival of a waitress to take their orders forced her attention back to Alec. She requested the shrimp salad, Alec a hamburger. As soon as the waitress was gone, Lauren bore down on him. "Is Roger Phelps a friend of yours?" she asked, not bothering to conceal her disapproval.

He opened his mouth to reply, then closed it. Obviously he could guess her opinion of Roger. He leaned back in his chair, pulled a toothpick out of his shirt pocket, and chewed on it thoughtfully. "I know him," he said at last.

"He greeted you as if you were his long-lost brother," Lauren said accusingly. "I thought he was going to haul you out of your chair and kiss you on both cheeks. Which would have been preferable to having him kiss *me* on both cheeks, but still . . ." She curled her lip.

"You don't like him?" Alec guessed.

"I think he's a scum bucket—pardon my French."

Alec chuckled. "The words I'd use to describe Roger Phelps would make the French blush."

"He's not your friend, then?" she asked, relieved.

Alec chewed on his toothpick for another minute, contemplating Lauren, gauging her. At last he leaned forward, removed the toothpick from his mouth and trapped her with his steady, probing gaze. "Can I trust you?"

"Of course," she replied automatically, then pressed her lips together and returned Alec's intent look. Whatever he was about to share with her was too important for her to respond in an automatic way. "Yes," she said, her tone earnest, her smile gone. "You can trust me."

He fell silent as the waitress delivered their lunches. Alone with Lauren once more, he ignored his hamburger and asked, "What can you tell me about Emily Spaeth?"

"Emily?" Lauren blinked in surprise. What did Alec know about her piano students? *Why* did he know about them? "I thought we were talking about Roger Phelps," she said warily.

"We are." Alec drenched his burger in ketchup, then lifted his eyes back to Lauren. "Emily studies piano with you, doesn't she?"

"She's one of my best students. She's extremely talented. Why do you ask?"

"She's a student of Roger's, too."

Lauren poked her salad with the tines of her fork. All of her students were also other professors' students. Given that Emily was a political-science major, it made sense that she would be taking a course with Roger Phelps.

Alec ate a bit, still staring at Lauren, measuring her. He seemed to reach some sort of internal decision. "This does not go beyond this table," he commanded in a low voice.

"Of course not," Lauren agreed, wondering what they were talking about.

"Does Emily have something going with Phelps?" he asked.

She stared at him, aghast. "If you mean what I think you mean—no. Absolutely not. No way."

"Why not?"

"She has a boyfriend. She told me...." Lauren swallowed to silence herself. What Emily had told her was that she was in love with an older man. "No," Lauren said, determined not to lend any credence to Alec's appalling suggestion. "No, Emily is a good girl. All her energy goes into her schoolwork, keeping her grades up so she can maintain her scholarship. She comes from a modest background, and staying at Albright means the world to her."

Alec digested Lauren's statement, his gaze shuttling toward Roger Phelps's table and then toward the window, scrutinizing the picturesque vista through the glass. She picked listlessly at her salad, too troubled by Alec's questions to eat.

"So, you think she wouldn't jeopardize her position at Albright by messing around with a professor?"

"I think she's too smart to do something that ridiculous," Lauren snapped.

Alec eyed her cautiously. "Is it ridiculous? I bet that sort of thing happens all the time, professors messing around with their students."

"Don't look at me," Lauren said loftily.

Alec chuckled. "Hey, this is an all-girl school. I don't think it would be your style, Lauren."

She wasn't amused.

He sighed, obviously aware of her uneasiness. "I haven't got any proof," he said. "Yet. But if something hasn't happened between the two of them, it will."

Lauren shook her head, as if that would make the entire concept go away. Of course professors had affairs with their students sometimes, and she supposed that at an all-women's school, sleazy male professors like Roger Phelps would be apt to try their luck with the students. And while in general Lauren would consider such behavior reprehensible but not earth-shattering, when it came to Emily Spaeth, her prize pupil, she simply couldn't abide the possibility.

"He's married," she muttered, aware that his marital status hadn't slowed him down when he'd made his unsuccessful passes at her.

"We both know the guy's a scum bucket," Alec reminded her. "The issue is, Mags thinks he may be abusing the power of his position at the college. I don't know what the deal is between him and Emily, but there's a rumor that last year he got a senior into law school in exchange for a roll in the hay. Now you're telling me Emily's under pressure to get her grades up so she can keep her scholarship and stay at Albright. I know she's doing special research for Phelps. I'd like to know what else she's doing to get an A from him."

"You're awfully suspicious," Lauren said reproachfully. While everything he said was factual, he had no way of connecting one fact with another and weaving it all into some grand, incriminating truth. Lauren *knew* Emily. Emily wouldn't sleep with a professor in exchange for a good grade. Lauren simply wouldn't believe that of her.

"Yeah, I'm suspicious," Alec agreed. "I used to be a cop—it comes with the territory. Mags asked me to come to Albright because I've got a background in investigative work. She thinks I can find things out for her that she can't discreetly investigate by herself."

Lauren dropped her fork, too dumbfounded to speak. Alec had said nothing outlandish—indeed, everything he'd said was perfectly reasonable. But she was still astounded to learn that Alec had come here on a specific assignment, that he was acting as a spy for the president of the college, and that he was telling Lauren about it, including her in his secrets.

He must have read her bewilderment in her face, because he reached across the table and closed his hand over hers. "Look, if you'd rather not know, just forget I said anything."

"No, that's all right," she managed.

"I wouldn't have laid all this on you, except that I'm worried about Emily becoming Phelps's next victim. And I thought, since you're her piano teacher..."

Lauren understood what he was getting at. "I'm not going to pump her for information, Alec. But I can certainly keep my eyes and ears open."

"That's all I would ask of you." He released her hand and smiled gently. "I don't want to put you in an awkward position, Lauren."

"No. It's fine, really. I don't mind. If I can keep Emily out of trouble, I'd like to help."

He scrutinized her, his smile remaining but his eyes growing solemn, intense with thought. "I know I can trust you," he said.

A strange, sparkling warmth filled her at his words. Just that morning she had told him as much about herself as she'd told Gerald in the nearly fifteen years they'd known each other. Over the weekend her body had told Alec things she hadn't even acknowledged in herself—her responsiveness, her insecurity, her deeply held beliefs about love and sex being inseparable. And every night, with her living room windows open to the cool evening air, her discordant piano playing told him things known by no one else but herself, things about fear and determination, about loss and courage.

He was more than just her friend, and she trusted him as much as he trusted her.

CHAPTER NINE

THEY ENDED UP having dinner together at his apartment. She'd already taken him out for lunch, had him over for supper and temporarily covered the bill for their one night out. This time he was determined to be a proper host—which, given his lack of culinary expertise, amounted to his spreading canned mushroom pieces across the top of the frozen pizza before he slid it into the oven. He spread them out evenly, at least, and folded two squares of paper towel to resemble napkins. The plates and the glasses matched. Lauren wouldn't have grounds for complaint.

She had told him over lunch that she was going to Boston the following day to have a specialist examine her hand. "My appointment with Dr. Nylander is at two o'clock," she'd said. "Just think, by two-thirty, I may have a whole new timetable for my recovery."

Her optimism was contagious. Alec wanted her visit with the doctor to go well. He wanted her to come back to Albright with a new therapeutic regimen and a rosy prognosis. He had resigned himself to the fact that he was involved with Lauren Wyler, but it was the involvement of friends, two people who trusted and helped each other.

"You can't just go to Boston, see a doctor and leave," he'd chided her. "All you know about Boston is Symphony Hall. Why don't you spend the day in the city and take in some of the sights?''

"I wouldn't know where to begin.''

"I'll tell you where to begin,'' he'd said. "Come to my apartment for dinner, and I'll mark up a map with a respectable sight-seeing tour.''

By the time they were seated at his kitchen table that evening, with hot, oozing slices of pizza and icy bottles of beer before them, Alec had come up with a better idea. "Why don't I drive into the city with you?'' he suggested. "We could get an early start, arrive in town by, say, ten o'clock—''

"No,'' she cut him off. She was smiling, but her tone was stern.

"Okay,'' he relented. "We could leave around noon, go straight to the doctor, and then go out for dinner afterward. There's this restaurant in the North End—as a matter of fact, there are about a hundred restaurants in the North End....''

She laughed and shook her head. "No, Alec. I want to go by myself.''

He knew what she was thinking—that his offer to accompany her was based on a desire to take care of her. After battling her manager over that very issue earlier that day, she was particularly quick to cut Alec off before his protective instincts ran away with him.

"Hey, it's not that I don't think you can handle it,'' he claimed. "The truth is, I left my coffeemaker in Boston and I want to pick it up and bring it back here.'' Her dubious look prompted a confession from him. "Well, I thought I could pick up my coffeemaker and provide you with moral support at the same time. Plus, I'm a terrific tour guide.''

"I'm sure you are," she granted. "But this is primarily a medical trip, and it's something I need to do by myself."

He backed down good-naturedly. "All right, then, go by yourself. But if the doctor's office is right near Mass. General, you're only going to be a few blocks from the Public Gardens. You've got to take a swan boat ride."

"A what?"

He took a swig of beer and shook his head reproachfully. How many times had she been to Boston, and she'd never heard of the swan boats, let alone ridden on one.

So he told her about the swan-shaped paddle boats that glided across the lake in the gardens, and about the elegant shops and hotels bordering the Boston Common. He described the esplanade along the Charles River, and the science museum just a few blocks from the hospital in the opposite direction, and the renovated Quincy Market with its boutiques and alfresco eateries, and Faneuil Hall, and Charlestown, where the *Constitution*—"Old Ironsides"—was permanently docked and open to tourists. "There's a whole lot to see, and you wouldn't have to go within a mile of Symphony Hall," he told her.

She laughed. "It sounds like a week's worth of sights—but write them all down for me, Alec. I'll try to visit as many as I can."

Satisfied, he let the conversation drift to other topics. As they worked their way through the pizza, she told him that Emily Spaeth had seemed preoccupied during her piano lesson that afternoon. "She left with fifteen minutes still to go in her hour," said Lauren. "I was surprised. Emily always takes her full hour—sometimes she even runs over. I don't mind because she's my last lesson for the day. But today she seemed kind of jumpy, and she was in a big rush. She said she had to be somewhere this evening.''

"Phelps," Alec informed Lauren. "She had an appointment with him for this evening."

Lauren looked startled. "How do you know that?"

He gave her a falsely modest grin. "Hey, I'm good at what I do."

"You're good at being a busybody," she muttered.

He recalled her fury at his having eavesdropped on her fight with Gerald that morning, and wondered whether she was still just a little bit peeved about that. "I'm not ordinarily a nosy person," he told her. "But if I sense trouble, I prick up my ears, okay?"

Lauren's smile was forgiving. "Sometimes being nosy isn't such a bad thing," she allowed.

"This morning—"

"This morning you acted on instinct." She toyed with a strand of mozzarella, plucking it from her plate, and arranging it on the pizza wedge. Her eyes remained focused on her food when she added, "I wouldn't have been bothered at all if I hadn't been so insecure about my ability to handle the situation myself."

"You handled it just fine," he said.

She lifted her gaze. "I surprised myself. I guess I surprised both of us." Her smile grew wider, expressing something far more complicated than simple forgiveness for Alec's having interfered that morning. It seemed to say that she and Alec both had learned something from the incident. They shared some profound understanding, and that special understanding rooted their friendship and nourished it.

"At this point," he said, "nothing you did would surprise me."

"Now there's a challenge," Lauren joked. She took a bite of pizza, swallowed and said, "So, how do you know Emily's spending the evening with Roger Phelps?"

"I was in his office when they made the plan. Did you know he's got a fat red couch in his office?"

Lauren wrinkled her nose. "She shouldn't be seeing him at night."

"The time of day doesn't matter, does it?"

Lauren sighed. "If I wanted to assume the best—and I do, Alec—then I'd say it's wrong for her to meet with him in the evening because it interfered with her piano lesson."

"And if you don't assume the best?"

She shook her head. "I don't care how much she wants an A—she wouldn't sleep with a professor just to get one."

"Are you sure about that?"

"She told me she was in love, Alec. If she's sleeping with Roger Phelps—" Lauren succumbed to a reflexive shudder at the mere possibility "—it would be because she thought she loved him."

"If her taste is that lousy, then why assume she's above trading sex for grades?"

"Taste is not the same thing as integrity. I know Emily, and I just know she wouldn't."

"You've known her for less than two months," Alec reminded Lauren.

She slumped in her chair, defeated. "It's all so . . . so sordid."

"It's real life, lady."

She shuddered again. "All right. Let's assume the worst. How am I supposed to question her? How am I supposed to interrupt a lesson to ask whether she's fooling around with Roger Phelps?''

"You don't have to ask her anything. Just be there if she wants to talk."

"Well, I'd like to help—not just you, but her. I don't want her getting caught up in something with that beast. He's married, for heaven's sake!"

"For heaven's sake," Alec echoed, amused by Lauren's high-minded indignation.

She permitted herself a sheepish smile. "I should be more blasé about these things. I've read your book, after all."

"Don't become blasé. It's refreshing to meet someone who can still get scandalized by a scandal."

"Maybe it's not a scandal yet," Lauren said hopefully. "Maybe Emily hasn't actually gone through with it. Maybe she's still safe."

"You want to protect her," Alec teased.

Lauren shot him a look of annoyance, then subsided with another sheepish grin. "I suppose I do. She's just a child, Alec. She needs protection."

"I'll see that she gets it," Alec promised. "I've got all these protective urges inside me. If I can't use them on you, I'll use them on her."

"With my blessings," Lauren said, raising her beer in a toast.

She left shortly after they'd finished eating. Alec understood that she wanted to hit the sack early, to rest up for her busy day tomorrow. He also understood that if she'd stayed too long in his home, he might have tried to persuade her to stay even longer.

Being friends with Lauren was nice, and the more practice he had at it the more natural it would seem. But for now, his best strategy was to avoid testing his willpower. Too much time in her company, and he would undoubtedly start thinking about kissing her, touching her, taking her into his arms . . . and that would destroy whatever chance they had to be friends.

He rose early Friday morning, threw on some clothes and went downstairs to see her off. Dressed in an attractive sweater-and-skirt outfit of forest green and sensible flat-soled shoes well suited for walking, she looked alert and cheerful. Her hair was brushed back from her face, and along with a small leather purse she carried her tote bag, which was packed with maps, the morning newspaper and an umbrella. "The weatherman predicted rain on and off today," she said, peering up at the overcast sky.

"Then skip the swan boats and go to the science museum," Alec advised.

Lauren grinned and let him take the heavy tote from her. "If your new book doesn't work out, you can become a travel agent," she said as they walked together across the leaf-strewn front yard to her geriatric Volvo.

"The new book's going to work out fine," he boasted. "It's got six murders and seven sex scenes in the first chapter alone."

Lauren snorted in disbelief. "I hope it isn't set in any of the places you've marked on the map for me to visit."

"It's fiction," he reminded her, placing the tote bag on the passenger seat and closing the door. "Of course, if you're really worried about your safety in the city, I could still come along with you."

"I'm not at all worried," she said serenely, letting him open the driver's-side door for her. She settled in her seat, fastened the seat belt and smiled at him through the open window. "You stay here and inflict fictional havoc on your beloved city. I'll dodge the raindrops and the bullets by myself."

"Yes, ma'am." He stepped back from the car as she started the engine. "Drive safely."

"That's the only way I know how to drive," she told him, then waved goodbye and pulled into the street.

Alec watched as she coasted down the block to the corner, turned and cruised out of view. The morning air was warm and humid, more like August than October. At his feet, fallen leaves lay limp and soggy.

He turned and shuffled back to the duplex, feeling curiously lonesome in her absence. He was pleased by her high spirits; he even shared her confidence that this new doctor would be able to accomplish something for her that the doctor in New York had been unable to do. Alec wanted to think that in time she *would* be going to Symphony Hall—to perform. For her sake, he wanted to believe that someday she would again stand on a concert stage with a grand piano behind her and an audience before her, cheering and demanding encores.

If that was what this trip to Boston was all about, he was glad she'd gone. And if what this trip was about was her declaration of independence, her most important solo performance, her chance to follow her own counsel and no one else's, he was even more glad she'd gone.

BY TEN-THIRTY that night he was showered and in bed, staring at the distorted reflection of a street lamp through the rain-streaked window across the room. He'd done a lot of work that day and he was wiped out, but he couldn't fall asleep. Not until Lauren got home.

During the day, his thoughts had occasionally wandered to her. He'd imagined her strolling through the

Public Gardens or the shops of Copley Plaza—or even better, rejoicing as her new doctor told her she'd be back to virtuoso status by New Year's Day. Alec had imagined her spending the afternoon following the Freedom Trail through Boston, tracking it into the North End, standing before the Old North Church with its simple brick walls and plain white spire, a stone's throw from Alec's Boston apartment. He'd imagined her in front of the boxy six-story building he called home, thinking of him as he thought of her.

In the evening, he polished off the leftover pizza and read the newspaper, then watched a silly detective show on television. But the drone of the TV couldn't fill the vacuum in his flat. Something was missing.

Her music.

Funny how he'd grown so used to her drills and practices. They were wretched—not because she played badly but because she came so close to playing spectacularly. Bad playing was laughable; almost-perfect playing was tragic. Yet Lauren's almost-perfect playing had become a part of his daily routine, a habit, a familiar presence in his life. Without it, his evening lacked some essential ingredient. The day didn't seem complete.

He waited up for her until the monotony of the television's offerings threatened to lull him to sleep on the sofa. He'd wanted to talk to her as soon as she got back, to hear how the day had gone and what the doctor had said, but by ten o'clock she still wasn't home, so he gave up and got ready for bed.

Lying awake, watching the raindrops shiver against the screen in his window, he tried to convince himself that she was all right. He'd listed so many places for her to see, maybe she'd decided to stay on into the evening and see them all. Maybe she'd decided to eat dinner in town—or even take a hotel room for the night so she could do more sight-seeing over the weekend. She was under no obligation to call and clear her plans with him.

On the other hand, what would be the harm in phoning one of his old buddies on the police force, just to be sure? To be sure of what? he thought irritably. What would he do, give the precinct house a buzz and ask if any beautiful young women with black hair and a malfunctioning right hand happened to have been mugged that day?

She was fine, he told himself. She was fine, and he was an overprotective idiot who'd lately been spending too much time immersed in the fictional environment of his crime novel. If Lauren so much as suspected that he'd been worrying about her, she'd bite his head off. And he would deserve it.

He eyed the glowing face of his alarm clock: a quarter to eleven. Where was she?

He heard a muffled thump below, the sound of her front door closing. A long breath escaped him and he felt his muscles unwind. He could get a full report on her trip in the morning. For now, all that mattered was that she'd made it home safely. He could stop stewing and go to sleep.

Relief washed over him like a wave, the undertow dragging him down into a relaxed slumber. Just as he drifted off, the dissonant clamor of her piano jolted him awake. He let out a groan as the noise shook his apartment. He was glad she'd gotten home, but he needed his sleep. It was much too late for her to start practicing now.

After a minute, he realized she wasn't practicing. She was banging on the keys, mauling them, flailing at them. The entire building seemed to rattle with the cacophony.

He cursed and tossed off his blanket. Whatever she was up to, it was going to have to wait until tomorrow. He had to get some sleep.

Swinging his legs over the side of the bed, he heard another sound—a crash. Not the piano, not the thud of a kitchen chair falling over but the sound of something shattering, something brittle and delicate smashing against a hard surface. A teacup, maybe. A china teacup colliding with the stone hearth of a fireplace.

He heard another smash. Then another.

He stepped into his jeans and was out the bedroom door before he had the fly closed. He barely broke stride to snatch his keys from the kitchen counter before he left his flat. Racing down the stairs, he heard more crashing noises, the distinctive crunch of china fragmenting. And then another haphazard bang on the piano, as if something heavy had fallen across the keys.

He shot out his front door and across the porch to hers. Through the open living room window he saw her remove a teacup from her collection and hurl it at the fireplace across the room. The cup cracked against the brass fireplace screen, knocking it against the wall. The floor was littered with shards of china.

"Lauren!" he shouted through the window.

Ignoring him, she lifted another cup from the shelf and flung it across the room. It struck the mantelpiece and exploded into tiny jagged slivers of white shrapnel.

She turned back to the shelf, and he caught a glimpse of her face. It was frozen into an expressionless mask, her eyes dull and her lips rigid. She was wearing the pretty green outfit she'd had on that morning, the gold wristwatch, the black flats on her feet. But her face was blank, as pale and lifeless as the cup she was pulling down from the shelf.

"Lauren!" he shouted. "Stop!"

She rotated and dashed the cup against the fireplace, watching impassively as it broke and the pieces sprayed across the floor.

Raindrops skittered over his naked back and chest, chilling him. His bare feet grew cold on the rough planks of the porch; his bad knee ached. He darted to Lauren's door, thumbed the doorbell several times and listened through the open window as the chime echoed throughout her apartment. He heard another cup crash into smithereens and groaned. "Lauren, let me in!"

Another crash.

He hurried back to the window. The shelves that had once held dozens of cups were now clear, and Lauren had returned to the piano. She lifted a thick book of sheet music from the ledge above the keys and tore a page from it. Then another.

Alec shoved his wet hair back from his face and examined the window. The screen's wooden frame was slick from the day's dampness, the old wood spongy. Six clamps held it to the building's outer wall. With a sharp wrenching motion, Alec jarred the screen from its track and yanked it off.

He shoved the inner storm window higher and climbed over the sill. Finally Lauren turned her attention to him. She stared at him as he advanced, her face vacant, her eyes flat. In her left hand she held the torn music book. Her right, Alec noticed, was contorted as it usually was, the two outer fingers twisted into her palm.

He had broken into homes before. He had cornered maniacs, and he had rescued victims. Right now he wasn't sure which of those descriptions fit what he was doing. Maybe both.

He took a cautious step toward Lauren, afraid of spooking her. Her lunatic demolition of her teacups and sheet music scared him. The emptiness in her eyes scared him even more.

"Lauren," he said quietly, consolingly. He inched toward her.

"Stay away from me." Her voice was as barren as her expression. She ripped several pages from the book and let them drift to the floor.

"Lauren—"

"Go away. Leave me alone!"

The edge of emotion in her voice was oddly reassuring. He took another step toward her and she hurled the book at him.

He caught it, but by the time he'd set it down on the piano bench she was across the room, yanking record albums down from the shelf next to her stereo system, tossing them heedlessly through the air, pulling more down, searching for something. With a dozen albums discarded she found what she was after—a copy of *Lauren Wyler Plays Chopin,* the record the librarian had shown Alec at the campus music library. The record he'd stared at long enough to develop a serious crush on the woman in the photograph on the jacket.

Lauren shook out the black vinyl disk and snapped it in two across her knee.

He darted through the room, swearing when he scratched the sole of his foot on a sharp piece of broken crockery, ducking to avoid being hit by a record that tumbled off the shelf. He manacled her wrists with his hands and she poked at his chest with the jagged edges of the broken record. He gave her a sharp shake and she let go of the two black semicircles. They hit the floor, creating twin clattering sounds. She tried to claw him with her fingernails instead, but they were too short to draw blood.

"Lauren."

"Let me go!" she wailed, struggling in his grip until she was able to yank one hand free. She swung her arm savagely across the shelf, knocking off the last few records and unhinging the dustcover of the turntable. Ignoring the records that hit him in their wild flight to the floor, Alec recaptured her hand and gave her another shake. She reared back and kicked his shin.

Grunting at the bruising blow, he recoiled from her. She spun away and knocked over her CD player with her foot, then returned to the piano, to the partially destroyed sheet music on the bench. She grabbed the book, attempted to tear several pages at once, and when they didn't give, whacked the spine of the book repeatedly against the keyboard, roiling the atmosphere with a chaotic jangle of sound that echoed painfully inside his skull.

Vaulting over the couch, he dragged her away from the piano and bound his arms around her, forcing the music book from her grip. He held her immobile, pinning her hands to her sides and enveloping her body with his, tightly enough that she couldn't wallop or kick him.

She twitched, squirmed, tried in vain to wiggle free. "Let me go!" she screamed, somehow managing to lift her knee toward his groin. He bent and twisted in time to deflect the blow with his hip. "Let me go! I hate you! I hate everything! I hate this!"

"Shh." He held her even tighter, praying that she'd burn out before she did any more damage.

In time she stopped writhing and wilted against him. Her shoulders began to shake. "I hate you," she moaned, less an attack than a lament. "I hate you."

"No, Lauren. You don't."

She gazed up at him, and the hard mask of her face seemed to disintegrate into a million crystalline pieces, like the china wreckage around them. Her lower lip quivered, her eyes welled up with tears. For the first time she seemed to know who he was, where she was, what was going on.

"Alec," she whispered, then crumpled against him and surrendered to a plaintive cry.

The fight had gone out of her, but he continued to hold her snugly, afraid that if he loosened his embrace she would fall. She trembled as great, wrenching sobs racked her body; her tears spilled hot and wet over his shoulder. Her hands fisted against his chest and the room filled with the low sound of her weeping, soft and mournful, each sob torn painfully from the depths of her soul.

It was hard to recall how strong she'd seemed yesterday morning, the last time he'd been in this room. She had stood up to her manager and to Alec then, fearless and independent. Now she felt fragile in his arms, breakable, her slender shoulders heaving and her fingers groping against the muscled wall of his chest as if searching for a handhold, something to keep her from collapsing.

"I've got you," he murmured, standing steady against the onslaught of her emotions. "I've got you, Lauren. It's all right, I won't let you fall."

"It's over," she groaned, her voice weak and tremulous. "Everything. Oh, God, my whole life, it's all gone. There's nothing left...."

"Shh." He stroked her hair, pulling it back from her moist cheeks, running his palm over the smooth black silk of it again and again in a soothing pattern. "It's all right, Lauren."

"It's not all right." She buried her face against his shoulder. "Nothing's all right. Nothing. I can't play anymore. I can't—he said—" Her voice disintegrated as she succumbed to fresh tears.

"I know, I know." She didn't have to go into detail; Alec could fill in the blanks. He could guess what she'd learned that day, what dismal truth the doctor had forced her to confront. He knew what she was going through. He'd been there himself, and he knew exactly how much it hurt.

Maybe it had been easier for him because, unlike her, he hadn't had any hope to begin with. From the moment he'd opened his eyes after a long, dreamless sleep to find himself in a glaringly lighted room, in an unfamiliar bed, he'd had no illusions about going back to where he'd been. His gradual return to consciousness had informed him of the tube threaded up his nose, his skin itching from his bandages, his lungs burning with every breath, his right leg throbbing and in his left no pain, no sensation at all. He recalled thinking he was paralyzed—and deaf because he couldn't hear anything. And then a woman in a white coat had leaned over him and said, "Well, hello there!" She'd been talking in a moderate tone, but her voice had exploded inside his head.

He'd lain there, not knowing what had happened to him, when it had happened or why. He'd known only one thing: he wasn't a cop anymore. What he'd been before he would never be again. Life as he knew it was over.

And then he'd realized something else: he wasn't dead.

Lauren didn't need Alec reminding her that she was alive. What she needed was for him to hold her and keep her from breaking anything else. He wished she had let him go with her to Boston today. She hadn't required protection from the big city, but she'd required protection from this, the truth. The rage.

"Lauren," he murmured, still stroking her hair with one hand, still hugging her with the other arm. She continued to cry, her tears streaking across his skin, her face warm and moist in the hollow of his shoulder.

"He said..." She sighed, shivering, clutching at him. "He said nerve tissue can't regenerate itself. He said he couldn't imagine why the doctor had told me I'd get any better. He said it was a miracle I'd improved as much as I had. He said..." She sighed again, a muffled, choking sound. "Oh, God, Alec—I can't play anymore."

"Yes you can."

"Not for people. Not the way I used to. It's all over. Everything in my whole life—"

"There's more to life than your piano," he assured her. "You may not believe that right now, but in time—"

"Time? In time? What time? I have *nothing.* There's no point anymore, no point to anything. I can't work. I can't play. I have nothing."

"You have me," he murmured. "Right now, you have me."

"Hold me, Alec."

"I'm holding you," he whispered.

She slid her arms up to his shoulders and tilted her head back. As pale as she'd looked before, now she was flushed, her skin feverish, her eyes bright with tears of despair and dread. "Don't let go," she begged.

"I won't."

She wound her fingers deep into his thick damp hair and guided his head down to hers.

FOR THE FIRST TIME in the hours since she'd left Dr. Nylander's office she felt alive again. Alec's mouth took hers, claimed it, opened to her, molded to her. She kissed him frantically, drinking in his strength, the heat and sensuality of him. If she could feel this, if she could share in it, maybe her spirit wasn't completely dead.

She had no future. She couldn't perform anymore; her hand was ruined. Dr. Nylander had told her it would be cruel to let her continue harboring false hopes. "Of course you'll always have your music," he'd said with an ingratiating smile. "You won't be able to play at the level you used to, but that doesn't mean you can't enjoy what's left."

What was left wasn't enough to live on. It wasn't enough to pay her way, to justify her family's sacrifices or her own. What was left was a great void.

No future.

She had no real past, either—nothing but a long, dreary chain of concert halls and hotel rooms leading to this moment, this sheer drop into nowhere. She had no background, no breadth, no knowledge of the world. No swan boats in Boston, no museums in London, no excursions to Stonehenge, no theaters in Tokyo, no photo safaris in the outback of Australia. What she had were teacups, dozens of small, charming, pretty, loathsome teacups. And now she didn't have them anymore, either.

No past.

All she had was the present, the warmth and power of Alec's arms around her, his mouth absorbing the anxious hunger of hers. She would take what she had, take as much as she could and hang on as long as she could, because after this there would be nothing.

Given her delirious state, it took her a while to realize he wasn't wearing a shirt. Her hands moved at first hesitantly and then avidly over the sinewy ridges of his shoulders, gripping, clutching, her palms wiping raindrops and her own tears from his skin. His arms around her were leanly muscled and graceful. His mouth was hard, demanding, his tongue sparring with hers. For a dazed instant she wondered what horrible thing he'd just endured that would make him want to kiss her as implacably as she was kissing him.

It didn't matter. All that mattered was now, the vibrant life inside him, the strength and shelter of his embrace. Even if her past and her future were nothing, *this* was something. It was breath and energy and need, hearts pounding and mouths clinging. It was Alec supporting her and making her feel, awakening her nerve endings with the promise of life, hope, something that could fend off the futility of the past and the bleakness of the future.

"Lauren..." Her name slipped from him on a ragged sigh as his lips glided over hers. His hands skimmed her back, then settled at her waist as he leaned away from her.

She tightened her hold on him, afraid of what would happen if she let go. Rising onto tiptoe, she fused her mouth to his again. Her left hand twined through the dense honey-colored hair above his ear, and her right drifted forward over his shoulder. Her inept outer fingers dragged through the golden curls that adorned the firm wall of his chest; her healthy fingers and thumb probed the warm, resilient surface of his skin. She felt his muscles flexing beneath her hand, his heart racing, his lungs pumping. Frantic, she deepened the kiss, stabbing his lips with her tongue, venturing beyond his teeth, pursuing him into his mouth.

She heard him whisper her name again, a protest, a plea, and then he brought his hands down to her bottom and cupped the roundness there, pulling her to himself. Sensation swamped her as he pressed into her, molten heat gathering below her belly as he rocked her hips to his. This was nothing like the easy pleasure she'd felt dancing with him. That had been delightful, exciting, heavenly. This was need, rampaging fear, the understanding that the only life left to her was what she was feeling right now.

Her hands continued to move on his bare torso as his moved on her. He gathered her skirt with his fingers, bunching it up around her waist. Then he caressed her thighs through her nylons, stroking her until her legs threatened to buckle.

In a single swift motion he lifted her off her feet and drew her legs around his hips. If she'd been capable of lucid thought she would have marveled at his ability to bear her weight. But she wasn't thinking. She was burning up, moaning as he kneaded the soft flesh of her derriere, as he centered her on his aroused manhood and pressed against her.

She still needed him, needed him immediately, fervently, with an intensity born of grief. But somewhere along the way, her need had become enmeshed within a more complex emotion. She desired Alec. She wanted him.

Without pulling his mouth from hers, he lifted her higher, enabling her to circle her legs around his waist. Picking his way through the devastation of her living room, he carried her to the hall, past the kitchen, past the study and into her bedroom. He strode directly to the bed and lowered her onto it, then followed her down, sinking into her arms.

His kisses were voracious, his tongue filling her, kindling heat in her throat, her breasts, her abdomen. Her tongue mimicked his, plundering his mouth with an aggressiveness she would never have recognized in herself. He shuddered as her hands explored the smooth expanse of his back, running down his spine and settling at the waistband of his jeans.

The only sounds in the room were his breathing and hers, the distant rattle of raindrops striking the window—and, abruptly, the rasp of his zipper as he opened it. The harsh sound forced her to acknowledge that this was more than just the present, more than mere sensation, more than simply a frenzied quest for something meaningful in her suddenly meaningless life. It was real, hot, physical. It was Alec's body and hers, and it was like nothing she'd ever known before.

But she couldn't stop. She wouldn't. The need was too great.

She pushed down the denim in back as he pushed it down in front, then felt his weight lift off her as he kicked the jeans away. His fingers moved deftly on her, easing off her sweater, peeling off her stockings, slipping off her skirt, plucking off her bra.

Once she was naked, he descended into her arms again, nibbling lightly over her lips and then slithering downward to kiss her throat, the fragile line of her collarbone, the swollen red tips of her breasts. He licked, sucked, nipped until she was moaning again, more desperate than ever—desperate for something she couldn't identify, something beyond her experience.

But then, her experience was pathetically limited. Her past was worthless, fruitless. She'd learned no valid skills, no simple way to make a living—and she'd learned nothing about the ferocious yearnings of her body, the agonizing tension Alec could create with his mouth on first one breast and then the other, with his hand roving across her navel, around the protrusion of her hipbone and into the dense thatch of hair between her legs.

His fingers slid over her flesh, probing the sensitive folds of skin and then entering her. She cried out, embarrassed by her wetness, by the reflexive clenching of her thighs, the quaking in her hips and the flood of sensation inside her. She almost begged him to stop. The insistent rhythm of his fingers against her hurt—and then felt good, so good, fearfully good. She lay still beneath him, wanting to abandon herself to the powerful pressure building inside her but afraid, afraid because she didn't understand it, because its allure was so strong.

With his free hand he gripped her wrist and steered her hand down until he could mold her palm around him. Her lame fingers balked, bending clumsily when her other fingers wrapped around him, but he wouldn't release her. His hand moved hers up and down, forcing her to accept him, to learn his size, his heat, the urgent strength of his arousal.

He rose back onto her, aligning his body with hers, skimming her lips with the top of his tongue. "Now," he whispered. Before she could question him, he pushed her hand away and spread her thighs with his knees. She felt him against her, poised, ready, but he didn't move. "Now," he whispered again, his voice taut but emphatic.

At first she didn't understand...and then she did. He longed for her as insanely as she longed for him, but he refused to act alone. She could no longer lie passively on the mattress, letting him guide her here and there. If she wanted him she would have to take him.

Timidly, uncertainly, she slid her hands down his back to the rock-hard surface of his buttocks and arched up, gasping at the shock of his invasion, then moaning as her body welcomed him in a rush of warmth. Evidently aware that she'd done all she could, he took charge, moving in a slow, subtle rhythm, stroking her as his fingers had stroked her. Each plunge pulled something tighter inside her, straining her, wringing her until her soul ached, until she was in agony.

His thrusts grew faster, harder. She wanted him to let up; she wanted him to keep going. She needed...relief. Release. Something she couldn't name.

He reached down and pulled her legs up around him, then forged deeper. His sweat mingled with hers, his mouth locked onto hers. She felt the tension in him. The muscles in his back bunched and stretched as his hips drove into her. One of his hands curved over her breast. Journeying lower, he massaged her hip, then wedged his hand between his body and hers, found her, touched her.

Like the daintiest of her teacups shattering against a hard surface, her soul shattered against him, exploding suddenly, exquisitely into shimmering fragments, pulses of energy coursing down through her flesh, through her veins, her cells, through her heart and soul. She heard

Alec groaning above her, his body wrenching, emptying into her.

After a long moment, he let out his breath and rolled over, bringing Lauren with him, cradling her in the bend of his arm and cushioning her head on his shoulder. She snuggled against him, listening to his erratic respiration, feeling his skin gradually cool and his muscles unclench.

Her past hadn't changed; her future remained a hopeless limbo. But she'd had this, this timeless present. For one idyllic moment in Alec's arms, she'd felt more alive than she'd ever felt before.

She'd had *this*—and it was enough to stave off the past and the future, if only for now.

CHAPTER TEN

WRONG, HE THOUGHT, staring up into the shapeless dark. No matter how much he'd wanted to make love to her—no matter how fantastic it had been—it was wrong. He should have heeded the warnings and steered clear of her.

In the curve of his arm she stirred, nestling closer. He ran his hand along her side, strumming her ribs, following the downward slope to her waist and the rise to her hip, unable to stop savoring the elegance of her body, the creamy smoothness of her skin, the pressure of her head on his shoulder, the brush of her knee against his leg, the warmth of her breath floating across his chest and the cool, slippery spill of her hair over his upper arm. He shouldn't be responding to her so strongly. Given how spectacularly he'd peaked just minutes ago, it didn't seem possible that he could be hard again, wanting her.

Nor was it right. He shouldn't have brought her to bed. Making love with her had been a mistake; he couldn't allow himself to make the same mistake twice.

He waited for her to say something. Sooner or later they were going to have to talk. But she only rested cozily beside him, her eyes closed, her head growing heavier and her breathing steadier. After a while he realized she had dozed off.

Sighing, he eased out from under her to pull up the blanket. In her sleep she mumbled an incoherent protest when he moved away, and like a fool he silenced her with a kiss. Her lips were too full, too sweet, and he kissed her again. In spite of the fact that she was asleep, she kissed him back. Maybe she was dreaming about his kisses.

He sighed again and pulled back. Her mouth settled into a delectable pout. He forced his gaze away, allowing himself one final look at her pale, magnificent body before he covered it with the quilt. Her breasts were so round, her waist so absurdly tiny, and that dark triangle of hair at the apex of her thighs...

He mouthed a silent curse at the insistent ache in his groin. Dropping back onto the pillow, he looped his arm around her and drew her to himself, allowing the quilt to settle over them in hills and valleys, like midnight snow.

Her body had bewitched him, thrilled him, intrigued him in an astonishing way. But it had also revealed the truth of her inexperience to him. She wasn't a virgin, but she might as well have been. She'd seemed bewildered by the depth of her pleasure, almost alarmed by it, as if it were all a complete mystery to her. She hadn't known what to do with Alec's body—although he had to admit her aimless, unskilled caresses had turned him on quite effectively. She'd been skittish about placing her hand on him; she hadn't known how to bring him to herself. She'd been so tight when he'd entered her, and when she'd climaxed she hadn't seemed to understand what was happening to her.

Except that it was glorious. Except that it was the ultimate joy. Her first time, probably, and she'd been blown away by it—and Alec had been a part of it, essential to it, just as blown away. It was theirs, something they shared, something they'd given each other. And it bound them irrevocably together.

He lay on his back, damning the night and his pitiful lack of willpower. Lauren had grabbed on to him like a shipwreck victim grabbing on to a bit of flotsam. She'd been drowning, and instead of holding her head above water he'd let them both be swept away by a tidal wave of sexual gratification. He'd wanted her so much he hadn't cared about the consequences.

And now he and Lauren were *involved*.

The last thing Alec wanted was to become involved with a woman in a situation as precarious as hers. The last thing she needed was to become involved with any man. Her life was complicated enough right now without a love affair thrown in. He should have resisted, should have kept his head, should have protected her— not just from him but from herself.

But she'd been raging with despair and he'd been raging with lust. So they'd wound up in bed. *Involved*.

"I'm sorry," he whispered, knowing she was too deeply asleep to hear him. "God, Lauren...I'm sorry."

She shifted, repositioning her head on his shoulder and sliding her arm down until her hand came to rest on the flat, lightly haired surface of his stomach. He covered her hand with his to prevent her fingers from drifting lower. If they did he would go out of his mind. He was already smoldering; one touch from her and he would ignite.

He was sorry for what he'd done. But in the thick, dark shadows of the night, with her naked body draped around his, he couldn't trust himself not to do it again.

WHEN LAUREN WOKE UP, she was alone. The clock beside her bed told her it was nearly six a.m.; a faint, milky haze crept over the windowsill and into her room. She felt dazed and disoriented, her body sore in unexpected places, the top sheet abrasive on her tender breasts. Where was her nightgown? Why was she naked?

Closing her eyes, she remembered. Everything.

She remembered her morning drive, the constant drizzle failing to dampen her spirits. She remembered parking in a public garage near Dr. Nylander's office and strolling in the rain, skipping playfully around the puddles as she wandered through the manicured lawns of the Boston Common. She remembered going to a café enclosed in greenhouse glass and lunching on fresh fruit and yogurt, and then strolling back to the doctor's office.

The anguish had been slow in building. She'd remained calm the whole time she was with Dr. Nylander, answering his questions, fisting and relaxing her fingers at his command, trying not to yelp when he pricked her fingertips with sharp objects, when he sizzled electrical currents into her muscles. She remembered nodding and thanking him and saying she understood what he was telling her. Then she'd walked back to the garage, paid the parking fee, climbed into her car and driven out.

She wasn't sure where she'd gone: over a bridge into Cambridge, over another bridge back to Boston, south into a ritzy shopping district and then east to avoid Symphony Hall. She'd meandered through Chinatown, past wharves and warehouses, along a road bordering the Charles River, south through a slum and into Brookline. She'd cruised down narrow streets of three-deckers, winding avenues of brick Colonials, drab blocks of tenements, rows of shops with their signs written in Spanish, Cambodian, Portuguese and Korean, some spray-painted with so much graffiti the signs were altogether unreadable. She drove, and the windshield wipers click-clacked, and the low clouds turned from light gray to slate to charcoal to black as a starless night spread like spilled ink across the sky.

She remembered arriving back in Albright late. The campus slumbered; the traffic lights at the major intersections had been switched from red-and-green to flashing yellow, creating a winking glare against the shimmering asphalt. The houses along Hancock Street were dark.

She remembered thinking, as she'd killed the engine and turned off the headlights, that she had reached a terminus, a dead end, a point beyond which she couldn't proceed. This was it. Final curtain call. No encore.

She remembered entering her apartment—and going berserk. And then...then Alec had arrived. He'd rushed in, grabbed her, carried her away from her misery. He'd touched her, filled her, loved her and made the pain disappear.

The last thing she remembered was Alec lying with her, his arm curved snugly around her, his hand sketching a delicate line up and down her back in a lulling tempo. Her last thought as sleep closed in on her was that he understood—that of all the people she knew in the entire world, he was the only one who truly understood what was going on inside her body and her mind.

Now he was gone. She sat up, modestly clutching the quilt around her even though no one was around to witness her nudity. Her skirt and sweater were spread haphazardly over a chair; her shoes lay on the rug near the closet door.

Then she heard the muted sound of someone moving around her living room. Glancing toward the bedroom door, she noticed a strip of light under it. Either Alec was still in her apartment or she was being burglarized. Hancock Street wasn't a high-crime district; she smiled at the reassuring thought that Alec hadn't run out on her.

She got out of bed and crossed to her closet for her robe. After tying the sash securely at her waist, she used her fingers to smooth the tangles in her hair, brushing it back from her sleep-warm cheeks. She padded barefoot to the bedroom door and took a deep breath to fortify herself before confronting the mayhem she knew was waiting on the other side of the door. Then she turned the knob and stepped into the hall.

The lamps were on in the living room, but when she reached it she was surprised to discover the room relatively neat. The screen was back in the window frame, her tattered sheet music was stacked on the piano bench and a paper bag full of broken porcelain stood propped against the arm of the sofa, beside it her kitchen broom. Her stereo components sat straight on their shelves. Alec knelt on the floor next to them, sorting through the scattered LPs and empty album sleeves, trying to match up the records to the jackets.

Obviously he hadn't heard her entrance. She gazed at him for a moment, taking note of the fact that he had on a shirt and sneakers. Last night he'd worn only his jeans. She recalled the athletic contours of his chest, the golden-brown swirls of hair adorning it, the solidity of his shoulders and the streaks of rain dampening his skin when he'd first grabbed her. She recalled his weight on her when they'd lain together, his male heat inside her, the intensity of his thrusts, the astonishing convulsions of her body cresting around him. Merely observing the powerful arch of Alec's back as he perused the label of a black vinyl disk caused an echo of sensation to surge through her flesh.

"Hello," she said quietly.

He flinched and twisted around, permitting his eyes to meet hers for a fraction of a second before he turned away. Standing, he brushed a residue of powdery white dust from the knees of his jeans and rolled his shoulders to loosen them.

"You didn't have to clean up," she said.

He rolled his shoulders again, this time with a shrug. "I didn't get it all. You'll still have to vacuum the floor. I picked up most of the big chunks, but there are lots of tiny pieces imbedded in the rug."

Why did this feel so awkward? Why did he address her as if she were a stranger, as if they were miles apart instead of a few paces?

"It was my mess," she argued. She wondered if Alec could hear the tension in her voice, the hint of anger. She wondered why they were discussing the chaotic state of her living room and her life instead of running into each other's arms and celebrating the miracle they'd experienced together last night. She wondered why Alec couldn't bring himself to look directly at her. "You shouldn't have cleaned up," she scolded. "I made the mess."

At last he did look at her, his gaze moving over her face, down her body to her bare feet and back up again, lingering briefly on her throat where it was exposed above the overlapping edges of her robe. "I think I made the mess worse,'' he murmured, raising his eyes briefly to hers again.

She surveyed the room. The shelves that had once held her teacups were now depressingly bare. The sheet music on the piano bench, however, didn't seem nearly as ruined as she would have liked. A few strips of clear tape would salvage most of the pages—as if that would do her any good.

"You prevented me from making the mess worse," she maintained, her voice still unnaturally low and taut. "I'm not sure whether I should thank you or curse you for that."

"Curse away," he said, a faint, mirthless laugh tinging his words.

She struggled to figure out what he was getting at. Why did he think he'd made the mess worse? He'd broken into her apartment when she'd been too deranged to let him in through the door, and he'd kept her from continuing her mindless trashing of the room. He'd let her vent her fury on him instead of her possessions—and then he'd transformed her fury into something different, something equally powerful but unspeakably beautiful.

So why was he behaving as if she were radioactive, as if getting too close to her would mean certain death? Why wouldn't he cross the room, take her in his arms and swear to her, as he had last night, that everything was all right, that he would hold her and never let go?

She took a step toward him and he indicated the couch with a wave of his hand. "Let's sit," he suggested, moving in his familiar uneven gait to the sofa and beckoning her to join him there.

They sat side by side, but he didn't sling his arm around her or kiss her cheek. She braced herself, knowing she wasn't going to like what he had to tell her.

It took him a while to begin. "I'm a jerk," he finally said. "I was way out of line last night. I wasn't thinking. I went on instinct, and . . . I was wrong."

Her mind told her he was referring to their lovemaking. But her heart told her that had been right, very right. Unable to accept his negative view of their intimacy, she chose to misunderstand him. "No harm done," she said with a weak smile. "So you broke the window frame. I see you were able to fix it."

"I'm not talking about the window," he said, refusing to acknowledge her mild joke. "I'm not talking about anything that happened in this room. I'm talking about the other part, in your bedroom."

She reminded herself that, compared to all the dreadful things Dr. Nylander had told her yesterday, nothing Alec said today could be that bad. She wasn't an accomplished lover, she knew that. But in her shy, fumbling way she'd somehow managed to please him. If he was going to complain about her technique, she would simply ask him to teach her how to do better.

If it wasn't her technique . . . then it was something worse. Something worse, even, than learning from the hand specialist in Boston that her concert career was over.

Swallowing, she studied her hands in her lap, the graceful, obedient left hand and the damaged right. "You didn't want to go to bed with me," she mumbled, figuring she might as well say it before he did.

"Oh, Lauren . . . I wanted to, more than you can guess." He sighed. "I wanted to so much I didn't stop when I should have. I took advantage of you, Lauren.

You were a wreck, and I should have been comforting you, and instead I took advantage of you in your weakness.'' He shook his head and stared at the pile of homeless records on the floor near the stereo. "I'm not sure I can forgive myself for that."

"What?" She leaned back, apprehension replaced by resentment. "You think you took advantage of me? In my weakness? Don't patronize me, Alec. Don't act as if I'm some sort of ninny who doesn't know what she's doing."

"You *didn't* know what you were doing," he countered, his tone as level as hers was shrill. "You were crazy last night, Lauren. You were out of your mind."

"I was—" she foundered on the truth in his words. She *had* been crazy. Not weak, not incapable of reason or unaware of Alec's intentions when he'd brought her to the bedroom, but... well, smashing cups and tearing books weren't exactly symptoms of mental stability. "I'll admit I was upset," she conceded. "But that doesn't mean—"

"You were more than upset. You were crazy, and you threw yourself at me, and..." He exhaled and gathered her hand in his, sandwiching her slender fingers between his leather-smooth palms. "I wanted you, so I took what you offered. I shouldn't have, Lauren, but I did."

"Don't apologize," she said wryly. "If it makes you feel any better, going to bed with you was the highlight of my day."

He closed his eyes and made a sound in his throat, part groan and part chuckle. "Oh, Lauren, it was the highlight of my year. But that still doesn't make it right." He laughed again, a sad, self-deprecating sound. "We didn't even talk about birth control—"

"Don't worry about it," she cut him off. "I've been on the pill since I turned twenty." Gerald had insisted on that, arguing that an unplanned pregnancy would destroy her career just as it was taking to the air. That she'd lived a celibate existence for most of the past decade didn't matter to him; whenever she contemplated letting her prescription lapse he would give her one of his lectures about "setting something up for her" if she ever felt the need for a healthy little romp between the sheets. "What's important is that you're always prepared, so there won't be any slipups. Your career comes first, Lauren. Always."

Not anymore, she thought with a sudden, staggering rush of bitterness. She had no career. She could stop taking her stupid pills right then.

Now there was an illogical thought, that if she could no longer play the piano she might as well not worry about an accidental pregnancy. Alec was right. She must be crazy.

"Lauren..." He ran his thumb over the dainty bones of her hand, tracing each slim line from her wrist to her knuckle and back again. "I like you," he said. "I care about you. I know you don't want anyone to try to protect you—but I can't help it. I worry about you. I don't want you getting hurt."

"Thanks a lot," she snapped. "My life is in a shambles, but one nice thing happened to me and you're worrying about my getting hurt. If you want to worry about something, worry about how in God's name I'm going to support myself for the next twenty years. Don't worry about the fact that you and I made love last night."

"We didn't make love," he said starkly. "We had sex."

Her heart stopped beating for a second. Her lungs froze. Her body went very cold. At last she understood what he was getting at: Love had nothing to do with it. The whole thing had been strictly physical for him. It was exactly as he'd described it: she'd thrown herself at him and he'd taken what she'd offered.

Her pulse resumed beating; she drew a breath into her lungs, and another. But deep inside her, in her soul, the coldness remained. Regardless of her unbridled rage and anguish last night, regardless of Alec's failure ever to broach the subject of romance or imply in any way that he and Lauren were anything more to each other than friendly neighbors, she had wanted to believe that love had been a part of it.

Alec was telling her that it hadn't.

And it hurt. Lord, how it hurt.

She closed her eyes and prayed for her tears to vanish before Alec could see them. Averting her face, she opened her eyes again and slipped her hand out from between his. "You don't have to protect me," she said, her tone hushed but steady. "I don't need anyone to protect me from myself or from what I do, from my decisions or the emotional fallout from them. I did what I did last night, and you don't have to feel guilty or take the blame or anything. I'm an adult, Alec, and whether or not you think I was crazy last night, I knew what was going on. I wasn't looking for love from you."

She was grateful for the sturdy quality of her voice, the plain rationality of her words. Most of what she'd said was true: she didn't want anyone protecting her, not Gerald and certainly not Alec. She was willing to assume the full credit for her actions, even if they were unwise.

As for the part about looking for love, well, that was almost true, too. She hadn't been looking for love when she'd come to Albright, when she'd met Alec, when she'd befriended him. She had agreed with Gerald that love would only dissipate her energies, and until yesterday, when all her effort had been focused on getting her career back on track, she had stoutly resisted anything that might detour her.

But when Alec had kissed her, when he'd held her and whispered that he wouldn't let her fall—love had been there. She hadn't been looking for it, but it had been there.

For her. Not for him.

If she could come to terms with the fact that her professional life was over, she supposed she could come to terms with anything, even this. She hadn't yet come to terms with either disaster, but in time she would. She had to. There was no alternative, no way to change what was. No way to heal her hand, no way to make Alec love her. No way to know for sure that when she'd kissed him last night she'd really been in love with him.

"I can't help thinking I made things worse for you," he said.

"Don't flatter yourself." She stood, pulled her robe tighter around her body and stalked off to the bedroom.

She rummaged through her closet for a pair of slacks and a sweater, then attacked her hair with her brush, stroking the bristles through the black strands with such vehemence her scalp tingled. All the while she tried to get a grip on herself, to stay calm, to persuade herself that last night was just one catastrophe colliding with another, a tornado ripping along the active fault of an earthquake. So she had no future and her heart was in shreds. What difference did any of it make? What was the point?

Tossing down her brush, she turned to straighten out the bed. She saw the twisted sheets, the indentation left by Alec's head in the pillow next to hers. Once more her body clenched in a memory of his lovemaking, his devastating kisses, the friction of his tongue on her breasts, of his fingers between her legs, the hoarse plea in his voice when he'd whispered *now*.

He'd needed her as much as she'd needed him last night. At that one instant, when he'd hovered above her, poised and tense, his desperation had been as great as hers.

He didn't need her anymore, though. And even if he did, need wasn't the same thing as love. Last night she'd been too inexperienced to tell the difference. This morning, though, she'd learned a painful lesson. Now she knew better.

Her long-suppressed tears welled over. Out of Alec's sight, she let herself weep. She didn't want him to know how badly he'd wounded her. If he knew, he'd keep worrying about her. He'd think she was weak and vulnerable and afraid, and he'd try to protect her. He'd step in and clean up the mess she'd made of her emotions, just as he'd cleaned up her living room.

She couldn't let that happen. She was determined to resolve everything—her future, her disappointment, her naive mistakes and her loneliness—without any help, without any white-knight ex-cop riding to the rescue. No one could protect her, no one could run her life for her. That was how it had to be.

In the privacy of her bedroom, alone with her grief, she let the tears flow. She didn't know how long she remained shut up by herself, crying, hugging her pillow, cleansing herself of every painful emotion. Eventually, her throat raw from her racking sobs, her eyes ran dry. Shaking her head clear, she pushed herself off the bed and stood; her legs trembled beneath her. She swabbed her face with a handkerchief and emerged from the bedroom.

Alec had left. She was all alone.

CHAPTER ELEVEN

ALEC TWISTED the cap off a Budweiser and took a swig, then wandered back to the smaller of the two bedrooms in his four-room apartment. He spied a few crumpled sheets of paper lying on the floor under the bridge table that served as his desk, but he didn't bother to pick them up. His trash can was overflowing.

He'd written a respectable number of pages in the week and a half since he'd gotten back to Boston, but not a single page worth saving. He'd held on to several pages to give him a sense of progress and productivity, but even on those he'd scribbled notes all over the margins and x-ed out entire paragraphs. He knew that in time they'd wind up in the trash can, too—or on the floor.

He took another swallow of beer, flopped into his swivel chair and stared at the inert typewriter keys until the sight of them made him sick. He pivoted in his seat and his gaze came to rest on the framed landscape print Rosie had bought for him at a flea market in Dedham last year. It was a bucolic scene of New England in autumn, rolling hills covered with brilliantly colored foliage, a stereotypical white spire protruding from the edge of a town green in the distance, a stereotypical red barn in the foreground.

It reminded him of Albright.

Groaning, he did a one-eighty and found himself eyeballing the dust jacket of *Street Talk,* which his mother had had professionally framed for him right after the novel came out. He scrutinized the bloodred background, the austere white letters, the photograph of him chewing on a toothpick and scowling.

He hadn't taken his book back from Lauren when he'd left. It was still in her possession, that photo glaring at her, his words taking up residence in her home—unless she'd gotten rid of the damned thing. Maybe she'd given it to a lucky student, or passed it along to one of her colleagues in the music department. Or maybe she'd tucked it into the fireplace, behind that swanky brass fireplace screen of hers, and put a match to it.

He wasn't obsessed with her, he really wasn't. If he thought about her at all, it was only to wonder how she was doing, whether she was coping successfully with the demise of her performing career and getting on with her life, whether she might someday learn to play the piano for nothing more than personal enjoyment. He was just curious about how things were going for her.

Like hell.

In the week and a half since he'd fled from Albright, he hadn't stopped thinking about her—and her career problems were the least of it. Whenever he let his mind roam, it traveled straight to her. He visualized her dark eyes, her darker hair, the faint quivering in her lower lip when she'd fought back tears that last morning and the admirable toughness in her voice when she'd dismissed him with a snappy rejoinder before stalking into her bedroom.

He recalled the sound of her broken sobs through the closed door, the despair she'd been too proud to let him see. Worse, he recalled what had preceded that despair, what he'd shared with her the night before he'd left her. He couldn't stop reminiscing about the petite dimensions of her figure, the birdlike delicacy of her bones, the surprisingly ripe contours of her breasts. The snug, humid warmth of her, the seething and throbbing of her body in response to him. Her astonishment that so much pleasure was possible.

He'd been astonished, too. He hadn't realized sex could be so intense, so powerful, so downright wonderful.

Damn. He had to quit torturing himself with memories. Setting down his beer, he plucked a toothpick from the open box on the bridge table and bit down on it hard, as if he were in agony and trying not to scream.

The radiator clanked and emitted an aroma of roasting dust. The toothpick broke in half from the force of his molars, and he discarded the pieces in the garbage pail, shoving the wads of paper down to make more room. He had to get back to work; he had to forget about Lauren.

His telephone rang. He leaned back in his chair and closed his eyes, counting the two rings before the click. His voice emerged from the answering machine's speaker. "Hi. This is Alec Fontana's answering machine. If you want to leave a message, go ahead."

"Alec?" his mother's voice blasted through the speaker. "Alec, please, if you're there pick up. I know you're there. Mags told me you're back in Boston. Come on, Alec, pick up."

She gave him a few seconds, but he didn't lift the receiver. He loved his mother, but at the moment he didn't think he could endure talking to her.

"All right," she conceded in her pitch-perfect Boston accent, all flat *A*s and lapsed *R*s. "Maybe you're not home now, but I know you're in town. Mags told me you left Albright over a week ago. And you still haven't called me. I'm your mother, Alec. I want to see you. Come for dinner, okay? Come and get a good meal."

The machine clicked off. Alec lifted his beer, took a drink, stared at his typewriter and cursed. Ten days in the city, and he still hadn't called her.

Ordinarily he tried to visit her every other week or so for dinner, usually when his sisters and their families would also be there. But the past week and a half hadn't been ordinary. He hadn't talked to anyone—not Rosie, not Mary-Beth, not his friends. During the day all he'd done was write pages of his new manuscript, reread them, wad them up and toss them onto the floor, gnaw on toothpicks and wish they were cigarettes. In the evening all he'd done was listen to the jumble of street noises outside his windows, watch TV and work himself into a foul mood. At night all he'd done was lie in bed and remember the last night he'd spent in Albright, in Lauren's bed, in her arms.

Maybe it would have been better if he hadn't left so abruptly. He'd waited for a while in her living room the morning after, hoping she would return so they could work things out between them. But she hadn't returned, and when he'd neared her door and heard her weeping, he'd had to restrain himself from charging through the door to comfort her again. The only thing that had stopped him was his knowledge of what had happened the last time he'd charged in and comforted her.

He'd done the wrong thing Friday night. Saturday morning he'd tried to do the right thing—and caused her even more misery. He'd hovered outside her door, his hand resting on the doorknob and his head aching with indecision.

If he went into her bedroom he'd kiss her. If he kissed her, he'd hold her, touch her, tear off her robe and make love to her all over again. So he'd left, in order to protect her—and maybe to protect himself, too.

That disturbing thought niggled at him late at night, after he'd finished tormenting himself by remembering how phenomenal sex with her had been. Maybe he'd left not because he was afraid of her becoming too attached to him, but because he was afraid of becoming too attached to her. What if she had turned to him only for a little help in getting through the night, and now she was done with him? What if she'd only been using him to distract herself from her professional dilemma for a while? What if he did something stupid like fall for her, and then she pulled herself together and marched off to conquer the world, leaving him behind?

What if she was the strong one, and he was the one who had wound up involved? Much as he hated to admit it, that might have been why he'd run for cover.

It hadn't taken him long to pack. Once he'd locked his suitcases into the back of his car, he'd driven around the block, away from the duplex so Lauren wouldn't come after him. He'd parked on Burke Street and hiked across the campus to the president's house to say goodbye to Mags.

The starchy maid guarding the front door of the Georgian mansion had tried to deny Alec entrance: Dr. Cudahy, it seemed, was hosting a tea for several members of the college's board of trustees. But Alec had wormed his way in and crashed Mags's little party.

He'd immediately regretted it. Thrilled by his unexpected appearance, Mags had insisted on introducing him to an assortment of silver-haired ladies in shirtwaist dresses and sensible shoes who were drinking more sherry than tea and who made a big fuss over his status as a bestselling novelist. Not until they'd cleared out of the president's house an hour later had he had a chance to tell Mags that he was going to have to leave Albright.

"What about Roger Phelps?" she'd asked.

"I'm sorry, Mags—I just can't deal with that whole scene right now. Maybe I can come back in a few weeks. But at the moment... I need some time away."

"Why? Is something wrong?"

For damn sure, he'd nearly answered. But he couldn't bring himself to admit to his aunt that what was wrong had to do with her celebrated visiting lecturer in music and Alec's unwise interference in said lecturer's agenda. So he'd fumbled and fibbed and finally, when he'd realized she could see right through his flimsy lies, he'd said he was having a personal problem and had to get back to Boston to straighten it out. Mags, bless her heart, had let the subject rest at that.

He sipped his beer, perused the last page he'd pulled from the typewriter, grimaced and crushed it into a ball, which he hurled onto the floor. He had until next June to deliver a manuscript to his publisher. At the rate he was going, he wouldn't have anything to send along in eight years, let alone eight months.

He reached for a fresh toothpick, then a fresh sheet of paper. He rolled the blank page into the machine, stared at it and cursed.

The telephone rang again. He listened to the two rings, followed by his tape-recorded message on the answering machine. Then the beep, and then: "This is Lauren Wyler...."

He sprang to his feet, knocking his chair over as he reached across the table and grabbed the phone. "Lauren!" he shouted, his voice resonating through the answering machine's speaker. His heart pounded, his breath quickened and his gloom miraculously dissipated. He didn't question why he was elated to hear from her. He'd consider the implications later. For now, he simply accepted it. "Lauren, don't hang up! I'm here."

"Oh." Her voice also emerged through the speaker, filling the room like sunlight.

"How are you?"

"I'm fine. I got your number from President Cudahy. I hope you don't mind."

"Of course I don't mind." *Tell me you missed me,* he silently implored. *Tell me you forgive me for walking away. Tell me you've been as obsessed with me as I've been with you these past ten days....*

"I wanted to tell you," she said, "that I'm really worried about Emily Spaeth."

Who? What? Alec stretched the telephone cord until he could reach his upended chair and right it. He sank into it, letting out a doleful breath as he absorbed the fact that this call had nothing to do with their brief affair.

"What about Emily Spaeth?" he asked, exerting himself not to sound dejected.

"She told me she's going to discontinue her piano lessons. She said she wants to devote more time to something she's doing for another professor. She said she needs to do it in order to qualify for some sort of special consideration on her scholarship renewal."

"Uh-huh," he grunted, wishing he cared.

"I'm troubled on a couple of levels," Lauren went on, sounding like nothing so much as a dedicated, rational teacher. "First of all, Emily is quite talented musically. I would hate to see her throw away that talent. And second..."

"The hell with her musical talent," Alec snapped. It bothered him that Lauren could discuss the Emily Spaeth situation as if it were the only thing that existed between her and Alec, as if she cared more about whether Phelps bedded her prize student than whether she and Alec were going to be able to mend things between them. What bothered him even more was the inescapable conclusion that she *didn't* care, that mending things was of no interest to her whatsoever.

After a pause, Lauren continued speaking, her voice even frostier than before. "I don't suppose you care whether she becomes a great pianist or not. But the rest of it—well, of course, no professor would ever demand that a student quit her music lessons in order to be considered for a scholarship. That's absurd."

Conceding that Lauren was determined to keep things impersonal, he asked, "Did Emily happen to mention Phelps's name?"

"No," she said. "I did."

"You did?"

"We were talking about a student recital that took place last Friday, and I said I'd run into Phelps's wife after the concert. I don't think I was too smooth about it, Alec—but I thought maybe it would jar a reaction from her."

"Did it?"

"No. I mean, not the reaction I expected. She didn't look shocked or horrified or anything."

"What did she do?"

"She said she was surprised Phelps's wife would have the nerve to show her face on campus. And I asked why, and she just sort of hedged and changed the subject. I don't know, Alec—I probably could have handled it better."

She probably could have, if she'd had a few years of police training in interrogation technique. "You did fine," he assured her.

"Well...what do you think? Is she in danger? Should I do something more? Maybe tell her about the student he was involved with last year?"

"That's a rumor, not a proven fact," Alec reminded Lauren. "I don't know if he did it. But if you think your student is in trouble now—"

"I do, Alec. I'm worried."

"Then I'll just have to do some more digging," he said. "I guess I ought to come back to Albright and check into it. If I can't pin last year's scandal on Phelps, at least maybe I can prevent this year's scandal from happening."

Lauren's tone brightened. "I was hoping you'd come back," she said, then quickly added, "Emily is a good girl. I think she's in over her head, but she's basically a good girl."

He sighed. He knew the message Lauren was trying to get across: that if Alec returned to Albright it would be for Emily's sake, not for Lauren's—or his own. That if he returned it would be to nail Phelps, not to insinuate his way back into Lauren's arms, into her bed.

He had promised Mags to do a job, and he'd abandoned that promise. Maybe one reason he was having so much difficulty getting any work done on his new book was that he felt guilty for having left Mags—and Lauren's air-head student—in the lurch.

"I'll drive back out tonight," he resolved.

"On Emily's behalf, I'm very grateful," said Lauren.

Not on her own behalf, Alec ruminated after saying goodbye and hanging up the phone. She sure as hell wasn't grateful that Alec "now you see me now you don't" Fontana was about to pop back into her life.

As he stalked to his bedroom, hauled a suitcase out of the closet, opened it across the bed and tossed clothing into it, he reviewed his conversation with her again and again. He couldn't come up with a single bit of evidence to prove that she had anything other than her student's welfare in mind in welcoming his return to Albright. From practically the first word out of her mouth it had been Emily, Emily, Emily. Not a hint of anything personal between her and Alec. Either she loathed him or she considered their relationship too insignificant to waste ten seconds of long-distance rates on.

He was in his car, heading west along the Massachusetts Turnpike, when he rethought that conclusion. If Lauren hadn't wanted any personal contact with Alec, she could have discussed her concerns with Mags and let Mags summon Alec herself. If Lauren hadn't wanted to talk to him she wouldn't have telephoned. If she truly didn't want to see Alec, she wouldn't have blurted out, when he told her he'd come to Albright, "I was hoping you'd come back."

He swore to himself that he could see Lauren without messing up. Her fragile beauty and sweet manner notwithstanding, he could deal with her without dragging sex into it. She'd been hoping for his return, and she would have it, and this time he'd behave himself. He would rescue Emily Spaeth from her own stupidity and collar Phelps, and he and Lauren would emerge from the encounter smiling instead of with her in tears and him fleeing for his life.

He shoved an old Doors cassette into the tape deck and cranked up the volume. Traffic on the Mass Pike was light, and he pushed the needle past seventy, figuring no state trooper would have the gall to ticket a retired city cop who'd been disabled in the line of duty. On the tape Jim Morrison growled at him to "roll, baby, roll," and he did. He was feeling good, feeling better every second. He was going to screw Phelps to the wall, save a damsel in distress who genuinely needed saving, do Mags the favor he'd pledged to do and repair the damage with Lauren. And then, when this was all behind him, every loose end tied up, he would return to Boston in the correct frame of mind and write the best damned second novel anyone had ever read.

He steered straight to the duplex. Mags had refused to take back his key to the apartment when he'd left Albright—he'd told her he would be back, after all, and she'd said she couldn't imagine that the college would rent the apartment to anyone else in his absence—so he didn't have to detour to the security office to pick up the key before driving to Hancock Street. Dead leaves crunched under his tires as he pulled to the side of the road and parked. The trees that less than two weeks ago had been flaming with color were now practically bare; the few leaves still clinging stubbornly to the branches were shriveled and brown.

The sight should have depressed him, but it didn't. His attention was riveted to the first-floor windows in the duplex. Lauren's windows. They were closed, her drapes drawn, but the lights were on inside her living room. She was home, inside that apartment, no more than forty feet away from him.

A wave of nervousness passed through him. What if he couldn't behave himself? What if one look at her caused all his resolutions to crumble? What if he saw her and wanted her so badly he was willing to risk everything—even an involvement?

Just be friendly, he cautioned himself. Just keep it simple. Just stay cool.

Climbing out of his car, he turned up the collar of his denim jacket to ward off the biting chill in the air. His stomach pointedly reminded him that it was well past his usual supper time. As soon as he unpacked his luggage he would ring up the pizza place in town that offered free delivery. He'd left some food staples behind when he'd taken off—half a can of coffee, some granola bars, enough to get him through breakfast tomorrow morning. After that he'd go out to the supermarket and restock.

He lifted the hatchback, pulled out his suitcase and his beloved coffeemaker, locked up and started toward the duplex, ignoring the cramp two hours of driving had spawned in his knee. Reaching the porch, he set down his things in front of the door on the right and dug into the pocket of his jeans for the key. His fingers closed around it and he started to pull it out.

Against his better judgment, he let his gaze drift to the door on the left. Against his better judgment, he extended his hand to her doorbell and rang.

An eternity passed, and then he heard the rattle of the bolt being released, and the knob being turned. The door opened and there she stood.

He drank her in. His gaze wandered from the coal-black hair that hung loose around her face to her face itself, the delicately sculpted cheekbones and dark brown eyes, the exquisite line of her jaw, the full, slightly parted lips. Her delectable throat. The play of her cream-colored cashmere sweater over her slender shoulders and waist and her firm bosom, the graceful proportions of her legs clad in brown corduroy slacks, her tiny feet hidden inside fuzzy wool socks.

He slid his gaze back up her body and was startled to notice that her right arm hung free at her side, the hand fully exposed. Even with him standing in front of her, inches from her, she made no move to hide it in a pocket. He studied the straight fingers and the crooked ones, the smooth, soft skin across her knuckles, her slender wrist. He didn't know why she was letting her hand show—but he knew it had to mean something.

Lifting his eyes to hers, he experienced a sudden swelling heat in his chest, in his gut, in his groin. He shouldn't have rung her bell. He shouldn't have come back to Albright. He shouldn't have answered his phone when he'd heard her voice on his machine.

He should have avoided Lauren Wyler with every ounce of self-preservation in his system.

Because now that he was with her, he had to kiss her. He couldn't help it. He was involved.

THE INSTANT her eyes met his she felt her carefully wrought control start to unravel.

After days of relentless introspection, brooding analysis and alternating bouts of hope and dread, she had finally begun to have faith that she was going to survive this crisis in one piece. She wasn't going to give up, she wasn't going to turn her back on life and purpose and joy. She would simply have to find a new purpose, a new way of living. She would have to derive joy from something other than perfectly executed arpeggios and standing ovations.

She'd been building up her emotional strength, performing mental muscle-building, psyching herself to face the world. What was past was past; it couldn't be changed. She saw no value in dwelling on who she had been or what she'd done.

Among the things she'd done had been making love with Alec Fontana. It had happened and now it was over, just one more aspect of her past that would have no bearing on her future. Sometimes, on good days, she could almost convince herself she didn't regret having done it, didn't blame him or herself. She could almost believe making love with him had been like playing the piano—it was behind her, history, over and done with, no longer relevant.

That belief evaporated the instant she opened her door and saw the multifaceted light in his eyes, speaking of so many unnameable things, the moment she saw him lift his hand to her cheek and slide it under her hair to the nape of her neck. The moment he drew her mouth to his.

His lips touched hers, pulled back and then crushed against hers as he abandoned any attempt at restraint. She couldn't restrain herself, either. The searing pressure of his mouth on hers eroded whatever resolve she had. She circled his waist with her arms, flattened her hands against his strong back and hugged him tight. Her lips moved with him, parted for him, opened fully for the sensual invasion of his tongue.

She felt more than heard his groan as their tongues met; an answering groan vibrated deep within her. Her knees trembled and her hips tensed in the same profound response that had been such a revelation to her the last time she'd been with Alec. This time she recognized it, welcomed it, delighted in it.

Only for a minute, though. For one twinkling minute desire eclipsed sanity in her mind—and then the darkness shifted, the shadows broke up and clarity returned. With a sharp shake of her head, she forced her arms away from him and retreated a step.

He was breathing heavily, his chest pumping in and out as he scrutinized her. "May I come in?" he asked in a gravelly voice.

She sent him a dubious glance, this time careful to avoid gazing directly into his hypnotic eyes. She focused instead on his unshaven jaw, the snug blue shirt under his jacket, his formfitting jeans and scuffed sneakers. If anything, the sight of his lean, virile body affected her as acutely as his eyes had. He had felt powerful in her arms, eager, compelling. For that one crazed moment when their mouths had come together she'd wanted him more than anything in the world.

She was afraid to let him in; she obviously couldn't trust herself around him. But she couldn't refuse to talk to him. She had asked him to come to Albright to help save Emily Spaeth from Roger Phelps. Since Lauren currently thought of herself as primarily a teacher, helping a student in trouble was the sort of act that defined her life these days.

"May I come in?" Alec repeated after her silence extended beyond a full minute.

"Only if you promise not to kiss me again," she replied quietly, rubbing the back of her hand across her mouth as if to wipe the taste of him from her lips.

He noticed the small gesture and frowned. Pulling a toothpick from an inner pocket, he stepped inside her apartment and closed the door behind him.

He surveyed his surroundings. Not much had changed since he'd last been in the living room. The asters on her dining table had been replaced by tawny marigolds, and the piano's keyboard lid was closed—permanently, as far as Lauren was concerned. She'd packed her sheet music into cartons and stored them in the study. The shelves that had once held her teacup collection remained bare; she hadn't yet figured out what to display on them. The rugs had been thoroughly vacuumed. Every last trace of her tantrum had been expunged from the room.

"How are you?" he asked.

If he was asking how she was holding up in the aftermath of his kiss, she wasn't sure how to reply. She chose to stick with inane generalities. "I'm fine."

"How's your hand?"

"How do you think?" she snapped, her patience fraying, her emotions much too close to the surface. "I can hold a pen. I can dial a phone. Grieg's *Piano Concerto in A-minor* is a little beyond me." Her anger subsided, replaced by the well-tempered stability she'd struggled so hard to acquire. "How was your trip?"

He appeared surprised that she would turn the spotlight on him and pose such a civil question. "It was all right," he drawled, his gaze narrowing on her. "Lauren, I'm serious. How are you? I've been worried about you."

"Have you?" She arched her brows and exhorted herself not to yield to the hostility simmering inside her. "I suppose that's why you took off without a word of farewell. I suppose that's why you ran away like a coward.'' Aware of the bitterness creeping into her words, she clamped her mouth shut.

Alec didn't flinch at her accusation. He let out a long, weary sigh and rolled his toothpick between his thumb and forefinger. ''I left because I thought you'd be able to work things out better if I wasn't around to confuse the issue.''

''How noble of you,'' she said loftily, starting toward the kitchen. ''I was about to make some tea. I haven't got any beer, so—''

He grabbed her arm and tugged her back around to face him. ''Lauren, I'm sorry. I still think I left for the right reasons. But you're right, the way I did it was cowardly. I'm sorry.''

His confession thawed her resistance—not enough for her to want to throw herself into his arms again, but enough for her to regard him as someone other than her enemy. ''It's all right,'' she said, lowering her eyes to the spotless rug. ''Maybe you're right, maybe it would have been harder for me to work things out if you'd been around.''

He relaxed his grip on her arm and slid his hand down to take hers. His long, thick fingers closed comfortingly around hers. ''Can I ask what you've worked out so far?''

It really wasn't any of his business. He had deliberately separated himself from her; he had no right to poke his nose into her affairs. Yet she needed someone to talk to. Bella Bronowitz was a good listener, but her greatest aspiration had always been to teach at a top-rate college, and she couldn't really identify with Lauren's grave disappointment at seeing her life-long dreams dissolve into dust. Alec could: not as a lover, not as a man, not as someone who had broken her heart, but simply as someone who'd been there, who'd gone through exactly what Lauren was going through.

Her indignation ebbing, she led him to the sofa and they sat. He automatically propped his left leg up on the coffee table, unintentionally reminding her of the injuries that had ended his career. His foot turned at the ankle as he relaxed, and his knee maintained a slight bend. At first glance it looked like any propped-up leg on any man—just as at first glance her hand looked normal. But the angle of his foot wasn't quite right, nor was the refusal of his knee to straighten fully.

Lauren wasn't the only person in the world with permanent scars.

As long as she concentrated on what she and Alec had in common she would be able to confide in him. "I've spoken to the head of the music department about renewing my contract here for another year," she said. "He was excited about having me continue teaching. He said he has to make sure the money is available, but if they can afford me, they'll keep me on."

"That's great."

She lifted her gaze to Alec's face. He watched her attentively, his eyes radiating only affectionate concern. "I've enjoyed teaching here," she admitted. "The work is challenging, my colleagues are nice and I feel as if I'm contributing something worthwhile. I don't know if I want to teach for the rest of my life, but it'll do for now." Encouraged by his gentle smile, she added, "If I've learned anything, it's that planning out your entire life is a stupid thing to do. I'm willing to plan as far as next year, and then I'll see."

He nodded. "What does Gerald think about all this?"

Lauren scowled. "I don't care what Gerald thinks anymore," she said sharply. "I've severed our relationship."

"Really? Isn't that kind of extreme?"

"It isn't extreme enough," she said. Her final encounter with Gerald was still much too vivid in her mind, much too raw.

She had called him on the Monday morning after her cataclysmic weekend, provided a succinct report on her visit to Dr. Nylander in Boston and told him she saw no reason to continue their professional arrangement. By Monday evening Gerald was in Albright, waiting for her on the front porch when she returned from campus.

"What are you doing here?" she asked with uncharacteristic rudeness.

"Come back to New York with me," he said, as if she hadn't spoken. As if she hadn't signed a teaching contract with Albright College—as if teaching wasn't the only positive thing in her life right then. As if he honestly believed he was still in charge, able to tell her what to do, expecting obedience and gratitude from her.

"You must be crazy," she blurted out. "I'm done. New York is done for me. It's over. I've got to get on with my life."

"That's exactly why I'm here," he countered, offensively calm, his eyes narrow behind his chic red-framed spectacles. "Lauren, you shouldn't have gone to see that other doctor."

"Why? Because I didn't clear it with you first?"

"It wasn't that." He seemed to wrestle with his thoughts for a minute. "I had a good reason for wanting you to stick with Dr. Hayes, Lauren. I didn't want you to lose hope. I was afraid you'd fall apart if you did. Dr. Hayes was also fearful about your emotional stability. He was going to break the news to you slowly, gradually, when you were ready to deal with it. You shouldn't have had to confront the truth this way."

"You mean—you mean Dr. Hayes knew all along that my hand wouldn't get better?" She was too enraged to mind the cold and the encroaching darkness. A chilly breeze swept over the porch, but Lauren's anger burned inside her like a fever. "Dr. Hayes knew the truth? And he kept telling me I'd improve?" As the full import of Gerald's words hit her, the fever rose to the boiling point. "And *you* knew! You knew all along! Gerald—I trusted you with my life, and you were lying to me!"

"For your own good," Gerald said smoothly. "I didn't think you were strong enough to handle—"

"So you protected me. I've got news for you, Gerald—I'm damned strong enough." It wasn't like Lauren to resort to even mild swearing, but she was too incensed to care about propriety. "You lied to me, damn it. You broke my wrist—"

"That was an accident, Lauren," he said, a glimmer of remorse shining through his words. "The roads were so icy—"

"And I suppose it was also an accident that you thought I was too weak to face the truth. Well, you were right, Gerald—facing the truth this way is even worse."

"That's why I wanted to cushion it for you." He took a step toward her and she recoiled from him. Sighing, he tightened his prissy wool scarf around his neck, shrugged his Brooks Brothers blazer higher on his shoulders and presented her with his most reasonable expression. "I wanted you to get used to the idea gradually, and in the meantime we could work out a new game plan. Maybe you can't concertize anymore, but there are other ways we can capitalize on your talent."

"My talent," she snorted, then waved her malfunctioning right hand at him. "My talent is gone, Gerald."

"You've got a splendid reputation," he explained, his calm tone only increasing her skepticism. "We can exploit that, Lauren. I've opened negotiations with one of the major piano manufacturers about having you become their spokeswoman. I've also investigated the possibility of some tasteful print ads. There's a premium cognac interested in you—an ad campaign that would involve you posing with a piano and a bottle, or some such thing—classy and sexy at the same time. There's money in it, Lauren, a great deal of money, six-figure money—simply because of who you used to be. And there are still the parties, the fund-raising galas. We can do well with that. We can keep you in the spotlight. You're still young and pretty. We can milk your background if we market you properly."

"Because of who I used to be," she murmured, her feverish rage waning as cold reality settled upon her.

"I'm telling you, Lauren, there's a lot of money in this."

"I'm making money as a teacher."

"Not as much as you could make—"

"As what? A huckster for high-priced booze?"

"It would be done tastefully. And they're willing to pay top dollar. We both know where you came from, Lauren. We both know how high you've risen. I don't want you to lose everything you've gained."

"I don't want to lose my integrity."

Her stubbornness seemed to exasperate him. "If you'd only trust me..."

"Trust you? After you lied to me—and arranged for Dr. Hayes to lie to me, too? How can I ever trust you again?"

"We go back so many years," he reminded her, his smile suspiciously placating. "I built your career. I worked as hard as you did. If it weren't for me, you would never have become a world-class pianist."

"Well, I'm someone else now," she said, and the reality no longer seemed quite so cold. This was the truth, *her* truth, and she wasn't going to let it upset her. "Who I used to be doesn't matter anymore, Gerald. All that matters is who I am now."

A few minutes later, he drove away. She stood on the porch, watching as the two red rectangles of his car's taillights receded into the night. Hugging herself for warmth, she reiterated to herself: *All that matters is who I am now.* At that moment she understood more clearly than ever before who she was: a strong, independent adult who could make her own decisions—and would. Who would set her own course and answer her own needs. Who would manage her own life without any interference from anyone.

"Maybe someday Gerald and I will be able to be friends," she told Alec. "But for now..." She exhaled, the very thought exhausting her. "I've hired a lawyer to handle the breakup. There are contractual and financial details to work out. It's more complicated than a divorce, I think."

"Just as sad, too, I bet," Alec murmured.

His sensitivity surprised her—and then, on second thought, it didn't. His explanation for why he'd disappeared that ghastly morning offered more evidence of his sensitivity. He'd left to give her the independence she needed. He'd left so she would be forced to stand on her own two feet, not to lean on him, not to let him take care of her.

That was one way to interpret his hasty departure. The other way was that he was a rat, panic-stricken by the thought that she'd gotten too close to him. He'd slept with her, and she'd started looking at him with love in her eyes, and he'd bolted.

She swung back and forth between the two interpretations. Maybe they were both right; she hadn't figured it out, yet. What she knew was that she'd been wrong to confuse sex with love—and that Alec could easily cause her to make that mistake again.

She couldn't think about it now, especially not with him seated beside her on the couch, close enough to kick—or to kiss. Rather than go insane trying to decide whether to despise or forgive him, she willfully shoved the entire dilemma out of her mind. "What are you going to do about Emily?" she asked.

Alec seemed bemused by her abrupt change in topic. He continued to envelop her hand in his, and she continued to pretend she considered his clasp nothing more than a gesture of sympathy.

He chewed thoughtfully on his toothpick, considering his response. Evidently he decided to follow her lead and turn the discussion from Lauren's emotional health to something neutral. "Well," he said, "the first thing to do is find out if Phelps is the professor pressuring her about the scholarship."

"Right."

"So," Alec continued, "I'll shadow Emily, find out where she's going, and when, and with whom. Phelps admires me, for some reason, so I might be able to get something out of him as well."

"What should I do?" Lauren asked.

"You?" His brows dipped in a fleeting frown. "Nothing."

She bristled. "What do you mean, nothing? Emily's my student."

"So? You're a professor, Lauren. You can't go skulking around campus, tailing your students."

"Yes, but—but I want to do *something*."

He contemplated her for a minute, his eyes glittering speculatively, the corners of his mouth twitching up into a reluctant smile. "You want to do something?" he repeated. "Okay. What you can do is be there."

"Be where?"

"Available. Be open to Emily if she wants to talk. Just keep listening. See if you can gain her confidence. See if you can get her to tell you what's really going on."

Lauren was disappointed. She would indeed have liked to skulk around campus a bit. That would have been exciting. She didn't want to be relegated to sitting around, waiting for her student to confess to adultery with her political-science professor. "How am I going to gain her confidence if she cancels her piano lessons?"

"Make sure she doesn't cancel. Change the schedule, do whatever you've got to do to keep her coming. Tell her you'll sacrifice your lunch hour to give her a lesson. I don't know, just make sure she'll keep seeing you."

"I'll try."

"As long as she's still meeting regularly with you, I think she'll stay out of trouble. You may be the best thing that ever happened to her, Lauren. You're good at opening people's eyes, making them see things differently."

That sounded like a serious overstatement to Lauren, but she accepted his lavish praise because he'd declared it so honestly. He wasn't buttering her up or trying to wheedle anything from her. He wasn't attempting to seduce her. He was merely voicing an opinion.

She wondered whether she'd opened Alec's eyes; she wondered what he saw differently. But to ask would be to drag the conversation back to the subject of their personal relationship, and she wasn't foolish enough to do that.

So she only smiled when he released her hand and stood. She nodded and accompanied him to the door when he said he wanted to get settled in upstairs. She braced herself for the fact that he was about to walk out of her apartment again—in another context, another mood than the last time he'd left her, but nonetheless he was walking out, and she knew her home would feel peculiarly empty once he was gone.

Opening the door, he stepped onto the porch and turned to face her. He seemed to be groping for the correct words, the proper way to say good-night to someone who'd responded insanely when he'd swept her into his arms, and then rejected him, and obviously remained utterly ambivalent about him.

"I'll see you," he said, his voice low, his eyes luminous as they wandered over her face.

"I'll see you," she echoed, then closed the door and leaned against it. Sure enough, the apartment seemed empty and cold. She felt woefully isolated.

She wasn't isolated, though. Alec was upstairs. She would once again hear his footsteps moving about above her, hear the muffled babble of his television and the on and off of his bathroom sink when he shaved. He would once again be a part of her world, his presence felt, his nearness something she would not be able to ignore.

He was back in her life, and he wanted her. God help her, she wanted him, too. What if she let him kiss her again? What if she yielded to the deep, aching need of her body, and then he left again? What if she acknowledged that she loved him, and he vanished like a wisp of autumn smoke? Where would she be then?

Right where she was now. Independent and unprotected. In love, and alone.

CHAPTER TWELVE

EVEN WITH A WOOL SWEATER on underneath his denim jacket, he was cold. Halloween was a few days away, but the evening air carried November's bluster. He shoved his hands into the pockets of his jeans and hunched his shoulders against the icy gusts of wind that tore across the campus, tossing the few unraked leaves high into the air and creating eddies of dust along the paved paths.

Nearing Emily Spaeth's dormitory, he slowed to a halt. At seven o'clock the ivy-covered brick building hummed with activity. Most of the windows were lighted, and the front door flapped open and shut as girls in down vests, their arms laden with books, set off for the library after dinner. Alec wedged a toothpick between his teeth and hovered in the shadow of a leafless oak tree, his gaze riveted to that incessantly swinging front door.

He had been back in Albright for four days, and in all that time he'd seen Lauren only once, the night he'd arrived. He'd spoken to her on the telephone a couple of times, the first when she'd phoned him to report that she'd talked Emily out of quitting her piano lessons.

Alec had been pleased by the news, but Lauren sounded glum. "I feel like I blackmailed her," she said.

"In what way?"

"Well, I told her I was sure she'd be getting an *A* from me, and that would help her keep her grade-point average up. She needs that for her scholarship." Lauren exhaled. "I feel bad about dragging her grade into it."

"Why? You weren't planning to give her an *A*?"

"No, she deserved the grade. But—I don't know, it just seems so... so manipulative."

Alec could have laughed at Lauren's ingenuousness. Hell, if she thought dangling an *A* over her student's head was manipulative, what would she think of the outright deceptions he had resorted to in his undercover assignments as a cop? He used to lie, misrepresent himself, say anything his target wanted to hear—as long as it worked. That had always been the bottom line: if it worked, he did it. The ends justified the means.

But he didn't laugh at Lauren. He smiled instead. Her idealism and honesty were kind of touching.

"Don't feel bad about it," he said. "Be happy she's going to continue her piano lessons."

"Yes, but she ought to continue them because she loves playing and she's good at it, not because she's afraid of losing her scholarship."

"Welcome to the real world, Lauren. You got her to agree to keep up with the lessons. Be thankful for that."

The second time he'd spoken to Lauren had been just that afternoon, after Emily's rescheduled piano lesson. Lauren had called him from her office within minutes of Emily's departure. "She seemed awfully high-strung, Alec," she reported. "I managed to get her to talk a little. I asked her if she was having problems with her boyfriend. She had told me a while ago that she was in love, so I figured it was all right for me to raise the subject."

"What did she say?"

"She got even more upset. She said she hated men, they were all after one thing and one thing only." Lauren sighed, a soft, plaintive sound that had a much stronger effect on Alec than the message she was relaying.

"I hope you set her straight," he said, an attempt at a joke.

Lauren didn't find any humor in it. "Given how little I know about men, I was in no position to correct her. Perhaps you could tell me what all men are after so I can enlighten her the next time I see her."

Alec stared at the floor. He knew she'd phoned from her office, but he imagined her below him, just a story away. If she had been downstairs, and if everything had been right between them, he would have hung up the phone and gone down. They would have talked face-to-face, person to person...and within seconds, he would want to kiss her.

Emily Spaeth understood men a hell of a lot better than her piano teacher did. Alec decided it was best to ignore Lauren's dig. "She didn't mention Phelps, did she?" he asked.

"No." Lauren sighed again. "I couldn't think of any way to sneak his name into the conversation this time. She was in such a state. She told me she was having trouble with two of her courses and she might get midterm grades of C in them, and if she couldn't get her average up she would lose her scholarship."

"Money's a big problem for her," Alec surmised.

"It seems that way. She said she'd do *anything* to keep her scholarship."

"Messing around with Phelps would fall under the heading of anything," Alec noted.

"She's naive," Lauren pointed out, apparently eager to defend her star pupil. "I don't think she realizes the implications."

"The implications of what? Whoring for a grade?" His voice was gruffer than he'd intended, but he didn't apologize. It annoyed him that Lauren could defend her student's moronic behavior, especially after she'd just insulted Alec, who was only trying to protect the moronic student from herself. If Lauren didn't know who was the good guy and who was the bad guy in this, she was as blind as her student.

She was obviously taken aback by his harsh language. "Emily Spaeth is a child, Alec. Barely twenty. You have no right to sit in judgment of her."

Once again Alec wanted to lecture Lauren about the real world. But he let it slide. What was the point in forcing her to view the universe through his perspective? What was the point in trying to forge a meeting of the minds with her? It wasn't as if he and Lauren were ever going to build any sort of relationship. She wasn't interested in him. She'd made that very clear the night he'd gotten back to town. And except for her two phone calls, she'd been avoiding him.

He'd stuck close to home since his arrival in Albright. Like a lovesick teenager, he'd tried to be where she could find him, just in case. But she'd never run into him when he'd loitered near the music building, or when he'd spent an inordinate amount of time on the front porch picking up his newspaper or his mail. She'd never even glanced up at his windows when she left the duplex in the morning or returned at night.

Not only hadn't he seen her—except for the glimpses he'd caught of her through his living room windows— but she seemed to have taken a vow of silence at home. Not once since he'd been back did he hear her moving around her apartment beneath him. Not once did he hear her pull her kitchen chair out to sit at dinnertime or push it in when she was done eating; not once did he hear the thump of her closet doors shutting, the whoosh of her drapes being drawn or the gurgle of her bathtub draining.

Not once did he hear her play her piano.

Perhaps she had resumed playing while he'd been in Boston. He knew she had little motivation to practice; it wasn't as if she were going to be performing onstage anytime in the next hundred years or so. But he wanted to think she would play anyway, just for herself, because it seemed unnatural for her to neglect something that had been such a significant part of her life for so long.

Either his presence was inhibiting her or else she hadn't yet come to terms with the truth about her music and her future. Maybe it was too soon for her to be able to play just for the fun of it. It had taken him a full six months after his assault before he'd been able to go back to his old precinct house, and when he'd finally visited, underweight by a good twenty pounds and wobbling on crutches, the experience had been as painful as any of the injuries he'd suffered. All his buddies had stopped what they were doing and gathered around; the ladies had kissed his cheek and the men had rushed forward with a chair and a cup of coffee, and they'd all fussed over him and given him such sympathetic smiles . . . and he'd recognized that he was a stranger there, someone who no longer belonged.

Another six months had passed before he could bring himself to visit again. By that time he'd written over half of *Street Talk* and hired an agent to negotiate a contract for him. He'd felt much better during that visit, because he had stopped thinking of himself as a cop by then.

How long would it take before Lauren stopped thinking of herself as a concert pianist?

How long would it take before Alec stopped thinking of her as a lover?

Her aloofness couldn't prevent him from dwelling on the last kiss they'd shared, analyzing it, recalling every nuance of it in his mind. That she'd kissed him with just as much ardor as he'd kissed her didn't count for much; she'd been the one to end it. She'd been the one to break away and say no.

He didn't blame her; he *couldn't* blame her. He'd abandoned her once. He'd handled everything wrong the last time. She had a right to protect herself, to keep her distance so she wouldn't get caught up in a momentary passion.

Alec was still caught up in the passion, though. He still wanted her. He still had trouble falling asleep at night. He still kept reliving the time they'd spent together in her bed, remembering how good it had been— and how much better it could be if they made love again, only taking it slow, savoring each moment, leaving the wild desperation out of it and aiming for pure pleasure.

If he'd been obsessed with Lauren Wyler back in Boston, returning to Albright only made it worse.

He wished there was some way to convince her that he'd never walk out on her again. But he couldn't even convince himself of that. Just because he was obsessed with her didn't mean he was prepared to make a life-long commitment to her. And even if he was, she'd probably turn him down. For all he knew, her detachment had nothing to do with self-protection. Perhaps he simply didn't mean anything to her.

She meant so much to him. Too much. He must have been crazy to think he could come back to Albright, nail Phelps's butt to the wall and make friends with Lauren. He must have been certifiably insane to think he could move back into the apartment upstairs from her and not be driven to distraction by her nearness.

The front door of the dormitory opened again, and two girls emerged. One of them Alec had never seen before; the other was tall and blond and buxom. He snapped to attention, instantly relegating all thoughts of Lauren to the back of his mind and focusing on the task at hand: finding out whether Emily was going to see Roger Phelps.

Shortly after he'd talked to Lauren earlier that day, Alec had given Roger a call at his office and suggested they meet for a drink that evening. The distinguished professor had sounded delighted to hear from Alec, but he'd declined the invitation, claiming he had an appointment with a student. "A sweet young thing has begged me for the opportunity to convince me she deserves a better midterm grade," he'd explained; Alec could almost hear Roger's smirk in his voice. "Let's do those drinks tomorrow night, instead."

Remaining in the shadows as Emily Spaeth and her friend walked down the path, Alec's mind echoed with those insipid words: *a sweet young thing*. If Emily was in fact headed to Phelps's office, she wasn't so sweet at all.

Emily and her companion strolled along the path until it forked. They both turned left, in the direction of the library—and Dwight Hall. As soon as they passed out of Alec's line of vision he emerged from the shadows and started after them.

They reached the library steps and paused. Thirty paces behind them, Alec paused as well. What if Emily went inside with her friend? No problem, he'd continue on to Dwight Hall anyway. Maybe some other dim-witted young woman was begging Roger for a good midterm grade tonight.

But Alec would rather Emily Spaeth be the one. One dimwit was the same as another to him, but Lauren had a personal investment in this one. Maybe he could earn some points with her if he rescued Emily from Roger's slimy clutches and her own foolishness.

After a few minutes of conversation, Emily's companion entered the library and Emily resumed strolling down the path. Alec trailed her, grateful for the darkness, the chatter of students sauntering about the campus and the rustle of dry leaves against the pavement. He noticed a cardboard cutout of a skeleton adorning a dormitory door, a carved pumpkin on the front steps of the Foreign Languages building, and then Dwight Hall loomed up ahead.

Only a few of the upstairs windows were lighted. Alec counted them to determine if Roger's was one of the ones illuminated. Not surprisingly, it was.

Emily entered the building. Alec marked time for twenty seconds, then followed her in.

The stairwell was unoccupied. He stole up the stairs, his sneakered feet noiseless on the linoleum floor. Nearing the top of the stairs he slowed down and peered surreptitiously down the hall. Emily was knocking on Roger's office door.

Alec pressed his back against the wall and listened to the door open, then slam shut. Then he leaned away from the wall and peered down the hall again. It was empty.

He glanced at his watch. He'd wait five minutes before interrupting the student-teacher conference. He wanted to catch Phelps in as compromising a position as possible, but not quite in the act.

He waited. He listened. The fluorescent hall lights buzzed; the ventilation system hissed. A student appeared from around a bend in the hallway and bounded past him down the stairs, sparing him a fleeting, mildly curious glance. He gnawed on his toothpick and waited some more.

He checked his watch. Four minutes had elapsed since Emily had entered Phelps's office. Long enough. Alec climbed the last few stairs, tossed his toothpick into the trash can on the landing and strode down the hall to Phelps's door. Drawing in a deep breath, he knocked.

He heard a brief, muffled exchange of voices inside. Then nothing.

He waited a few seconds and knocked again. More muffled sounds from inside.

"Hey, Roger!" he hollered. "Come on, man, open up. I thought we had a beer date." Their "beer date" had been set for the following day, but Alec figured Roger would be more likely to open the door if he was aware that it was Alec on the other side—and if Alec made enough noise out in the hall to embarrass him.

In another minute, the door opened a few inches. Roger positioned himself in the doorway to block Alec's view of the office. He was dressed, but his attire was incriminatingly rumpled. His hair was mussed, his shirttails untucked, his shoes missing.

"Alec," he said with a faint smile, although his voice was as smooth and confident as always. "I thought we'd made that plan for tomorrow night."

"Did we?" Alec did his best to look befuddled. "I'm all confused now. I thought it was tonight." He leaned casually on the door. Roger's grip tightened on the knob, holding the door immobile against Alec's weight. "Well, come on, I'm thirsty," Alec declared. "You know how we famous writers can be. Hitting the booze is part of the verisimilitude."

Roger's eyes narrowed on Alec. "Give me ten minutes?" he half asked.

"Sure, I can wait," Alec replied agreeably. Noticing that Roger's death grip on the doorknob had relented, he gave the door a quick, sudden kick. It swung back to reveal Emily seated on the decadent red couch, her blouse obviously unbuttoned beneath her sweater, her feet bare, her jeans unsnapped and her eyes glassy with panic.

A long, painfully awkward minute passed in silence. Emily wrapped her arms tightly around her waist and doubled over, hiding her face behind a curtain of golden hair. Roger examined Alec with a calculating gaze. Alec pulled another toothpick from his pocket and toyed with it, waiting for one of them to speak.

At last Roger did. "As you can see, you've come at an inopportune time."

"Better now than a few minutes later," Alec commented wryly.

Roger offered a cloying smile. "Well, yes, I suppose that's true."

"She's a student, for God's sake," said Alec. Emily flinched and tightened her grip on herself.

"She's of legal majority."

"So what?"

"So... I suggest you take your leave, and we'll have that little drink tomorrow."

"What about her grade?" Alec persisted.

"What about it?"

"Is this the way students convince you to raise their grades?"

Emily suddenly erupted, her blue eyes flashing angrily. "*He* asked for this, you know. He told me I was special, and he promised to help me keep my scholarship. I didn't come here to convince him of anything. I came because he said I had to if I wanted him to help me stay in school. He promised!"

Roger looked extremely uncomfortable. Alec scowled. "You may be of legal majority, sweetheart, but legal age and maturity are two different things. Fix your clothes and get out of here, okay?"

"Don't you tell me what to do!" she ranted, venting her anger at Alec. "You have no right coming in here. This is between Roger and me."

Her wrath bounced off Alec. "Do you know what it's called when you trade sex for money?" he asked, his tone impassive.

Her cheeks turned a bright crimson. "He made me do it! Not for money, for school! He made me!"

"I never forced her," Roger retorted indignantly. "She came here of her own free will."

"I used to think you loved me." Emily's hostility found its rightful target at last. She snapped into action, smoothing her blouse under her sweater and tucking it into her jeans, then yanking on her socks, all the while railing at Roger. "And then I found out you were married, and you did this to another student last year. She's in law school now, at Harvard, and you pulled this on her. You pick your students and tell them they're special, you soften them up and then you hit them with this deal. You told me if I wanted your help I'd have to show you my appreciation. You said I had to spend more time with you, even if it meant having less study time in the evenings, and less time to practice the piano. You said I had to be properly appreciative, remember?"

Roger's eyes burned with rage. "I can see how appreciative you are, too," he countered in a low, tense voice. "Do you realize who I am, Emily? Do you realize that I'm considered a foremost expert in my field? I've been on television, I've consulted with Presidents. And you're just a lazy undergraduate who doesn't exercise her intellect, who doesn't want to earn high grades through hard work and study. You *should* be appreciative to have someone of my stature paying attention to you."

"Uh..." Alec didn't want to hear any more of this. It was one thing to catch Roger and Emily on the verge of hanky-panky, and quite another to listen to them hurl ugly accusations at each other. "Emily, clear out of here, would you?" he urged her. "It's over. Just go. I'll take care of Phelps."

"It's not my fault," she said, stepping into her shoes and running her fingers jerkily through her tangled hair. Her voice sounded querulous now, less incensed than anxious. "It's not my fault. He did it. He promised—"

"*Go,*" Alec commanded.

Emily lifted her books from the floor beside the couch and stood. Pushing past Alec to get to the door, she cast him a quick, frantic glance, one colored by both hatred and fear. And then she was gone.

He turned to Roger, who smiled with barely a trace of contrition. "These things happen," he said, as if completely confident that Alec understood. He appeared at ease, almost complacent, as he perched on the edge of his desk, his arms crossed and his eyes glittering with amusement.

Alec had nothing more to say to Roger. He'd accomplished what he'd set out to do. He'd found out what his aunt needed to know and he'd saved Emily from whatever tawdry fate Roger had planned for her. He could leave this simpering, sniveling philanderer, just walk away and wash his hands of the whole sordid scene.

Something held him back, though: a picture of Roger's attractive, demure wife. The flash of anguish in Emily's eyes before she'd raced out of the office. And Lauren, who had been exposed to one of life's most bitter lessons yet had never let the bitterness rub off on her. Lauren, who had been denied her lifelong aspiration, and had plunged headlong into a new career, worrying about her student with the same intensity as she once worried about her music.

For Lauren, for the goodness inside her, Alec had to say something. "These things don't just happen," he muttered, giving Roger a scathing stare, deriving some small pleasure from watching the man's smug expression fade. "People make them happen."

"Oh, come now," Roger argued. "This isn't a good-versus-evil scenario. She was quite willing—"

"She's a kid. Young enough to be your daughter."

"Old enough to know her own mind," Roger countered.

"You have power over her, Phelps. You were the one who said people become professors because they want the power. Well, you have the power, and you've used it in a real sick way."

"No, Alec—"

"You disgust me," he said. "Put on your shoes. We're going to have a chat with the president."

"Ms. WYLER?" The voice on the telephone was shrill and breathless. "Ms. Wyler, I'm sorry to call you at home. This is Kitty Forsythe. You don't know me, but I'm a friend of Emily Spaeth's."

Lauren tightened her grip on the phone. It was eight o'clock. She had heard Alec leave the duplex earlier, just as she heard everything he did, listened for it, imagined his every movement as the sound descended into her room. He'd gone out about an hour ago, and now a friend of Emily's was calling her, seeming close to hysterical.

"Yes?" she said.

"Well, I hate to bother you, but—"

"That's all right. What is it?"

"Well, it's Emily. I know she takes piano lessons from you, and you're the only professor she really likes, and she's...well, she's packing. She says she's going to leave Albright, drop out and leave school, and I think she's like freaked or something. She refuses to talk to the dorm adviser, and she's locked herself in her room and I thought, well...I know it's late, but—"

"I'll be right over," Lauren said at once. "Which dorm is it?"

As soon as she hung up, she grabbed a jacket and her keys and left the apartment. Something had happened tonight. She'd known it would; she'd felt it in the air, in her gut. Emily had been so edgy during her lesson today, jumpy and uneasy, her playing choppy and riddled with errors. Lauren had felt awfully nosy questioning her about her love life, but she'd been eager to get Emily to open up somehow.

Maybe nothing had occurred between Emily and Roger Phelps tonight. Maybe Emily had simply had a fight with some other, legitimate boyfriend and was heartbroken about it. Maybe that was why she wanted to leave school. Twenty-year-old girls—especially those without someone like Gerald Honan keeping their emotions firmly in check—could be mighty melodramatic.

Jogging down Hancock Street to the campus, Lauren tried to persuade herself that Emily had had a lovers' quarrel with her beau—but she knew that wasn't what her friend's call was about. Alec had gone out that evening. Something had happened, something with Roger Phelps. And now Lauren's most gifted student was, in the terminology of her classmate, freaked.

By the time Lauren reached the dormitory, her cheeks tingled from the brisk night air, and her breath escaped her in visible puffs of white. She charged into the building and identified herself to the on-duty student in the entry hall: "I'm Lauren Wyler. I teach in the music department, and I'm here to see Emily Spaeth."

The girl nodded and lifted the receiver of the dorm phone. "I'll telephone upstairs."

"Ask for Kitty Forsythe," Lauren told her.

The girl rang upstairs, talked to someone on the other end for a minute, and then gestured toward the stairs. "It's the third floor," she said. "Go on up."

Lauren did. At the second-floor landing she heard the cheerful babble of young voices gossiping and giggling, the splattering rush of a shower, the infectious beat of a rock and roll tune. She continued up to the third floor, where a pale, wide-eyed girl in a baggy gray sweat suit was waiting for her.

"This way," the girl said, hurrying Lauren down the hall. "I'm Kitty. I live across the hall from Emily. She's, like—it sounds like she's crying or something in there, and cursing and stuff. I don't know, if she was into drugs I'd think maybe she just took something she shouldn't have, but Em's always been straight-arrow. She doesn't even drink wine."

"Do you think it's her boyfriend?" Lauren asked, prepared for a negative reply.

"What boyfriend?"

"She implied during her lesson today that she's really down on men. I thought she and her boyfriend might have broken up or something."

Kitty shook her head. "She doesn't have a boyfriend. She used to have this major crush on one of her professors. She wouldn't tell me who he was, because it was supposed to be this big secret. She said he was in love with her because he'd picked her out for special attention and all this stuff, and I'm like, yuck. I mean, a professor? Nothing personal, Ms. Wyler, but a professor?"

"So she didn't really have a boyfriend," Lauren confirmed.

"All she had was him. She was gonzo over him. And then, recently, she began to say she realized he didn't really love her or anything, but he was just using her and damned if she wasn't going to use him right back."

Lauren winced. "Was she having an affair with him?"

"I don't know. All I know is, she said she was going to get what she could from him, because he didn't really love her anyway, but he could do things for her and she might as well follow through. I could never get a straight story from her, but I thought she knew what she was doing."

Whoring for a grade, Lauren thought, recalling Alec's blunt description of what Emily was doing. Her stomach knotted; her heart sank. She acknowledged that, despite the evidence, despite Alec's cynical wisdom about such affairs, she had secretly hoped he'd been wrong about this. She'd hoped Emily hadn't really gone to Phelps. But Alec had been right all along. *Welcome to the real world, Lauren.*

"Is this her room?" she asked as Kitty drew to a halt in front of a closed door.

"Yeah. Emily?" Kitty yelled through the door. "Ms. Wyler is here."

"Go away!" Emily's voice emerged.

"Emily," Lauren said, as gently and patiently as she could. "Open up, please. I'd like to help you." In fact, she wanted to shake Emily, scream at her, berate her for being such a ninny. But Lauren was a teacher now. What she would do was serve the needs of her student.

A minute ticked by before the door opened to reveal Emily, her hair snarled and her eyes red-rimmed. Behind her a suitcase lay open on her bed. A footlocker stood on the floor next to the bed, its lid propped open. Clothing was scattered about the room.

Issuing a quiet thank-you to Kitty, Lauren stepped inside and shut the door behind her. Emily shrank back, allowing Lauren to cross the room and sit in the ladder-back chair beside the desk. "Kitty tells me you're thinking of leaving school."

"I've got to," Emily moaned.

"Because of financial problems?"

"Because my reputation is shot." Emily crumpled onto the bed and wiped her tear-streaked cheeks with a tissue. "It'll be a scandal, I know."

"You had an affair with Roger Phelps," Lauren said.

Emily shot her a startled look. "How did you know? Oh, God, if you know everybody must know."

"Nobody knows," Lauren swore.

"This friend of his knows. He caught us. I'm so stupid, it's all my fault—"

"*Your* fault? Emily, Professor Phelps was the adult in this thing. He should have known better. He took advantage of you."

Emily wept, her tissue growing soggy as she mopped her face with it. Lauren spotted a tissue box on a shelf and passed it to Emily, who accepted it with a silent nod and plucked a fresh tissue from it.

"At first, I thought he really cared for me," Emily admitted, her voice quivering. "I was so flattered, Ms. Wyler, I thought—wow, this older man really likes me, and he's really handsome, and he's paying all this attention to me and asking me to come to his office all the time, and . . . and then he said he'd be able to guarantee me my scholarship. I really thought he loved me."

"And you loved him?" Lauren asked.

Emily shrugged, then nodded.

"Did you know he was married?"

"Not at first." It was barely a whisper. "Then I found out, and he told me to grow up. He told me we could help each other. He said he likes to help his students as long as they're willing to help him. He can get them scholarships, he can get them into graduate schools. I can't even think about graduate school, Ms. Wyler. I can't even afford to be here at Albright.''

"If you're worried about college costs, Emily, there are plenty of ways for you to raise money. You can take a loan or get a job. In fact, I can think of a terrific job for you—giving piano lessons. You could advertise in town. I'll bet there are youngsters in Albright who'd want to study with you. I would write you a recommendation if you'd like.''

Emily peered at her through watery eyes. "You would?''

"There are proper ways to finance your way through school. Having sex with a professor isn't one of them.''

Emily groaned. "They'll probably expel me.''

"No. I won't let them," Lauren promised.

"They *should* expel me. This is a school for smart girls. I'm an idiot.''

"You aren't an idiot, Emily. You got yourself into a mess, but fortunately you've gotten yourself out of it.''

"No I didn't. That guy, Roger's friend, he got me out of it. He stopped Roger before it was too late. He barged into the office—it was almost like he knew what was about to happen. He didn't even look surprised. He just came in and got me out of there.''

Lauren considered telling Emily that Alec was no friend of Roger's, but she decided not to. It didn't matter who Alec was. All that mattered was that he'd saved Emily before it was too late, as Emily herself had said.

"Tomorrow," Lauren resolved, "I'll go with you to see the dean of students. We'll straighten the whole thing out.''

"She'll think I'm too stupid to be at Albright College.''

"She'll think," Lauren assured her, "that you were innocent and inexperienced, and you made a mistake. Sometimes, when a woman hasn't had much experience, she gets confused. She reads more into a man's actions than he intends. She sees love when all there is is lust. That's not stupidity, Emily. It's a part of growing up. We learn from our mistakes."

"You, too?" Emily's eyes widened; apparently she could tell Lauren was speaking from her heart. "Something like this happened to you?"

Lauren smiled sadly. "I never got involved with a married professor," she said. "But I once was in love, and the man didn't feel the same way. I..." She sighed. "I was playing a rhapsody, and he was playing rock and roll." She swallowed the lump in her throat and forced her smile brighter. "But I learned from it. And you will, too. It's part of becoming a woman."

Once she'd extracted a vow from Emily not to do anything rash in exchange for her own promise to accompany Emily to the dean's office the following morning, Lauren gave Emily a comforting hug and left the room. A blast of frigid air greeted her as she emerged from the dormitory into the overcast late-October night. She buttoned her jacket and tucked her hands into the pockets. As chilly as it was, she was in no hurry to go home.

She ambled slowly through the campus, reviewing her conversation with Emily. She thought she'd handled Emily's predicament well, calming the student and teaching her, leading her to new insights. That was what teachers were supposed to do.

Yet she'd been dishonest with Emily. She'd told her she had learned from her own mistakes with a man. But she wasn't sure that was the truth. If it had been a mistake to fall in love with Alec, then she hadn't learned a thing.

He had moved to Albright to help out his aunt. In spite of his disapproval of Emily, he had helped her. And he'd helped Lauren, even when she hadn't believed she'd needed any help, even when she'd resented him for it. He hadn't done any of it for money, or for power, or to improve his own status or feed his ego. Coming to Albright hadn't made him a better writer or healed his knee.

He had never lied to Lauren, whether the subject was her hand or her future—or his feelings. Unlike Roger Phelps—and unlike her manager, Gerald—Alec had never misled her, exploited her, acted dishonestly.

He had never pretended to love Lauren. He'd made love with her only because she'd wanted him to, invited him, all but demanded it. The instant he'd seen the direction her emotions were taking, he'd broken away from her—not to hurt her but to spare her from further pain.

God help her, she loved him. More tonight than before, she loved him.

She had told him she didn't want him protecting her, and she'd meant it. As she made her way slowly back toward Hancock Street, though, she found herself wondering whether she would ever be able to protect herself from the pain of loving a man who didn't love her.

CHAPTER THIRTEEN

ALEC RANG THE BELL at the front door of the president's house with his left hand; his right was planted firmly on the sleeve of Roger's professorially tweedy jacket. He didn't really think Roger would try to bolt, but he wasn't going to take any chances.

The distinguished professor appeared to be sulking. His eyes were averted; his mouth arced downward. Although Alec was only a couple of inches taller, Roger looked tiny to him, shrunken, defeated.

When the maid didn't answer the doorbell after a minute, Alec rang again. A sound above him caused him to back up a step, dragging Roger with him. Mags was fidgeting with a second-story window, unlatching it and drawing it open. "Yes?" she called down. "Who's there?"

Alec suppressed a laugh. Shouting from an upstairs window was classic Cudahy behavior. When Grandma Cudahy had lived on the third floor of a three-decker, she'd always responded to her doorbell by throwing open a window, hollering "Who's there?" down to the street and, if her visitor passed muster, tossing down the front-door key so the visitor could let himself in. Alec wondered whether Mags was going to toss down the key to the president's house.

"It's me, Mags," he shouted up to her. "I brought someone with me. We've got some business to take care of."

Lighted from behind, Mags's face was shadowed, but Alec could envision her frown as she stared down at the two men on the semicircular brick porch. He could imagine her sizing them up and deducing their reason for coming to see her. "I'll be right down," she said.

A few seconds later, she heaved the massive front door open. She had on a plush flannel dressing robe, fleecy slippers and her reading spectacles. A smudgy ink stain ran along the outer edge of her pinkie, and her blondish-gray hair fluffed in a disorderly halo about her head. Her gaze moved directly to Roger and stayed there, even though her words were intended for both men. "I hope you'll forgive my informal appearance. I usually don't entertain guests at this hour, but this looked important."

"Not so important that we have to rouse you from bed," Roger said obsequiously.

"I wasn't in bed," she said. "I was working on the speech I'm supposed to give to the Chicago chapter of the alumnae association next week." She angled her head to view Roger's face, which he promptly ducked. "Something tells me this is going to be worth putting the speech aside for. Come in, gentlemen."

They followed her into the house, through the great room and into the small parlor with the fancy antique furnishings. Alec's knee was sore, but he remained standing as Mags sank comfortably into her armchair and Roger stiffly lowered himself onto the edge of one of the sofa cushions. "I think Professor Phelps would like to discuss his job performance with you," Alec said.

Roger winced. Mags peered at him over the rims of her eyeglasses, then glanced up at Alec. "How bad is it?"

"They weren't completely undressed when I broke in on them."

She let out a long breath, then tapped her fingertips together and ruminated. "Who was the student?"

"Emily Spaeth," Alec told her. "A junior, I think. She was worried about her grade. Roger here was generously offering her the opportunity to get it up, as it were."

Roger grimaced at Alec's pun. Mags's grim smile was tinged with disgust. "What about last year's incident?" she asked.

"Miss Spaeth mentioned that she knew all about it," Alec replied. "I haven't exactly gotten a signed confession from good ol' Roger here...."

"Emily was quite upset," Roger cut in. "She didn't know what she was saying."

"She knew damned well, pal. And we've got corroborating evidence."

Roger blanched. "What evidence?"

"A letter."

"From the girl's best friend," Mags added.

Roger squirmed. "In other words, you're willing to take the word of a student over that of a faculty member."

"When the faculty member is you, yeah," Alec drawled. "Now, Roger, you can make this easy by confessing, or you can make me work up a sweat getting the truth out of you. We *law-enforcement officers* are good at that kind of thing, so..."

"What do you want me to say?" Roger blurted out, obviously cowed. "You want to know what happened last year? It was her idea, not mine. *She* came to *me.* She knew I had connections at Harvard Law School, and she propositioned me.''

"And you were just so overwhelmed, you didn't know how to say no,'' Alec muttered sarcastically.

"It's the truth. When a young woman with such irresistible allure presents herself to a healthy man... I'm sorry, Margaret,'' he mumbled. ''I don't expect you to understand.''

"I understand just fine,'' said Mags, glowering at Roger through her spectacles. "If you're telling the truth about last year—a big *if*—am I to presume this nonsense with Emily Spaeth is all her fault, too? You're just a defenseless man under siege from all these oversexed undergraduates, is that right?''

"Well...'' Roger couldn't deny his claim sounded preposterous. Much as he loathed the man, Alec suffered a stab of sympathy for him. He knew what it was like when a woman offered herself, a woman so desirable, so lovely the man couldn't turn away.

Then again, he hadn't bartered with Lauren. He hadn't paid her off. He hadn't made love with her so he could feel powerful, or demanded anything but her own pleasure in return for his.

Still, he could understand the impulse Roger had acted on. Not the act, but the desire. He might be a better man than the sniveling professor, but not by much.

"Why don't you go get yourself a drink, Alec?'' Mags suggested. "Before we drag in law-enforcement tactics, I think I'd like to confer with Dr. Phelps alone. The kitchen is just past the dining room, down the hall and on the left.''

Alec nodded and left the parlor. He was shaken by the possibility that he might have anything in common with Phelps. Whatever they had in common, though, a huge difference loomed between them. Not because Alec hadn't pressured Lauren, not because he hadn't dangled some tangible reward in front of her, but because he cared so damned much about her. He had cared then and he did now. He cared in a deep, relentless, overwhelming way.

Following Mags's directions, he passed a dining room large enough to host a banquet for fifty guests—something the president of Albright College was no doubt called upon to do every now and then—and located the industrial-size kitchen across the hall. Two large refrigerators stood side by side; he opened one and found a six-pack of Budweiser chilling on the shelf.

He pulled out a bottle, twisted off the cap and took a long drink. Mission accomplished, he thought, picturing Roger and Mags shut up in her fancy parlor, hashing out the facts and weighing the repercussions. It was over now, all but the closing moments. The denouement, his editor called the final unwinding of a story. Alec supposed that as an author he ought to know the technical terms.

Maybe this was the denouement of Roger's story, but even the beer couldn't get Alec to unwind. He wasn't ready to type "the end" and go back to Boston. There were still loose ends, unresolved conflicts. There was still Lauren Wyler.

They were all wrong for each other; Alec knew that as well as Lauren did. She was a princess, delicate and dainty and beguilingly innocent. She had no use for a jaded ex-cop with overprotective tendencies. She'd turned to him once, when she'd been at her weakest. Now she was strong. She didn't need him.

He didn't need her, either, he told himself. He was strong, too. Just because he was attracted to Lauren, just because she intrigued him, just because she haunted his every thought and starred in his every fantasy didn't mean he ought to get involved with her.

A short, humorless laugh escaped him. He washed it away with a long sip of beer.

Mags's and Roger's voices drifted down the hall to him, soft and indistinct. He left the kitchen, curious to hear how they were coming along. Halfway along the hall he stopped; the door to the parlor was opening. Roger exited the room. Storming into the hall, he spotted Alec and froze.

The two men stared at each other. The suave, well-cultivated creases in Roger's face seemed to have evolved into deep grooves, slashing his high forehead and cheeks like underlines and exclamation points. His eyes were hard, his lips thin, his hands furled into fists.

Alec tried to think of something to say. *Sorry. Have a good life. Thanks for praising my novel.* None of them adequate, or necessary.

Roger's jaw flexed as he too appeared to be searching for something to say. Like Alec, he thought better of it and marched off in silence.

By the time Alec reached the parlor, the house was reverberating with the loud thud of the front door slamming shut. Mags lounged wearily in her armchair, her head rolled back and her eyes closed, her feet propped up on the coffee table.

"That's a Chippendale, Auntie dear," Alec scolded. "Put your feet down."

She opened her eyes and lifted her head. The smile she gave him was baleful. "I've got a better idea. Why don't you come on in and put your feet up? I don't know about you, but I feel destructive."

Alec flopped onto the couch near his aunt and handed her his beer. She took a sip.

"I demanded his resignation," she said, answering his unspoken question. "It was either that or I'd have to fire him, and when I laid out the alternatives he decided to resign. Unfortunately I have to keep him on till the end of the semester. I can't just boot him out when there are so many students taking his classes. It wouldn't be fair to them."

"What about replacing him?" Alec asked.

"I can bring a replacement to Albright for the spring semester. I've already got someone in mind—a doctoral candidate at Yale. I think she'll be able to handle it."

Alec was impressed that his aunt could have scared up a replacement so quickly. "Does she want the job?"

Mags grinned and took another sip of beer. "I haven't talked to her yet. I was waiting to see what you'd find out about Roger. But she'll come," she said confidently. "She's an Albright alumna. Out of respect for her alma mater, she'll come."

"The old-girl network," Alec muttered, although he was also grinning.

"You bet."

"What about the kid—Emily? What are you going to do about her?"

Mags's smile faded. "I have to talk to her. I expect this has been a traumatic experience for her."

"*I* expect she didn't exactly get railroaded," ~~Alec~~ pointed out. "She knew what she was getting into, Mags."

"I'm sure she did. We admit only intelligent girls into this school, so if she's here she must be intelligent. That's not to say she's immune to trauma, however. Even smart girls can do foolish things and get hurt." She gave her head a tired shake. "Roger said he was only taking what the girl offered. Heaven knows how many girls have offered him something, and how often he's taken it. We only know for sure about this one and the pre-law student last year."

"They aren't blameless," Alec contended. Just as in his family—like Albright, a bastion of femininity—he felt obligated to present the male viewpoint fairly.

"No," Mags concurred. "They aren't. I can't say for sure who offered what or who made the first move. But I *can* say that just because a woman offers something doesn't mean a man has to take it. Sometimes—I suspect it goes against a man's nature—but sometimes he simply has to say no, because saying no is the right thing to do and because to say yes would ultimately hurt the woman. Even if this student threw herself at Roger Phelps, he should have known better. He should have said no."

Mags couldn't have meant for Alec to take her words personally, but he did. Long after he left the president's house and walked home through the frosty night, they echoed inside him, eating at him, chastening him.

The hell with it. Whatever had occurred between Lauren and himself, whoever had offered, whoever had taken, whoever should have said no—none of it mattered anymore. He was done in Albright. Wishing otherwise didn't change a thing. He'd always been good at facing reality, and this was his reality now. Lauren had pushed him away; she'd kept her distance. She'd limited all their conversations since his first night back to the subject of Emily Spaeth and Roger Phelps. She didn't play her piano anymore. A long time ago, he'd asked her to play—for him. But then he'd left her, and by the time he'd come back she no longer wanted that connection with him. She no longer wanted to send her music into his life.

Reality: she didn't want him around. It was time for him to leave.

The downstairs half of the duplex was dark when he arrived there. It was nine-thirty, a bit early for her to have turned in for the night—but when she went to bed was none of his business. He exerted himself to ignore her door. Unlocking his own, he let himself in and trudged up the stairs.

He was restless. He showered, put on fresh jeans and a sweater, and pulled out his suitcase, thinking he might as well start packing. The sooner he left town, the better.

He opened the suitcase on his bed and stared at it. He couldn't pack. Tomorrow, maybe, but not now. His brain was in overdrive; he couldn't waste his energy on something as dreary as packing.

He wandered into the den. He hadn't written a word since he'd returned to Albright four days ago. Tonight, he felt ready to burn off all his excess energy at his typewriter.

He rolled a clean sheet of paper into the machine and began to type. He'd gotten pretty adept at typing with his index fingers and thumbs—bad form, but it worked. In little time he'd warmed up and was moving along at a decent pace. The words flowed. He filled the page, pulled it out, scanned it and decided it was a keeper. He inserted a second sheet of paper into the roller.

The typewriter clacked loudly. Outside, the wind buffeted the trees, causing them to creak. He jiggled his right foot, propped his left on a crossbar under the typing table, shoved up the sleeves of his sweater. He started on a third page.

Solve the crime, lose the girl. That was how this book was going to work. That was the shape of it, the plot, the bittersweet irony. Back in Boston, when he'd been tossing every single page he wrote into the trash can, he'd been trying to force the story in a different direction, trying to make it come out with the hero not only solving the crime but getting the girl, too. And it just didn't work that way. Some endings just weren't destined to be that happy.

Now he knew. Now it was fitting together, making sense, getting written. Solve the crime, lose the girl. That was Alec's story.

He was hammering so hard on the typewriter, he almost didn't hear the music at first. Only when he reached the bottom of the page and pulled it out of the roller was he aware of the sound.

A few hesitant notes on the piano. One, then another, random and tuneless.

He ought to disregard it and continue writing. He had finally figured out where his story was going and how to get it there. This wasn't the time to stop.

He reached for a clean sheet of paper and rolled in into the machine. He lifted his hands to the keys and tried to concentrate.

A chord. A second chord, pitched above the first, and then a third, an unexpectedly jazzy progression.

What the hell was she up to? This wasn't her beloved classical music, the prim, stodgy stuff she always played. Abandoning his typewriter, he went into the living room where he would be able to hear better.

She was improvising something slow and bluesy. When she missed notes she didn't bother to go back and play them correctly; the clashing harmonies and fouled-up fingerings only added to the gutsy quality of her improvisation. At first she seemed to be avoiding the high notes, those she would have had to play with the two lame fingers of her right hand. But after a while, she started letting those notes creep in. She missed a note but didn't stop. She missed another note and slurred over the passage. She picked up the tempo, experimented with a bass riff, pounded some rock chords against it, then let the music smooth out again into something soft and dreamy.

It was the most beautiful music he'd ever heard. And he admitted to himself, with an acute pang of self-awareness, that he wasn't willing to lose the girl.

SHE PLAYED because he was typing. She played because she wanted to prove to herself that she was strong enough to mend herself. She'd survived the end of her career; she had to assure herself that she could survive her relationship with Alec.

She had hiked around the campus for a long time, trying to sort her thoughts, until the cold had closed in on her. Reluctantly she'd returned to Hancock Street. The first thing she'd noticed was that the second-floor windows were filled with light.

That light had told her he hadn't left town yet. No doubt he would, soon. He'd completed his assignment. There was nothing to keep him in Albright any longer.

She had let herself into her apartment, locked the door and reflexively tuned in to Alec's movements upstairs. All she'd heard was a faint tick-ticking sound. It had taken her a minute to identify the ticking as his typewriter.

She had imagined his fingers flying over the keys of his instrument. Her gaze had drifted intuitively to *her* instrument. She hadn't touched her piano since...

Since the night she and Alec had made love.

She had pulled off her coat and tossed it onto a chair. As she'd approached the piano, a shiver of doubt had rippled down her spine, but she'd fought against her fear. If she was ever going to get over Alec, she would have to start by lifting the lid off the keyboard, sitting down and attacking the keys.

So she'd taken a deep breath, lowered herself onto the bench, slid the lid up and back along its tracks and studied the familiar pattern of white and black keys. Her pulse had drummed in her temples; her eyes had blurred with tears.

Welcome to the real world, she had whispered to herself, and then she'd begun to play.

She'd deliberately refused to run her scales and drills. She'd avoided her favorite pieces, the old familiars with which she'd established her no-longer-relevant reputation. She had forced her fingers not to tremble, forced her ears not to listen. Her only aim had been to prove to herself that she was strong enough to endure.

After a while, her pulse returned to normal and her vision clarified. The slick surfaces of the keys felt curiously comfortable against her fingertips; their smooth, clean action soothed her. The bloopers and blunders didn't trouble her; she accepted the clumsiness of her weakened right hand.

Music was different now. It was something she made not for money, not for fame but simply because it was there, an essential part of her.

She let the melody lead her, let the harmony follow its own logic. She played nothing in particular, just notes, pretty sounds, swinging sounds, jagged, jarring sounds. It felt good, like tasting chocolate after a long diet or diving into a lake after a day beneath the hot August sun. It felt good.

She wasn't sure what made her look up. When she did, she saw Alec standing on the porch outside her window, watching her.

The intoxicating effect of the music slowed her reflexes. Her hands lay quiescent on the keys as she absorbed his presence. Silence filled the room.

His gaze held hers. His eyes probed, questioned, pleaded. Wisps of vapor escaped from his mouth with his every breath. He had on only a sweater and jeans, no jacket, yet he didn't shiver, didn't hug his arms to himself for warmth. He just stood there, watching, waiting.

Letting him into her house might be the biggest mistake of her life. Yet she couldn't bear not knowing what it was he was trying to tell her with his eyes. As if under a spell, she rose from the bench, walked to the door and opened it.

"Thank you," he said, stepping inside.

She inched back, aware of the danger in letting him get too close to her. "You must be freezing."

He shook his head, then laughed and rubbed his hands together briskly. "I guess I am. I was out there a long time."

That startled her. How long had he been spying on her? How deeply had the music bewitched her that she hadn't noticed him? Why did having him in the same room with her make her feel helpless and giddy and out of control? Why, when she knew it would only lead to heartache, did she wish he would sweep her into his arms, as he had the last time he'd appeared on her doorstep, and kiss her?

"I thought you'd be getting ready to leave Albright by now," she said quietly.

He nodded. "I took out my suitcase. I was going to start packing, but I couldn't bring myself to do it. Not without saying goodbye to you."

That was it, then. He'd come downstairs to say goodbye.

"And then you started playing," he continued when she didn't speak. He took a step toward her, and she bravely held her ground. "And I realized I couldn't say goodbye," he concluded.

"Why not? You're all done here, you accomplished what you set out to do."

"The first time we kissed, you told me you couldn't get involved with me." He dared to slide his hand under her chin, along her jaw, around to the nape of her neck. She willed herself to resist the friction of his thumb against her skin, the flutter of heat it ignited deep inside her. "And that was okay, because I wasn't looking for an involvement, either. But then, I was never really looking for a career as a writer, and it found me. And you were never looking for a career as a teacher, and it found you. And—" he moved closer yet "—I think an involvement found us."

His lips caressed hers, so lightly, so tenderly she wanted to weep. "Alec," she whispered, desperation battling with desire inside her. "I can't make room for you in my life and then have you walk away when you're done. I've lost a lot already. I don't want to lose any more."

"Then don't lose me," he murmured, brushing his mouth over hers again, pausing to nibble her quivering lower lip. "Make room and let me stay."

Just as her fingers had responded to the tactile pleasure of the keyboard, so her lips responded to the tactile pleasure of Alec's kiss. They moved, softened, parted for the sweet invasion of his tongue.

She wasn't sure how she and Alec wound up in her bedroom. All she knew was that suddenly they were there, standing next to her bed, still kissing. One of Alec's hands combed through her hair and the other roamed her back as his mouth conquered hers, his tongue surging deep, his desire feeding hers. A heavy warmth settled in her hips, just as it did every time he kissed her, every time she thought of him. A matching heaviness settled in her soul, convincing her that even if she didn't survive losing Alec it would be worth having his love tonight.

She slipped her hands under his sweater and up, shoving the knitted wool out of her way so she could touch his chest. He groaned and pulled back slightly. "Let's not rush this time," he whispered, even as he leaned toward her, inviting her sensual exploration. "Let's make it last."

She nodded in agreement. But her hands contradicted her, yanking the sweater up and over his head. He tossed the sweater aside, then smiled as she twined her fingers through the golden hair of his chest.

She skimmed his nipples and they stiffened into points. Delighted by his visible response to her touch, she let her hands rove down to the waistband of his jeans—and felt his entire body stiffen in arousal.

He kissed her again, a voracious kiss that sent waves of heat through her flesh. Her hands stilled against the taut muscles of his abdomen; she was scarcely aware of his fingers dancing down the front of her blouse, plucking open the buttons, easing the fabric over her shoulders and down her arms. Her brassiere followed the blouse onto the floor, and then his lips left hers to graze her throat.

Turning her, he backed up to the bed and sat, bringing her breast to his mouth. Her body went limp as he licked, sucked, scraped his teeth with exquisite gentleness over her flushed nipple. Just when she felt she couldn't stand any more of his sensual assault, he turned his attention to her other breast, feasting on it, teasing and tasting until her legs gave way.

Alec tumbled backward, pulling her down on top of him, sliding her higher so his mouth could mate with hers again. She felt the hardness of him through what remained of their clothing, felt the ferocious need of him in the rocking of his hips against hers, felt his eagerness in the deft motions of his hands on the waistband button of her slacks, on the zipper, on her underwear as he stripped her naked.

Her own fingers weren't nearly as dextrous; she fumbled with his fly and he laughed softly, his lips vibrating below hers. Brushing her hands aside, he made quick work of removing his jeans.

Once he'd kicked his pants off the bed, he guided her down onto the mattress next to him. His hands journeyed over her tingling skin, lingering at her waist, savoring the sharp edges of her hipbones, dipping briefly, tantalizingly into the dark curls of hair below. "Tell me what you want," he whispered, his eyes coming into sharp, silvery focus as he gazed down at her.

Everything, she wanted to reply. *You. Your body. Your love. Forever.* "I don't know," she confessed, afraid to ask for more than she could have.

He studied her face for a moment longer, then bowed and touched her lips with his. Rising onto her, he slid downward along her body, dropping light kisses over her shoulders, over her breasts and belly. His tongue darted into her navel and she laughed, partly because it tickled and partly because she was nervous.

He shifted lower, settling between her legs, sprinkling more kisses along the edge of her hair and along the inner surface of her thighs. "Alec?" she whispered, anxiety stringing her body taut.

"Don't be afraid," he said, his voice a soothing purr. He shifted yet again, cupping his hands around the soft flesh of her bottom and lifting her to his mouth.

She heard a strange, strangled sound—her own tortured moan as his tongue made love to her. Her hips writhed and tensed; her heart stopped beating; her lungs stopped drawing breath. Her hands clutched at the blanket as her back arched, and she moaned again, astonished by the shocking force of her body's surrender. Fiery spasms racked her, tore through her, rendered her unable to do anything but feel, and love.

"Alec..." It was a sob, a helpless cry. She was defenseless against such overwhelming intimacy, against the devastating joy he had brought her. All she could do was try to give him a joy to equal it.

She recalled the way he had pressed her hand to him the last time. As he rose onto her she reached for him, this time without his having to coax her. He was already hard, but she caressed him to an even greater arousal, her fingers tight around him, her confidence increasing as she saw the delight in his face, heard it in the raggedness of his breath, felt it in the flexing of his hips. Instinctively she knew when he needed more than just her hand. She guided him to herself, rising as he thrust into her, taking him as deep as she could.

"Oh, Lauren . . ." His voice dissolved into a sigh as he held himself motionless inside her. She sank and rose again, wanting only to please him. He gasped and closed his eyes, and she moved again, drawing him into the pulsing heat of her. He groaned, obviously thrilled by her assertiveness. After a moment he took over, adopting her tempo, advancing and retreating, surging and ebbing, stroking her until she felt the renewed pressure inside her, intensifying, increasing until she had no choice but to surrender to its blissful power once more.

"Yes," he breathed, his thrusts fierce and quick, building to a feverish peak as he strove to join her in ecstasy. He surged, shuddered in release, and sank into her arms with a weary sigh.

For a long time afterward neither one of them moved. They simply clung to each other, trembling, struggling for breath. When Alec finally stirred, Lauren reflexively held him tighter. The first glimmerings of thought filtered through her benumbed mind—and they told her he was leaving.

"I'm not going anywhere," he said, as if he could read her thoughts. "Just getting the blanket." He wiggled it out from under them and drew it up over their cooling bodies. Then he cuddled her close to him, cushioning her head with his upper arm.

His face was less than an inch from hers. He gazed at her with the same attentiveness as he'd watched her through her window earlier that evening. His eyes, so recently glazed with passion, now seemed uncannily clear and sharp in the room's shadows.

"I can write in Albright as well as in Boston," he pointed out. "It doesn't matter. Wherever you want to be."

She understood what he was saying, but she was afraid to believe it. "For how long?" she asked warily.

"As long as you'll have me."

His words gave her courage. "What if I wanted to have you forever?" she asked, worried by the possibility that she was pressing him too hard, forcing a commitment she had to have but he might not be able to make.

"You've got me forever," he swore, brushing a long black strand of hair back behind her ear and then leaning forward to kiss her temple. "You're not the same woman I met a month ago, Lauren. You haven't got your whole future worked out anymore. But whatever it turns out to be, I want to be there. I don't know if that's asking too much...."

"No," she assured him, brushing her fingers over his lips. "Whatever my future is, I want you in it."

"You don't need me anymore. You're stronger, now, in charge of your destiny. You're independent. You don't need me."

"I do," she argued. "I love you, Alec."

His smile spread warmth through her. "I love you, too."

"You're right, I don't know what my future is going to hold. But then, neither do you. Things change. Circumstances change."

"This won't change," he whispered, molding his hand to her hip and urging her more snugly against him.

He kissed her again, a slow, languid kiss that sent a shimmering tide of warmth through her, both exciting and comforting her. "I want you to meet my family," he said. "My sisters are the biggest busybodies in the world, and if my mother finds out you cook food in a wok, she's going to think you're undernourished. My Grandma Cudahy is going to give you a lecture on sex, and—"

"I know your aunt," Lauren reminded him. "If she's representative of your family, I think I'll like them just fine."

"We can have Thanksgiving together," Alec suggested.

Lauren smiled. What a marvelous idea. She had been cut off from her family for too long, and Alec's family sounded so close-knit, so affectionate. She'd love to celebrate a real Thanksgiving with a real family—not with a few professional friends at someone's apartment, eating turkey teriyaki and radicchio at a buffet, but a genuine Thanksgiving with yams and stuffing and cranberry sauce. With loud, nosy relatives and whining children and glasses of beer.

With Alec.

"You were wrong," she told him, tears of happiness burning her eyes. "I *do* need you."

"You've got me," he whispered, covering her mouth with his again.

Yes, she had him. But things did change. They would. She knew better than to believe it could be forever.

CHAPTER FOURTEEN

LAUREN CAME TO A STOP in front of the row house. Its redbrick walls were drab, layered with a century's worth of city grime, but the rectangular first-floor windows glowed with light, warm and welcoming in the frigid November night.

She tightened her grip on Alec's hand. "Are you sure this is all right?"

"Positive."

She glanced at him in his corduroy slacks, ribbed sweater and denim jacket. Clad in a Fair Isle sweater and a below-the-knee skirt, she wasn't exactly dressed elegantly, herself. It had been Alec's idea that they dress casually. "If everything else turns out to be a bust," he'd rationalized, "I don't want to have to be stuck wearing my suit, too."

Someday, she thought, giving his hand one more anxious squeeze and then strolling with him up the three concrete steps to the wood-plank porch, she was going to have to see him in his much-maligned suit. Perhaps they would take in a concert at Symphony Hall. One of her old friends from Juilliard was scheduled to solo with the Boston Symphony Orchestra in January. It would be fun to bring Alec to the concert. He'd dragged her to a rock club; one good turn deserved another.

Assuming, of course, they were still together in January.

She had no reason to think they wouldn't be. But some thoughts defied reason, and some events couldn't be predicted. A year ago she wouldn't have imagined that she would be negotiating a second year on her teaching contract at Albright instead of immersing herself in rigorous preparation for a resumed concert schedule. She wouldn't have imagined that she'd find such deep satisfaction in teaching, that she'd take such pleasure in persuading a student like Emily Spaeth to change her major—from political science to music— and to rededicate herself to her education. Lauren certainly wouldn't have imagined that she would have fallen deeply in love with a man like Alec Fontana—or any man at all.

She didn't doubt that Alec loved her, but she had learned through painful experience that it was a mistake to place too much faith in the future. It was a mistake to plan ahead too far, to expect everything to remain as it was right now. She wasn't exactly worried about the possibility that Alec would walk out on her, but she understood that nothing was ever permanent. Life was full of traps and unforeseen dangers. No matter how much she and Alec loved each other, everything could change in an instant, in a single flash of fate.

All she could do was enjoy what she had and not think too much about the ice patches that might lie ahead, waiting to send her dreams into a fatal skid.

At the front door she hesitated again. Alec peered down at her. "What's the matter?"

She succumbed to a bout of nerves. "It's just—I feel like a stranger," she explained in a small, tight voice.

"It's family," Alec reassured her.

"For all I know, they don't even want me here."

"They want you."

She longed to believe him. "Do you really think so?"

He bowed and gave her a quiet kiss. "I know it. Everything's going to be fine." Before she could stop him, he pressed the doorbell.

THE MINUTE he'd climbed out of his car and filled his lungs with the sour city air, he'd felt totally at home. It was a proud working-class neighborhood, a lot like the South Boston neighborhood of his childhood. Cars were parked bumper to bumper along the curbs; the houses huddled together in a dreary facade of soot-stained brick, but they were well lighted, with vest-pocket gardens, flower boxes below the windows, gourds decorating front porches and Indian corn hanging on front doors.

He had intended to put up a calm front in order to counteract Lauren's obvious anxiety. But as they waited for someone to answer the door, he realized he wasn't putting up a front at all. He honestly felt relaxed.

He instantly recognized the woman who opened the front door. Her black hair was streaked with silver, and she wore it pulled smoothly back from her face rather than loose down her back. But her eyes were Lauren's eyes: dark and almond-shaped, angled above delicately sculpted cheekbones. Although she had to be somewhere in the vicinity of fifty years old, her skin was surprisingly smooth and clear, as creamy as her daughter's.

Her smile was hesitant as she held open the screen door. "Hi, Lauren," she said, kissing Lauren's cheek and then stepping aside to let Lauren and Alec in. Her gaze rose to him. "You must be Alec. It's nice of you to come."

"My pleasure, Mrs. Wyler," he said, presenting her with the bouquet of autumn-hued blossoms he and Lauren had purchased for her.

"Oh, my." Lauren's mother seemed overwhelmed by the flowers. Color rose in her cheeks and her eyes shone with pleasure. "How sweet of you. They're so pretty."

An awkward moment passed as Lauren and Alec lingered in the front hall with her. Alec rubbed his icy fingers together to warm them up; Lauren uncoiled her scarf from around her neck. Mrs. Wyler concentrated on the bouquet, gingerly peeling back the green tissue paper and sniffing the flowers. Her hands, Alec discovered, didn't resemble Lauren's at all. They were thicker, the cuticles red and ragged, the skin of her knuckles rough and dry. Definitely not the hands of a pianist. They looked like hands that spent a great deal of time in dishwater.

Through the arched doorway into the living room came the babble of a televised football game. The air was rich with the aroma of roasting turkey.

"Richard?" Mrs. Wyler called into the living room. "Lauren and her fellow are here. Come take their coats, will you?"

Lauren's father appeared in the archway. Like her mother, he was slight in build, dark-haired and dark-eyed. He had broad, well-muscled shoulders, though, and a smile that seemed to come easily to him. Dressed in a plaid flannel shirt and brand-new jeans, he immediately won Alec's heart when he shook his hand and said, "You look like you could use a beer."

In the living room, Alec met Lauren's brother, Ricky. He too wore a plaid flannel shirt and jeans, as well as heavy leather work boots. He stood several inches taller than his father, but he had the same fine-boned physique and cleanly defined features as the others. "How ya doing?" he greeted Alec, giving him a quick, bemused appraisal and then glanced toward the TV screen, as if eager not to miss any of the game. Maybe his reticence had nothing to do with the game, though— maybe he was just shy.

"Who's playing?" Alec asked.

"Philadelphia." Evidently Ricky didn't consider the other team worth mentioning.

Lauren's father entered the living room with a frosty mug of beer. He handed it to Alec, giving him another smile. "You want something, Lauren?"

"Not right now."

"Some wine, maybe? I haven't got any fancy stuff, but—"

"No, thanks," Lauren said, shooting him a quick, nervous smile. "Maybe later."

Her father shrugged and resumed his seat in an overstuffed easy chair. Ricky's eyes shuttled between Lauren and Alec. "So, how ya doing, Lauren?" he asked.

"Okay. How are you?"

"Hanging in there." He eyed Alec with a sheepish smile, then turned back to the television.

It occurred to Alec that he fit in better with the Wyler family than Lauren did—at least as far as drinking a beer and catching a televised football game on Thanksgiving. If he and Lauren had gone to his mother's house instead of the Wylers', he would have been doing exactly what he was doing right now.

He indicated the sofa with a wave of his hand and asked Lauren, "Shall we?"

"You sit," she answered. "Enjoy the game. I'm going to see if my mother needs any help in the kitchen."

Alec followed her out of the living room with his eyes. He had noticed the pallor of her skin, the tension tugging at the corners of her mouth. He'd also noticed that she had hidden her right hand in the pocket of her skirt. He hadn't seen her do that in ages. Obviously she felt sensitive and insecure today.

He joined Ricky on the couch and pretended to take an interest in the football game. But his gaze darted about the room, searching for clues about Lauren's family, her background, the first fourteen years of her life—anything that would tell him how Lauren had come to be the woman she was, the woman he loved. The room's furnishings were old, bordering on shabby, but impeccably clean. Not a trace of dust marred any surface; not a speck of lint sullied the faded gray carpet. Two framed still lifes hung on the wall; a built-in shelf held college graduation photographs of Ricky and another girl—Lauren's sister, Alec assumed. Instead of a graduation shot of Lauren, her parents displayed a photograph of her in the magnificent black gown with the snug bodice, the scooped neckline and the full floor-length skirt that she'd worn on the cover of the Chopin album. Her hair brushed loose and her face discreetly made up, she posed in front of a concert grand piano on a curtained concert stage.

A piano. Why wasn't there a piano in the room? How could Lauren have become a famous pianist if she'd spent her formative years in a house without a piano?

There *had* to be a piano somewhere—unless her parents had gotten rid of it after they'd gotten rid of their daughter. What if they had? What if they'd removed the piano from the premises the instant Lauren had moved to New York? What would that imply about their feelings for their world-famous daughter? What would it mean if they'd erased all the obvious traces of her life from their world?

He had no right to jump to conclusions. As far as he could tell, her parents and brother were nice, normal folks. Maybe they'd sold the piano for desperately needed cash during one of her father's layoffs. Maybe the piano had broken, or they'd donated it to a school in Lauren's name. Maybe they regretted the distance between themselves and her as much as she seemed to.

That distance was real. Lauren hadn't wanted to come here for Thanksgiving. She'd wanted to spend the holiday with Alec's family, and at first he'd wanted to, too. But over the past few weeks he'd reached the conclusion that they belonged in Allentown with the Wylers for the holiday. The thing that had separated her from her family for so many years—her professional devotion to her music—was no longer applicable. If ever she was going to build a bridge to her family, now was a good time to begin.

Lauren's father cleared his throat and gave Alec an assessing gaze. "Are you a musician, Alec?" he asked.

Alec had expected the obligatory paternal inquisition. "No," he answered amiably. "I used to be a cop. Now I write books."

"No kidding? I thought...well, when Lauren said she wanted to bring a fellow home for Thanksgiving, well, we just figured you'd be...you know."

"A world-famous musician like her," Alec concluded.

Her father smiled modestly. "Well, yeah."

Hoping to put him at ease, Alec returned his smile. "I used to be able to play the spoons, but it drove my mother crazy."

Lauren's father nodded. "So, you're a former cop, huh? State, city, what?"

"City. I was with the Boston P.D."

Mr. Wyler digested this. "And you're off the force now?"

Alec nodded. "I hurt my leg and had to retire."

"I see. And now you write books?" At Alec's nod, Mr. Wyler asked, "What kind of books?"

"Novels."

"Any money in that kind of stuff?"

"If you're lucky," Alec told him. "So far, I've been lucky."

Mr. Wyler accepted his answer with a grin and turned back to the television. The Eagles had just intercepted a pass, and the loud cheering on the television was seconded by louder cheering from Ricky. "So, you write books," Mr. Wyler speculated. "All three of my kids got a good education, I'm proud to say." Abruptly he silenced himself, as if he considered it in poor taste to boast about his children.

Lauren came back into the living room and Alec forgot the TV and Mr. Wyler's painless cross-examination of him. His mind shut out everything except her. Even though her expression was inscrutable, her eyes blank and her mouth neither smiling nor frowning, he was dazzled by her regal beauty, by the way the room's atmosphere seemed to brighten in her presence.

Who would have guessed, just a couple of months ago, that he would be so wildly in love with anyone—let alone a woman like Lauren? Who would have predicted that Alec would be so happily *involved* with someone, so willing to go to the ends of the earth for her, so ready to make eternal commitments? Once it had been a miracle that he'd awakened after a long, critical coma. Now he found himself contemplating an even greater miracle: waking up next to Lauren for the rest of his life.

He tamped the thought down into the deeper recesses of his heart. He might be ready, but Lauren wasn't. Whenever he so much as hinted that he was thinking about their future, she would retreat. "You can't plan for the future," she would say. "I did that once, and look at me now. You just can't make those kinds of plans."

At her entrance he rose to his feet. His chivalry brought a faint smile to her lips—her father and brother scarcely acknowledged her presence with fleeting glances. She crossed to the sofa and sank into the cushions, pulling him down beside her. He arched his arm around her shoulders.

"My mother didn't need me," she said.

He knew she meant that her mother didn't need her help in the kitchen. Even so, her choice of words disturbed him with their mournful resonance. In his mother's house, the women always collaborated on dinner while Alec and his brothers-in-law watched football. After dinner, the guys were in charge of cleaning up the kitchen, while the women sat around the dining room table drinking Baileys Irish Cream and gossiping and the kids ran amok in the basement. Everyone helped everyone; everyone needed everyone.

Alec kept his thoughts to himself. "Where's your sister?" he asked.

"At her boyfriend's house," Lauren told him. "They'll be here in time for dinner." She nestled closer to him, not so close that her father and brother would comment on it but close enough for Alec to feel the tension in her.

He twined his fingers through her hair, a physical way of telling her he was as close as he could be. God help him, he wanted to protect her.

He grinned at the notion of what she'd do to him if he ever admitted that, but he felt sad inside. There was no way to protect her from what she was going through right now, no way to make her feel needed by her mother.

Her father tossed a swift look at them, smiled cryptically and turned back to the television. At the next commercial break, Ricky eyed them with curiosity. Other than the constant din of the television broadcast and the occasional clank of a pot in the kitchen, the room was silent.

Could this truly have been the home of a brilliant musician? Alec was hard-pressed to believe it.

A rattle at the door alerted them to the arrival of Lauren's sister. Everyone in the living room stood in unison to greet the newcomers, who swept into the house on a gust of cold night air and laughter. "We're here!" Lauren's sister bellowed. "Better late than never!"

Cheryl could have passed for Lauren's twin, except for the superficial differences: the short, blunt-cut hair, the sultry eyeliner edging her lashes, the hip leather aviator jacket and the black boots. Her boyfriend's hair was blond, but exactly the same style and length as hers. His jacket was a male version of hers, and his boots were identical in style. "The Doublemint twins strike again," Ricky joked.

Cheryl playfully socked Ricky in the arm, then gave her father an exuberant hug. Unzipping her jacket, she turned to Lauren and her smile grew diffident. "Hey, Lauren," she said meekly. "Good to see you. This is

Don," she introduced her boyfriend. "Don Scoley, my sister Lauren and..." She peered questioningly at Alec.

"Alec Fontana," Lauren supplied as Alec shook Cheryl's and Don's hands and voiced the appropriate courtesies.

"So..." Cheryl slid off her jacket, her beautiful dark eyes still fixed on Lauren. "So, what's up?"

"Not too much," Lauren said. A flat-out lie, but Alec didn't call her on it. She knew better than he did what she could and couldn't say to her family.

"How's New York?"

"I'm living in Massachusetts this year," Lauren reminded her.

"Oh. Yeah. Right." Cheryl's smile grew poignant; she seemed to realize, more than the others, how far apart Lauren had grown from her family. "How's Massachusetts?"

"I like it," said Lauren.

Cheryl's gaze wandered to Alec, and her expression regained its charming humor. "I'll bet you do," she said knowingly. "Come on, let's go help Mom set the table."

Don took Lauren's seat as she trailed Cheryl out of the room. Alec ached in sympathy for her. This was much harder than he'd thought it would be—on him as well as on her. Maybe he shouldn't have forced the issue and insisted on visiting her family for Thanksgiving. Maybe he should have brought Lauren with him to his mother's house, where they would have had a happy, tranquil time of it.

But family was important. He believed he wouldn't have come through his injuries and survived his losses as well as he had without the loving support of his family. Lauren still had a lot to survive, a lot to work through. He wanted her to have what he had, to find the kind of contentment he'd found at the end of his struggle.

He loved her, but he was only a man. He wanted to be everything to her, but he couldn't, and he knew it. Every now and then he would come downstairs to the first-floor apartment after a day at his typewriter and find her sitting at the piano, flexing her right hand, obviously afraid. He would try to comfort her, try to encourage her, and she would give him a faraway look, as if he couldn't possibly know what she was going through. All the love he felt for her couldn't make the pain go away.

The pain wasn't merely her broken wrist, her damaged nerves, her inability to play. The real pain was what she'd sacrificed on her way to success—and what her family had sacrificed in her behalf. If she was ever to recover fully, the healing had to start here, in this brick row house in Allentown, Pennsylvania.

"Dinner's on," Mrs. Wyler sang out from the dining room.

The family gathered around the long table, at the center of which stood a milk-glass vase holding the flowers Alec and Lauren had brought. They sat together on one side of the table, facing Ricky, Cheryl and Don. Mr. and Mrs. Wyler took their places at the head and foot of the table. Mr. Wyler recited grace, then made a big production of sharpening the carving knife and slicing up the bird. Plates were passed, serving bowls, a pitcher of apple cider and a basket of warm rolls. The sounds of knives scraping dishes and glassware clinking mingled with brief expressions of praise:

"Great stuffing, Mom."

"Meat's real juicy, hon."

"Could you please pass the gravy?"

After a while the noise leveled off. Lauren bowed over her plate, holding her knife in her distinctively awkward manner as she cut a piece of meat. She speared the piece with her fork, but instead of lifting it to her mouth she let her hands fall to her lap and gazed about the room. "I have an announcement to make," she said.

Everyone stared at her. Alec stared, too. He had no idea what she was about to say.

"I'm not going to be playing concerts anymore," Lauren declared. "My career is over."

Stunned silence met her. Again, Alec reacted as her family did, although his amazement was based not on the news itself but on the fact that she hadn't informed her family before this moment.

"What are you talking about?" her father finally said.

"My hand isn't going to get better. It's healed as much as it can—which isn't enough to sustain my career. I can't play anymore, not professionally."

They all erupted at once: "What do you mean, it isn't going to get better?"

"But that doctor in New York—"

"I thought Mr. Honan promised—"

"But it's your whole life!"

"My whole life has changed," Lauren cut them off, her voice faltering only the slightest bit. Unable to look directly at her family, she focused on the arrangement of orange and tan flowers at the center of the table. "I know you all gave up so much for me, and..." Her tone wavered; her eyes glistened with tears. Alec reached under the table and pulled her right hand into his lap, sandwiching it between his, warming it, trying to impart strength and confidence to her. "It was like..." She swallowed and forced herself to continue. "I always believed I was doing it for all of you—the performing, the recording, all of it. I wanted to do it for you. You all gave me so much, and I wanted to give back as much as I could, and...and now I can't. I can't repay you. I can never make it up to you...."

Her voice cracked. She lowered her eyes to her plate.

"Oh, Lauren." Her mother rose from her chair and edged around the table to Lauren. She patted her shoulder and gave her a tentative hug. "You worked so hard, all these years. It's such a shame."

"I don't mind that," Lauren insisted. "We all work hard. And now I'll work hard at something else. I'll probably keep teaching. I..." She sighed. "It's just...I've let you all down."

"No," her father protested. "You've always made us very proud."

"It's not like you wanted this to happen or anything," Cheryl pointed out.

"And hey," Ricky teased, nobly attempting to leaven the mood, "now that I've got my Corvette, I guess I won't need any more loans for a while."

Lauren managed a feeble smile. "I'd like to think—" She sighed again, and exchanged a long, meaningful look with Alec before addressing her family once more. "I'd like to think that since I won't be traveling so much anymore, touring and all that, maybe...maybe I can spend more time here with you."

"That would be real nice," her mother said. Her fingers flitted over Lauren's shoulders once more, and then she backed off and returned to her seat, as if embarrassed about becoming too sentimental.

Lauren seemed embarrassed, as well. Sliding her hand out from between Alec's, she pushed away from the table. She appeared on the verge of crying, and she clearly didn't want to fall apart in front of her family. "Excuse me for a minute, please," she mumbled, placing her napkin on the table and hurrying out of the room.

Alec hastily excused himself and chased after her. She darted through the kitchen and then down a flight of stairs leading into the cellar.

Alec followed her down into a finished family room. The bluish fluorescent ceiling lights glared off the whitewashed walls and linoleum floor, giving the room a hard, chilly atmosphere. The furniture was old and ratty—a plaid couch, a few vinyl chairs, shelves full of bowling trophies and boxed games, framed diplomas and a piano.

It was an old spinet, its veneer scratched and the gold letters of its brand name peeling off. Frowning, Alec wandered over to inspect it more closely. The keyboard lid was closed, the bench pushed in. Like everything else in the house, it was immaculately clean.

His gaze sharpened on the shelves beside the piano. Not all the trophies were for bowling, he realized. The cup-shaped ones were for playing the piano, and they had Lauren's name engraved into their stands: first place in a statewide competition, first place in a regional, an award for unique achievement in music from the local school district. The framed parchments weren't all diplomas, either. Many of them were certificates of merit, citing Lauren for her accomplishments in music. All of them were framed, displayed in honor.

Spinning around, he found Lauren seated on the dowdy plaid couch, staring at him. Tears streamed down her cheeks, but she didn't wipe them, didn't turn away. The sorrow in her eyes reached out and gripped his soul.

"They're really proud of you," he murmured, moving across the room to join her on the couch.

"Yes." Her voice dissolved in a sob, and Alec quickly offered his handkerchief. She dabbed her eyes, then sank weakly against him. "They're proud of who I was. But I'm not that person anymore."

"Why did you wait so long to tell them? You've known since last month you weren't going to go back to performing."

"I couldn't tell them," she moaned. "I didn't know how to break the news. I knew how upset they'd be."

"They're upset for *you,* Lauren. Not for themselves."

"They don't have to be upset for me," she argued. "I'm fine. I'm heading in a new direction, and I feel good about it. But... but they wanted me to be a concert pianist. That's what they worked so hard for, and now I can't. I can't."

Alec gathered Lauren into his arms, cradling her, massaging her trembling shoulders. "I think they're fine, too," he murmured, brushing his lips against the crown of her head. "I think they'll get used to it just like you have. You've given them as much as they've given you, Lauren. Don't feel you've let them down."

She shuddered, then grew still. He continued to stroke her hair, her back, the nape of her neck. He continued to hug her.

"I've been lonely for so much of my life," she whispered, her voice raw from weeping. "I had friends, I had Gerald, but I always needed something more."

"Your family," Alec guessed.

"My family." She glanced up at him, her eyes no less bewitching for their tears. "And someone to love," she added.

"That's also family," he noted, then touched his mouth to hers, lightly, lovingly. "Marry me, Lauren. Let me be your family, too."

She lifted her hand to his cheek and traced the edge of his jaw, as if she were touching him for the first time, as if her fingertips could tell her what her eyes couldn't. "Are you sure that's what you want?"

He smiled. "If I didn't want it I wouldn't have asked."

"What if—" she drew in a tremulous breath "—what if things change again, what if I find out I can't teach anymore, or I don't like it, or I have to decide all over again—"

He silenced her with another kiss, this one quick and firm. "What if you're in an accident? What if I get beaten up on the streets of Boston? What if, what if? We can't always control what happens to us, Lauren. Maybe my next book won't sell like my last one. Maybe I'll run out of things to write about. A few years down the road, we could be broke. And then I'll find a job that you don't need a good left knee for, and you'll find a job you don't need a good right hand for, and we'll make a life of it." He kissed her again, then pulled back and smiled. "We love each other. The rest is just details. We can work it out as we go along."

She frowned slightly. "If I got married, Alec, it would be forever. How can we make promises about forever? Those 'what ifs' can change the future."

"They can't change how I feel about you," he argued. He rubbed the tiny dent between her eyebrows with his thumb, wanting to smooth away her sadness and fear. "What's the problem? You don't love me?" His casual tone couldn't disguise the very real anxiety welling up inside him at her failure to accept his proposal.

"I do love you," she murmured. "More than I've ever loved anyone or anything."

"Even your music?"

"Even that." She sighed. "My music was something I *did,* something I worked at. You're...you're here. A part of me. It's like—like you're always right above me, moving around, and I hear you, and I know where you are."

"I'm not above you," he whispered. "I'm with you."

"Yes," she agreed, sliding her other hand—her bad, beautiful right hand—along his cheek and into his hair, pulling him to her for a deep, consuming kiss. "I can face anything the future throws at me as long as you're with me. I'll marry you, Alec. I love you."

He returned her kiss, letting her glorious words echo inside him. If he hadn't had to breathe, he probably would never have ended the kiss. When he did she gave him a smile so sweet and enchanting he nearly kissed her again.

One more kiss and they would undoubtedly wind up making love on this sagging couch in the cool, windowless cellar while her family gathered at the kitchen door and wrung their hands. "We'd better go back upstairs," he whispered, unable to keep himself from brushing her brow with his lips. "I think you've got another big announcement to make."

"My poor parents," she said with a faint laugh. "One shock after another."

"That's what life is all about."

"At least some shocks are happy ones."

"Mmm." One last kiss. He shouldn't, but he couldn't help himself. He covered her luscious lips with his, sliding his tongue over hers and feeling her tremble in response. With a groan, he stood, took her hand and pulled her to her feet. "Come on," he said in a passionately husky voice. "Let's go give the folks a happy shock."

Lauren handed him back his handkerchief. He dabbed a few stray tears from her cheek, stuffed the linen into his pocket, tightened his arm around her and walked with her up the stairs, where her family, the future, and a feast of Thanksgiving were waiting for them.

Harlequin Superromance®

Come to where the West is still wild in a summer trilogy by Margot Dalton

Sunflower (#502—June 1992)
Robin Baldwin becomes the half owner of a prize
rodeo horse. But to take possession, she has to travel
the rodeo circuit with cowboy Matt Adams, living
with him in *very* close quarters!

Tumbleweed (#508—July 1992)
Until she met Scott Freeman, Lyle Callander was about
as likely to settle in one spot as tumbleweed in a
windstorm. But who *is* Scott? He's more than the
simple photographer he claims to be . . . much more.

Juniper (#511—August 1992)
Devil-may-care Buck Buchanan can ride a bucking
bronco or a Brahma bull. But can he win Claire
Tremaine, a woman who sets his heart on fire but
keeps her own as cold as ice?

**"I just finished reading *Under Prairie Skies* by
Margo Dalton and had to hide my tears from my
children. I loved it!"** —A reader

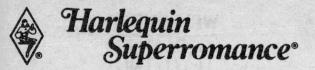

Harlequin Superromance®

Coming in August from
Harlequin Superromance
A new novel from the author of
BRIDGE TO YESTERDAY

IN GOOD TIME
By Muriel Jensen

A mad but cunning killer is stalking Paula Cornell.
Reluctantly, Paula must place her faith—and her life—
in the hands of bodyguard Dane Chandler, a man ten
years her junior.

In their secluded mountain hideout, Dane and Paula
fall in love. But unless Paula can overcome a tragedy
in her past, she will never be able to be the wife and
partner Dane needs her to be.

IN GOOD TIME
A story of hope and renewal
Superromance #512

IGT92

WELCOME TO

The quintessential small town where everyone knows everybody else!

Finally, books that capture the pleasure of tuning in to your favorite TV show!

GREAT READING...GREAT SAVINGS...AND A FABULOUS FREE GIFT!

Each book set in Tyler is a self-contained love story; together, the twelve novels stitch the fabric of the community. The covers honor the old American tradition of quilting; each cover depicts a patch of the large Tyler quilt.

With Tyler you can receive a fabulous gift ABSOLUTELY FREE by collecting proofs-of-purchase found in each Tyler book. And use our special Tyler coupons to save on your next TYLER book purchase.

Join your friends at Tyler for the sixth book, SUNSHINE by Pat Warren, available in August.

When Janice Eber becomes a widow, does her husband's friend David provide more than just friendship?

If you missed *Whirlwind* (March), *Bright Hopes* (April), *Wisconsin Wedding* (May), *Monkey Wrench* (June) or *Blazing Star* (July) and would like to order them, send your name, address, zip or postal code, along with a check or money order for $3.99 (please do not send cash), plus 75¢ postage and handling ($1.00 in Canada) for each book ordered, payable to Harlequin Reader Service to:

In the U.S.

3010 Walden Avenue
P.O. Box 1325
Buffalo, NY 14269-1325

In Canada

P.O. Box 609
Fort Erie, Ontario
L2A 5X3

Please specify book title(s) with your order.
Canadian residents add applicable federal and provincial taxes.

TYLER-6

HARLEQUIN SUPERROMANCE®

IF YOU THOUGHT ROMANCE NOVELS WERE ALL THE SAME...LOOK AGAIN!

Our exciting new look begins this September

Harlequin has a bold, sophisticated new look to whisk you into the world of Superromance...compelling, contemporary and always emotionally involving, these romantic stories are hard to put down.

Watch for a sneak preview of our new covers next month!

HARLEQUIN SUPERROMANCE— Simply sensational!

HST